Bluestown

Bluestown

Geoffrey Becker

St. Martin's Press
New York

Design by Ellen R. Sasahara

Library of Congress Cataloging-in-Publication Data

Becker, Geoffrey.
Bluestown / by Geoffrey Becker.
p.   cm.
ISBN 0-312-14223-4
1. Fathers and sons—New York (N.Y.)—Fiction   2. Rock
musicians—New York (N.Y.)—Fiction.   3. Young men—New York
(N.Y.)—Fiction.
I. Title
PS3552.E255B58   1996
813'.54—dc20   96-4269
CIP

First Edition: May 1996

10 9 8 7 6 5 4 3 2 1

For my sister

———————————

I want to thank the following people for reading, comments, and support: Fred Leebron, Steve Rinehart, Anne Dubuisson, Reagan Arthur, and especially Lynda Leidiger.

I got to keep movin'
blues fallin' down like hail
And the days keeps on worryin' me
there's a hellhound on my trail.

ROBERT JOHNSON,
"Hellhound on My Trail"

Part One

I

W hen I was fifteen, my father showed up at our high school and stood outside the door of Mr. Margin's history class wearing his leather jacket, waving a pink piece of paper. It was a September afternoon, sunny but not too hot, the sky bright blue. I had been alternately staring out the window and making eyes at Lucy Westbrook, who sat opposite me and had probably the nicest body in the whole school. Mr. Margin stopped lecturing (the subject was, I think, slavery) and went to the door, then gestured for me to step out into the hall with him.

"You're excused, Spencer," he said. "It seems you've forgotten something."

I didn't know what he was talking about, but the prospect of getting out of that stuffy classroom was an unexpected gift.

"Your doctor's appointment, Spence," said my dad, pointing to his watch. "We're late already." He had this concerned, fatherly expression on his face, and looked at Mr. Margin in commiseration. "I knew he'd forget. He's known about this for weeks."

"It's my experience," said Mr. Margin, "that given half a chance, these kids will forget anything. Get a move on, Spencer—read the next chapter for tomorrow's class." He gave me an affectionate smack on the shoulder.

"Kids," said my dad to him, then led me down the hall. When

3

we got to the front entrance, he looked both ways, then began to run. He took off across the front lawn, past a group of students sharing a joint, nearly tripping over a girl who was stretched out in the sun. I ran after him, thinking that this time he had finally, truly lost it. When I caught up with him at his car, a '67 Buick station wagon with a wired-on front bumper, I could see the back was loaded with equipment, all his guitars, an amplifier, and a suitcase. I got in the passenger side as he started up the engine.

"What's going on?" I asked when I'd caught my breath.

He slipped on a pair of aviator sunglasses. "It's way too nice a day to hang out in school," he said.

He loved to break rules. This was part of the reason he'd been banished, several years before, from the small ranch house where my mother and I still lived along with Hal, her boyfriend. My dad, a few gray traces just beginning to appear in the hair that fell over his ears, now stayed in a small apartment downtown, over Angelo's Pizza and Calzone. I saw a lot of him, more than my mother would have liked. He was only supposed to get me one day a week, but I'd go over to his place after school and hang around listening to albums, or playing cards. Since his work, when he had any, was at night, he was home afternoons. He liked to talk about the old days, when rock and roll was still counterculture and not just something else to show on TV. We'd sit on his secondhand sofa bed, albums and cassette tapes strewn across the floor, the smell of pizza wafting up through the floorboards, and he'd tell me how he was never really cut out to be a family man. Possessions and responsibilities made him nervous, he claimed, even things like his stereo and television. Even so, whenever he did get some money, he'd spend it on a new toy, a phase shifter or a compressor, or maybe a graphic EQ, and together we'd spend hours fooling with the knobs and buttons.

He played me albums, everything from T-Bone Walker and Lightnin' Hopkins to Jimi Hendrix and Duane Allman. Guitar, he said, was the only instrument on which you could really play

4

the blues, and by now I was an expert. I knew Texas from Chicago (where it seemed all the players were named either Milton or Melvin), understood that Robert Johnson had been just as much of a genius as Thomas Edison. I fully believed I knew what it meant to have the blues. In school I covered my notebooks with drawings of guitars and amps. My prize possession was a Muddy Waters T-shirt he brought me back from New York once, and which I wore so often my mother had to swipe it from my room just to get it washed. With my friends I smoked cigarettes and kept my hands plunged deep into my pockets, nodding in time to an imaginary beat. What I liked above all things was the tortured sound of a guitar string, bent almost to the point of breaking.

I asked about all the equipment, and he explained that he had an audition in Montreal for a gig with a new band that had backing, a recording contract, everything but the right guitarist. This seemed major, and there was an intensity on his face that I hadn't recalled seeing. When I asked him how they happened to come up with *his* name, he just smiled and said "a friend of a friend." My dad had a lot of friends.

He made a living as a guitarist, more or less. It always seemed he was on the verge of real success when something would happen. My mother said he brought it on himself, but as far as I could see, he just ran into a lot of bad luck. For a while he'd pinned his hopes on a local woman named Maddie Kelso, an emaciated redhead with an enormous, whiskey-steeped voice. He worked with her for about a year, but she got born again and moved to Wisconsin. Another time he left his car unlocked and all his stuff was stolen, so for months he had to borrow equipment. But he stayed optimistic, full of plans, and even my mom, on the uncomfortable occasions when she would run into him at the supermarket or the drugstore, found it hard to be angry with him. She didn't like us spending time together and said he was a bad role model, but he could always do something dumb, like wiggle his eyebrows at her, or juggle a couple of avocados, and at least get a laugh.

5

We went to the Dairy Queen and had black-and-white milkshakes. That was where the greasers hung out, and the parking lot was full of them: slicked-back hair, big combs sticking out of the back pockets of their polyester pants. They leaned against jacked-up cars with blaring radios, smoked cigarettes, ignored the girlfriends who lounged next to them, all hairspray and lip gloss. In his leather jacket, worn-out jeans, and shades, my dad was easily the coolest-looking person there. I liked the way we could just hang out together on the hood of the Buick, feeling the hot metal under our legs, sipping a cold shake.

"Jimi," he said. It was something we'd done since I was little, calling each other by the names of dead guitarists. I was Jimi and he was Duane, after Duane Allman, who was definitely the closest thing to a hero in his life. Nobody'd ever played slide like Duane, or ever would.

"They sent me expense money," he said.

"Great," I said. "That means they're serious."

He shrugged. "I guess. The way I see it, if I drive up, it costs me next to nothing and I pocket the difference. What do you say? Feel like a road trip?"

I could think of nothing I felt like more. An image of the two of us cruising north through New England flashed through my mind like the trailer for a sixties road movie. But, I pointed out, my mother was going to be a problem.

He lowered his voice. "We won't tell her. We'll just leave a note saying you're with me, and when we get back, I'll take all the heat."

A note from him wasn't going to get me out of anything, but I wanted to go, so I convinced myself it was a workable plan. After all, it would just be a couple of days.

"It feels a little like running away from home," I said, enjoying the idea. A friend of mine, Nicky Dormer, had run away from home for four days the year before, and afterward he'd seemed to me years older.

"Jimi, my man," he answered, massaging my shoulders, "it is impossible to run away from home with your own father."

My mom was still at work. We drove by the house and I ran upstairs to get a toothbrush while he stood in the kitchen penciling a quick note in his peculiar handwriting, an angular sort of chicken scratch. When I came back down he was still laboring over it. It was odd seeing him there, back in the house for the first time in years. He looked uncomfortable, out of place. I looked at what he had written, but it wasn't until we were in the car and heading out of town that I asked him about it.

"Hey, Duane," I said, "how come you put down that we were going to Virginia?"

"Just a precaution," he said. "In case she decides to call the cops, it'll buy us some time."

As soon as we were on the road, he slipped in a cassette of the Allman Brothers doing "Statesboro Blues," and I kicked my feet up on the dashboard. The music almost seemed to be powering the car. I'd seen pictures from back when I was only about three or four, when my dad practically *was* Duane Allman. He wore his hair all the way down his back and had the same mutton-chop sideburns. The day after Duane died on his motorcycle, my dad managed to get into an accident on his. He broke a leg and an arm, but he also got an out-of-court settlement that was enough to buy our house, as well as a good PA system and a couple of guitars. He was twenty-five years old, a high school graduate with a wife, a kid, and his own place. Things started to happen. Weird people would come over in the middle of the night to hang out, and in the morning there'd be spilled beer and cigarette burns in the carpet. My mom and he would fight, then he'd disappear for a couple of days at a time. Afterward he'd always try to make up for it by doing something real normal, like mowing the lawn, or taking the three of us out to the movies.

Finally, she just told him to move. I was nine. "Buddy," he said to me, "I'm not going anywhere." He wrote his new phone number on the inside of a book of matches and put it in my hand.

We stopped for gas at a turnpike service station and he pulled out his wallet. It was stuffed with bills, more money than I'd ever seen him with at one time. He removed a ten and gave it to me. "Candy bars," he said, solemnly.

I got change and pushed quarters into the machine until I had extracted four Snickers, our favorite. Then, on impulse, I also bought a pair of cheap amber-tinted sunglasses that were aviators like his. They were small on me and rode high on the bridge of my nose. They cost six dollars and were probably worth about forty-nine cents, but I bought them anyway. When I got back to the car, he lifted them off and bent the flimsy frame across the middle, just slightly, then put them back on me. "That's it," he said. "Now you're cooking."

As we drove, we talked about Canada. Neither of us had ever been, so we made a list of things it was famous for.

"Canadian bacon," I offered.

"Salmon," he said.

"The Expos."

"Draft dodgers."

"Niagara Falls."

"That's in America."

"Only part of it. The other part is Canadian."

He looked over at me. "Who figured that out?"

"It makes sense. It's a natural divider. That's how they always divide up countries. States, too." When he didn't say anything, I fell silent for a little while, thinking about how things divided. How did they know exactly where Canada stopped and America began? It was all just water—there couldn't be any clear line like on a map. I thought about me and my dad: I was halfway to thirty, and he was halfway to seventy. I always had

8

an idea that when I turned eighteen I would experience some obvious transformation into adulthood, but now that I was getting closer, I wondered. The twenty years that separated me from him suddenly seemed like nothing at all, not if you looked at the whole picture.

We crossed the Vermont border around sunset and stopped for burgers at a place with two enormous trucks parked outside. It was a classic roadside diner, but somehow not quite real; everything in it was brand-new, though styled to look mid-fifties. It was someone's idea of what a diner should have looked like— lots of chrome and mirrors and a big, colorful jukebox. I put a quarter in and selected two songs.

"If they like you, does that mean you'll have to move to Canada?" I asked, coming back to the table.

"Could be," he said. "I don't know. It all depends."

I pictured his apartment over the pizzeria, tried to imagine someone else living there. It just didn't seem a real possibility. "I'd miss you," I said. "Where would I hang out?"

He tapped the tabletop with his fork. "Well, let's not count our chickens. They may not want me at all. I'm getting kind of old for this line of work."

"How can you say that? Look at the Stones. Look at . . ." I tried to think of someone else. "B. B. King. He's still going, and he must be about sixty."

He yawned. His eyes were rimmed red from all the driving. Under the fluorescent lights, his skin was the bluish color of skim milk. "I don't know," he said. "The way I see it, this may be my last shot. If it isn't happening, I may just try to get into something respectable."

"Like Hal?" Hal was in insurance, and we had a fair amount of fun at his expense. Both of us thought insurance was about the most boring thing you could possibly do, and that by having Hal move in, my mother had not so much found a mate as taken out a policy. In fact, I kind of liked him. He never tried to be my father, he was just Hal. He left me alone when I didn't want to be bothered, and he cooked great Chinese meals every Tuesday night.

"Exactly. How do you think I'd look in a suit and tie?" He picked up his glasses and pointed them at me. "Let's talk coverage," he said in a salesman's voice. "You tell me you play in a band? Fine. Say one day you get up there on stage, put a hand on your guitar, the other on the microphone. And let's just say that system isn't properly grounded. In one blue flash you get zapped right into the next state. What about your wife? Your kids? Who takes care of them? The musicians' union? You say you're not in the union? Well, I have a little policy designed just for you. We call it the Guitar Player's Friend—it provides all-purpose coverage for you and your loved ones, and it's issued by the Chuck Berry Mutual Accident and Life Insurance Company, a name you've known and trusted for years. Believe me, you won't want to plug in without it."

The waitress interrupted him with our food. I waved a french fry. "Brilliant," I said. "You could be rich."

"Yeah, maybe," he said, modestly. "I'd like to think I'll be able to leave you something someday." He sipped his coffee. "If you had all the money you could ever want, what would you do?"

I chewed and thought. "I don't know, I guess I'd buy about ten guitars, a small recording studio, and some video equipment."

He nodded. "And live where?"

"Hawaii maybe. The Swiss Alps."

"Good choices. A little romantic, but you're supposed to be romantic at fifteen."

"So? What would you do?" I asked.

"I believe," he said, "I'd do exactly what I'm doing right now."

He was tired and didn't feel like driving much more, so we started looking around for a place to stay. Since we were in Vermont, he said, we ought to find one of those quaint country inns where you slept under thick goose down comforters and they served you up a big New England–style breakfast in the morning. We must have spent an hour driving around trying to find one. Eventually we settled on a motor court with a sign of a blinking neon sheep jumping over the name: TRAVELLER'S REST. The parking lot was empty, and my dad kept shaking his head over the fact that the one time he actually wanted to spend some money he couldn't find a way to do it, but I was happy. This was much more the kind of place I imagined crashing for the night, and as for the rest of that stuff, it wasn't really cold enough for a down comforter, and I supposed I could live without breakfast.

Our room was hooked up with cable television, and I found an old British vampire movie with lots of gore and women nearly tumbling out of their bodices. My dad spent ten minutes going back and forth to the car bringing in his guitars. It seemed a little odd to me that he'd bothered to take all of them along, but I didn't say anything. This was a very big audition for him, and I figured he needed the extra confidence. He took a pint bottle of Chivas Regal out of his bag, went into the bathroom and returned with two tissue-wrapped glasses. I'd never had Chivas, but I remembered reading on an album cover that it was John Lee Hooker's favorite drink. I squinched over to make room for him on the bed, then took the glass he handed me. He turned down the sound on the television.

"Your mother called me last week," he said, after a moment. "Says you're messing up in school."

"That's not true," I told him. "Just one class. I'm getting Bs in everything else. Anyhow, why should she call you?"

"She wants us to stop hanging around together so much, at least till your grades pick up."

We almost never talked about school, except in the most general way, and having him speak to me like this, father to son, when we were now hundreds of miles from home, seemed a kind of betrayal.

"That's stupid," I said.

He nodded.

"I hope that's what you told her."

"I didn't tell her anything," he said. "I wanted to talk to you first."

I was suddenly angry at my mother for trying to interfere so blatantly with my life, and behind my back, too. I wasn't a kid anymore. I had been thinking about calling her, just to let her know I was all right, but now I felt like letting her stew a little.

"You know," he said, lying back on the bed and crossing his legs, "she's probably right. I'm thirty-five, still kicking around the same town I grew up in, still trying to land a steady gig. Being with me isn't going to help you become CEO of General Motors."

"Come on," I said. "You're my dad." I sipped at my drink, which made my eyes water.

"Okay." He studied me. "I just wanted to make sure."

A question occurred that I was almost afraid to ask. "Could she do something? Something legal, I mean?"

"I don't know. It's a possibility." He got up and went into the bathroom.

I made a promise to myself that regardless of what happened, things would continue on between us the way they always had. It was hard to imagine my mother actually doing something so drastic, but taking off without her permission had already given me a sense of power. Things could be any way I wanted them to be, I thought. What were they going to do, put me under armed guard?

"How long do you think we'll stay in Montreal?" I asked when he came back.

He looked through the blinds out at the parking lot. "Not long. A couple of days, tops." Then he slapped a hand down on my leg. "What do you say we head out and see if there's any nightlife around here?"

I jumped up and turned off the set.

We drove around until we found a little roadside place called Mother's that had pickup trucks parked outside and a flashing red Miller sign in the window. There were maybe twenty-five people inside, not counting the band, five bored-looking guys in checked shirts playing sleepy country tunes. The guitar player didn't look much older than me, in spite of an attempted mustache. When we walked in I immediately sensed hostility, but I just followed my dad. He went to the bar, took a seat, ordered us drinks, and helped himself to a handful of peanuts from a bowl they had out. I reached in and grabbed a couple, too. The bartender pursed his lips and considered me for a moment, then shrugged and uncapped us two long-neck bottles of Bud.

"Never order anything fancy in a strange bar," said my dad, tipping back his bottle. "The first thing people notice about you in a place like this is what you're drinking."

I nodded. We sat for a while. Then I got up to go to the bathroom, and when I got back he was in a conversation with a fat guy he introduced as Al. Al worked as a mechanic, he said. He had huge, grease-blackened hands.

"This your kid?" asked Al.

My dad smiled proudly and I stood there feeling like a prize hog. I wished I were still back in the motel room watching television.

"I got a kid," said Al. I waited for him to say something else, but for Al, the statement was a complete thought, and he just turned and faced the bar.

The band shuddered to a halt and went on break, and my dad ordered a round of shots for them, digging into his stuffed wallet and tossing a twenty onto the bar. Then he left me and Al sitting together, went over and got talking to the guitarist and bass player. I thought about all the bars in our town where he'd played. He was always in trouble with the club owners for showing up late, or mixing up dates, but he could smooth-talk them and manage to get hired again regardless. One time he got himself booked into two different places with different bands on the same night, and rather than cancel, did half of one gig, then drove to the other and finished up the night there, using me as an excuse. "You came down with a convenient case of the mumps," he explained the next day. "I could never have made it without you." For two days after that, I walked around faking a cough and trying to look weak, just in case someone should want to check out his story.

Al wasn't much of a talker, so I drank my beer and tried to pretend that hanging around in a bar was the most natural thing in the world for me. I counted the bottles of liquor lined up next to the cash register.

"Jimi," my dad said, coming over and poking me in the side. "We're going to sit in next set. What do you say?"

I looked into his eyes to see if he was kidding. I played a little guitar, but not very well, and never in front of people. The prospect terrified me, and I could see he was serious. "You go ahead," I said. "I'll watch."

"Come on, we'll do some blues." He smiled encouragingly.

"I can't," I said. "Really."

"Sure you can," he told me.

I felt something close to panic, but at the same time it didn't seem that I had any choice. They had an extra guitar on stage for me, and the band's guitarist handed his over to my dad. When he did that he gave me a little smile that made the few dark hairs spread out on his upper lip. I took it as a sign of encouragement and plugged in. My dad called out "Red House," a Hendrix tune he knew I knew, and started playing. I tried to follow along, but after a few seconds I realized something was off.

My guitar was tuned a peculiar way. The chords I formed were one disaster after another. My dad kept giving me furious looks, as if I was deliberately screwing around. Everything I played came out wrong. He leaned over and shouted something to me that I could not hear above the music. I could see the band's guitarist leaning against the bar, laughing. I did the only thing I could think of: I stopped playing. Or rather, I pretended to play, damping the strings with my left hand so that no sound came out. My dad shook his head, turned away and began to sing the first verse.

14

The song seemed to go on forever. After a while, he picked up an empty Budweiser bottle and ran it along the strings for a slide, while I mimed along, numb, waiting for it to be over. When it was, finally, we got hoots of approval and applause, but I barely heard them in my rush to get off.

The band's guitarist said something to me as he took the instrument out of my hands. I jumped down, ignoring the amusement in his eyes, and went and stood next to a shuffleboard table while my dad talked to some of the locals, bearded men in checked wool jackets who clapped him on the back and offered to buy him drinks. Finally he came over to me.

"Let's go," I said.

It was cold in the parking lot, the air smelling of pine, the muted sounds of the bar mixing with the swell and hush of the wind in the trees. My dad walked me to the car and unlocked it.

"It was in open tuning," he said, finally. "Set up for slide."

"Yeah?" I said. "How was I supposed to know that?"

"You know about open tuning. All you had to do was think."

"I *couldn't* think!" I practically shouted. "Nothing sounded right and I didn't know what to do!"

"So what?" he said. "You just quit? You can't let yourself get beat like that."

"I didn't."

"Well, what do you call it?" He was glaring at me, and I could see that he was really upset about this, more so even than I was. I'd grown three inches in the past year, and at five-eleven, I was now nearly as tall as him, but it hadn't really struck me until just now.

"I didn't quit," I said quietly. "I stayed up there with you."

We drove in a silence that I was afraid to break; the longer it went on, the more permanent it felt. He wouldn't look at me. He was speeding too, I noticed, but I wasn't going to say anything.

15

Then, about a mile from our motel we got pulled over by the cops.

As the officer shined his flashlight into our faces, I thought about the note we'd left. If my mother really had reported us to the police, this was probably it. I wondered what, if anything, they could do to him. I suspected he could get in a lot of trouble. Mostly, though, I was worried he might not get to the audition, and that it would somehow be my fault. I sat frozen in anticipation, the cold night air flowing against my face from the open window, hoping as hard as I could for nothing bad to happen.

"Been doing a little drinking tonight?" asked the policeman as he examined my dad's license.

"Yes, sir," he said. "Two beers. But I'm sober."

The cop pointed his flashlight in my face. "Who's that?"

"My son."

"Is that right?" He turned the light away from me and back at my dad. "Taking a little vacation, are you?"

"You might say that."

"Please, get out of the car, Mr. Markus."

I had to sit for ten minutes while they ran him through a series of tasks to determine whether he was drunk. It was hard to watch. He walked a straight line four times, and counted backward from fifty twice. They made him balance on one leg, then the other. All the while, another cop sat behind us, just a silhouette under the flashing blue light, speaking into his radio. They were checking on us. They didn't believe he was my father.

Finally, they wrote out a ticket and let us go. Just like that. This seemed incredible luck to me, and as soon as we were back under way, I let out a little whoop.

"Man," I said. "That was close."

But he still wasn't talking. In fact, he wouldn't even look at me. I wanted to tell him it didn't matter, to just forget it, but I couldn't. He didn't say anything at all until we got back to the motel. He put out a hand and tugged at the top of my head, then ran it down the back of my neck.

"You could use a haircut," he said.

When I woke the next morning, he was in the bathroom, shaving. I went and leaned against the door, watching him slide the razor carefully along the contours of his throat. He put a finger on his nose and pushed it comically to one side to get at his upper lip, turned and made a face at me. I liked seeing him shave. Getting my toothbrush, I fought him for sink space. When he pushed back, I pushed harder, then scooped water out of the sink and splashed him. He dropped the razor, picked up the can of shaving cream and advanced toward me, his face spotted with islands of foam. I ran, but he cornered me by the television and emptied half the can onto my head before I managed to wrestle it out of his hands. We stood there for a while, the two of us covered in shaving cream, laughing. Then he took the can from my hands, flipped it once in the air, and went back into the bathroom.

We reloaded the car and checked out. He paid cash for the room and asked the guy at the desk where we could get a good breakfast. He recommended a place about three miles away that turned out to be one of those country-style inns we'd been hoping to find the night before, and had in fact driven right past. We were both starved, and my dad told me to order a dream breakfast—anything I thought I could possibly eat. I had four eggs, home fries, sausages, waffles, toast, orange juice, and coffee. He had steak and eggs with fried onions. The waitress looked a little hassled bringing out all that food—there was barely room for the plates—but we got a kick out of being so extravagant, and we tipped her heavily when we were through. After all, it wasn't our money.

We hit the road about eleven, windows open, tape deck turned way up. We sang along with some old Traffic and Santana, and I beat out rhythms by banging one hand on the glove compartment and the other against the roof of the car. It was a perfect day to be driving, and north seemed the only direction possible. The Buick's big engine hummed powerfully in front of us, and even the air tasted like Canada, cool and fresh and full of promise.

"Hey," I said to him. "What do you say after Montreal we just keep on going? We could set a record. First station wagon to reach the North Pole."

"Bad idea," he said, adjusting his glasses with his forefinger.

"Why?"

"Because. Too much competition. The North Pole is swarming with guitarists already."

I kept quiet.

He closed his eyes for a moment. "They've got this little town up there. It's jointly owned by all the major record companies."

"Not a very pleasant place to live," I said.

"That's the whole point, it's a miserable place to live." He reached over and turned the stereo down. "Bluestown," he said. "Most of the greats are up there, on salary, just biding their time. Muddy Waters, Jimi Hendrix, Duane Allman, Elmore James. All of them hanging out, drinking, jamming, and trying to keep warm."

"So what you're saying is that they're actually still alive?"

"That's exactly what I'm saying. Where do you think they keep getting those 'previously unreleased' recordings from? The blues wasn't selling, so they figured this would be a good way to stir up interest. And let me tell you something, a couple of years from now the world is going to be in for one hell of a surprise. Because they're coming back, all of them."

"Return of the Killer Guitarists," I said in my best coming-attractions voice. "When is this going to happen?"

He shrugged. "Who knows? When we're ready for them, I guess. When everyone has had enough of the crap they play on the radio."

"Bluestown." I flipped through the road atlas. "You know, it's not here on the map."

"It's there. Trust me. You just go to Chicago, then head due north."

"But," I pointed out, "the North Pole is due north of everywhere, not just Chicago."

"Hey," he said. "Don't argue with your father."

I nodded off for a while, imagining a town built entirely of ice, with fur-bundled shapes walking up and down the streets carrying guitar cases. I kept thinking, How do I know these people are who they say they are if I can't see their faces? Then we got off the highway and I woke up. We were a little south of St. Johnsbury. My dad said he wanted to take a few minutes and look at a typical New England town. The place was called Denton, and it was truly quaint: tree-lined streets, big old houses with well-kept yards, two neat white-steepled churches only a couple of blocks apart. It was one of those picture-postcards of a town, and I thought it probably didn't look any different now than it had fifty years ago. I couldn't imagine what people there did for a living, but everyone we saw looked reasonably well-off. We drove up and down its few streets, looking at the houses, just enjoying the simplicity of the place. In the center of town, he pulled over by the bus station and put the car in neutral.

"How about a couple of candy bars before we get going?" he said.

I was still stuffed from breakfast, and I couldn't believe that he was actually hungry again, but I said sure and hopped out of the car. He stuck his hand out the window with a five-dollar bill in it. I took the money and went inside.

It was a tiny bus station, just a window, a bench, and two vending machines. The guy at the window was out of singles, and I waited while he counted the whole five out in quarters, nickels, and dimes. Then I bought two Snickers bars. With them in my hand, I stepped back out into the bright sunlight.

He was already gone. I could see the tailgate of the station wagon bouncing away from me down the street in the distance.

I stood there watching him go, thinking that any moment now he would turn around and come back. It had to be a joke. But he kept going until the car disappeared over a crest.

I stared after him down the street. I was standing alone in the middle of a tiny Vermont town with two chocolate bars in my hand and no idea what to do next. Then I stuck my hand in my jacket pocket and felt the wad of money. He had slipped it there somehow without my noticing, and when I took it out I counted nearly eight hundred dollars, most of it in fifties and twenties. I sat down right where I was on the curb.

It took a little while to collect myself. I walked up and down the main street looking into shop windows, kicking at loose stones on the street. I opened one of the candy bars and took a bite, but dropped the rest of it in a trash can. I took out the roll of money again, fanned through it. This time, a small slip of yellow paper fell out from between two of the fifties. Picking it up, I saw that it was a withdrawal slip for just over a thousand dollars from my father's bank, and on it in a teller's handwriting were the words "Account Closed."

I stood for a while feeling the sun on my face, looking up at a solid blue sky that extended, unbroken, right up to the Canadian border and beyond. There was no audition, I realized. There had only been, for a brief while, an idea about the two of us starting over again someplace else. I thought I understood what it felt like to look at your own future and see nothing but disappointment and failure stretching out like a series of clouds toward the horizon. The thing was, if he'd asked, I would have kept going.

Taking all the change I had in my pockets, I began feeding the parking meters of downtown Denton, Vermont, pumping each one hard until it would take no more, then moving on to the next. After a while, when I ran out of coins, I stepped back into the dark little bus station and paid for a one-way ticket home.

2

J *ust before Christmas*, a carton of steaks arrived from the
Tru-Pak Meat Company in Omaha, Nebraska. They were
tenderloins, round and thick, packed in dry ice. Why he thought
this an appropriate present I can't say, but at least they were a
kind of communication. My mother and Hal had recently gone
vegetarian, and though I doubt they would have eaten them
anyway, I ended up working my way through the box myself.
Sometimes I'd come back from a party at two or three in the
morning, foggy from beer, and fry one up, fearing that I would
wake the whole house as it hit the center of the heavy black pan
and the hissing sound exploded in the quiet of the kitchen.

I called Tru-Pak to see if I could get his address, but the secretary explained company policy was not to give out that information. She asked me how I liked the steaks, and I said fine.
She suggested I might want to try the sausage and cheese as-
sortment, too.

I had a cheap electric my dad had given me the year before,
a blond, single cutaway, and while in the past I'd only goofed
around with it, now I carried it around all the time, played it
constantly. The more I worked, though, the more convinced I
became that I was basically clumsy. I wanted a stinging vi-
brato—to be able to bend notes and make them sing. I squeezed
tennis balls to strengthen my hands, practiced scales from a book
I found in our basement called *New Rockin' Rhythms for Guitar*

that featured a man in a suit with perfect classical posture playing an electric with a paisley pick-guard while a miniskirted
woman looked on.

Instead of listening to my teachers, I drew guitar necks and
filled them with notes, counted half-tones, tried to find the
logic in how they repeated themselves from string to string.
Lying in bed at night, I'd visualize my fingers forming some simple chord—E, or A—then decide what pitch each string was
sounding. The relationships began to make sense to me, the flat-
ted thirds for minor chords, the different kinds of sevenths. I
spent much of my waking time humming intervals.

I began hanging out more with Nicky Dormer. The two of us
haunted the shadowed landscapes of corporate office parks,
smoking gold, Colombian dope from a pipe he'd made out of
brass plumbing fittings. Nicky was black, but lived in our neighborhood, which was almost entirely white and middle-class.
His skin was pale enough that the other black kids called him
names, "Deerskin" and "Bleach-boy." He played guitar, too,
and could do Hendrix solos note for note. Sometimes, after
school, I'd just sit in his bedroom and watch him, his tiny practice amp cranked for maximum distortion. He was odd in other
ways, besides being a loner. Until very recently, he'd still been
staging funerals for his G.I. Joes that died in combat. He buried
them in his backyard, marking their graves with small, carved
Popsicle sticks.

Nicky bought most of his drugs from Dwight, one of the
counselors at Flight Three, the third floor of a house near our
school where kids could go and hang and supposedly stay out of
trouble. The place was often empty, and we'd sit around the living room, read magazines, argue about music. Nicky believed the
whole Western tonal system was a scam perpetrated on us by
the Renaissance, which he thought of as a conspiracy on the
order of the Mafia or pro-football owners. He'd gotten this idea
from European history, which he'd taken the year before, and

it had grown in him ever since like a tumor, pressing out almost everything else.

It was late afternoon, February, and the light was nearly gone. What there was fell in short shafts through the dirty blinds. I'd just made Nicky listen to my cassette of *Robert Johnson: King of the Delta Blues*, and now he was looking at me oddly, as though I were playing a joke on him.

"Might as well give up right now," he said.

"Pretty incredible, isn't it?"

"If that guy could make a record," Nicky said, "anybody could."

There were two guitars up there, a cheap Yamaha acoustic and a no-name plywood thing with a red, white, and blue pick-guard. I picked one up and chunked out a simple rhythm for him to solo to. He played a couple of things, then stopped, shaking his head.

"Twelve-tone." This was his shorthand comment for all that was wrong with the world. He applied it equally to a poor piece of music and a bag of pot that was all seeds.

"Just listen to yourself," I said. I was worried about him. Lately, he didn't even bother to finish his sentences. "Stop thinking so hard."

He put the instrument aside, fumbled for a cigarette, spent nearly a minute smoothing out all the creases and dents until it was a nearly perfect white cylinder. We were alone upstairs; Dwight had left to get cigarettes a few minutes before, having sold Nicky ten dollars' worth of something that Nicky paid for with a five, two ones, and a handful of change. It was very quiet. Someplace in the distance I could hear the sound of children's voices shouting and playing.

There was a creak of a door opening downstairs. Nicky held a finger to his lips. "Fire escape," he said.

I followed him to Dwight's office. We climbed over his desk and out the window just as the officers came into the other room. We had to jump the last six feet or so because the ladder didn't reach all the way to the ground, and as we ran I looked back and saw two police cruisers parked out front. Nicky was shedding evidence as we moved: a film canister full of pot, a plastic bag with something wrapped in tinfoil inside.

"Split up," he said when we'd gone a block.

We were on the other side of the fence from an abandoned playing field. He took his brass pipe and flung it as far as he could out into the dirt, then turned and sprinted north, toward his favorite area of woods by the Unitarian church.

I went the other way, cutting through backyards whenever possible. After a few minutes I went back out to a sidewalk and cut my pace to a leisurely stroll, doing my best to appear to have nothing to hide and not to be out of breath. I ran a mental inventory: I wasn't carrying anything illegal, though I had smoked a joint a few hours earlier and probably still looked a little high.

I got a Coke at the pizza place in the shopping center, just generally tried to be invisible for a while. When I finally wandered into the house it was nearly six. My mother came into my room and stared at me, hands on her hips, eyes tired. She'd been in bed all day with a cold. In her blue robe, her nose red from blowing, she looked like some kind of bird.

"Tough afternoon?"

There was no use denying it. My eyes were pink as a rabbit's, despite the Visine I'd squeezed into them.

She sat in my desk chair, put one hand over her mouth, and considered me with the same tired look she often gave to the avocado plant by the front door that had been dying for the past eight months. "Why are you being like this?" she asked.

"How do you mean?"

"Like *him*. You're acting just like Dan at his worst. I refuse to believe it's genetic, so I'm left thinking that this is a choice on your part."

I stared at my shoes.

"The police were by, asking about Nicky Dormer. They seemed to think that you'd know how to find him."

"What did you say?"

"I didn't say anything. I told them I'd ask you, and if you knew anything, you'd give them a call." She picked up a pencil, put it back down. "Please don't come home this way again." She sighed, stood up, and left me alone, closing the door softly behind her. I flipped on the radio and hunted for something good, congratulating myself on a clean getaway.

Nicky, too, had gotten away, but a week later he was arrested downtown while shoplifting a carton of cigarettes at the WaWa market. He had his guitar with him at the time, a sanded-down Gibson SG Special which he carried in a canvas sack since he had no case for it, and when he tried to run, it was no contest. The arresting officer called for backup, and after sprinting less than two blocks, Nicky found himself looking into a police revolver. They put him on the ground, stepped on him, handcuffed him. At the station, they found a sheet of blotter acid in his boot. The guitar was presumed stolen property and confiscated.

"They can't do that," I said when he told me about this over the phone. "That's yours. Don't you have a receipt or something?"

"Hell, no," he said. "I'll never get it back."

He spent two weeks at a juvenile detention center before being returned to his mother's custody. A few days later, the police released the instrument to him, its neck broken in two places, the tuning pegs bent into useless positions. Nicky took a screwdriver and removed the pickups, bridge, and other salvageable hardware, then set the body ablaze in his living room fireplace atop one of those wax logs that burns different colors.

A girl at school, Judith Horner, began following me around with a pitying look in her eyes. I'd known Judith since the first grade—until the fourth we'd been in the same class together— but over the past few years, by unspoken agreement, we'd become strangers. She'd grown into a gawky teenager, thin, flatchested, all neck, with pale skin that was just beginning to bounce back from a two-year bout with acne. She wore plaid skirts fastened with big safety pins, got excellent grades, hung out by herself a lot. I didn't know what she wanted, but one night she called me. I pretended, just for a moment, not to know who she was.

"Judith *Horner*," she said. "Please meet me tomorrow after school. There's something I'd like to show you."

We met by the front arch. It was raining lightly, and when she asked if I had an umbrella and I told her no, she produced a second one from her canvas book bag. "It's sort of embarrassing, but I usually carry two. They're always blowing inside out on me." She was going out of her way not to meet my eyes with hers. "Would you like a mint? I mean, well not a mint, exactly. They're Altoids. They're pretty awful, really, but I sort of like them. I don't know. Here." She held out a small tin.

" 'Curiously strong,' " I said, reading the label.

"Funny, isn't it? Like they were surprised when they tasted one."

She didn't live that far from me. Her street was a narrow, twisting lane that I'd walked past many times, but never turned down. It was thickly planted with maples and oaks, and in the rain they seemed to lean inward and whisper to each other, the silvery undersides of their leaves turned up to catch the water and the wind. Judith's house was boxy and brown, with a square garage on one side and a cement stoop. There were wind chimes clinking by the front door. She grabbed the mail and we went inside, where we were met by a large malamute who immediately began sniffing my knees.

"Toby, cool it," she said. "Coke?"

"Sure." I walked around the living room, accompanied by Toby, looking at things. There was an old KLH stereo, an extensive collection of jazz albums. On a shelf next to the stereo sat a wooden bowl filled with polished stone eggs. I picked one up and rolled it around in my hand.

"Here." She brought me a drink and I swallowed about half of it. I felt nervous. I had no idea what Judith wanted. I scratched

Toby's head and he responded by wagging his tail for me, then heading out into the kitchen where I heard him begin to eat something crunchy.

"He always eats when people come over," she said. "I've never figured out why, exactly. Either he thinks if he doesn't eat his food you will, or else it's just that he's hopelessly neurotic. We got him at the pound, though supposedly he's a purebred, so my vote is for neurotic. Not that I blame him, being abandoned and all."

We went out into the garage, which had space for two cars. Only one was there now, an old Volvo with rusting fenders. The front end of the garage was a work area, with shelves on which neatly labeled glass jars containing nails and washers and screws were lined up. There was a small lathe and a table saw and a bunch of wood leaning up against the far wall.

"My dad likes to build things," she said. "At least he tries. He made the dresser in my room. He's learning to do a chair. He says that's the real challenge, a chair, even though it seems like it would be so simple. It has to support a lot of weight and still look good."

I nodded, walked around looking at the tools, pretending a kind of professional interest.

"This is where it happened," she said.

I put my hands in my pockets and waited.

"Dad was up in Boston on a project—he's a landscape architect—and he still hadn't gotten back. I woke up early and heard the car running. I didn't even think about it at first, but after a while, when it was still running, I got up. She was just sitting there in her bathrobe. She'd put on makeup and everything. Her eyes were closed and I almost thought she was visualizing. She always had to sit for a minute and picture the route she was going to take. Anyway, she'd run a hose."

"Your mother?"

"We tried to keep it quiet, but even so, kids at school heard. Stuff gets around. This was nearly three years ago."

I stared at the side door of the Volvo, which had a subtle dent in it, as if it had been punched. I wondered why she was telling me this. A dry husk of a bug lay overturned near my foot and I kicked at it. "What did you do?"

"I turned off the car, of course. Then I called 911."

"Do you know why she did it?"

She shook her head. "Not really. Depression, I guess. She wasn't a happy person, even though she took a lot of happy drugs. They just made her crazy. I once watched her peel an entire onion, one layer at a time, while listening to the Brandenburg Concertos. By the end of that onion, she was a complete mess, crying like a baby." She paused. "Your dad was some kind of musician or something, wasn't he?"

"My dad's alive and well," I said. "He just left town, that's all. Business reasons."

"You don't have to pretend with me, you know. I understand. It's lousy and selfish and you spend a long time getting over the fact that someone you thought you knew could be so inconsiderate, but you do get over it. Eventually you heal. I never even went to therapy, though they said I could."

"I'm not pretending," I said. "He's alive. He just moved to Canada."

She took a step back. "I'm sorry. Some kids were talking and it sounded like, well—oh, God. I feel really stupid now. You must think I'm a first-class idiot."

"I don't think that."

"But something happened, right?"

"We went on a road trip. My mom freaked and called the cops. It was a big misunderstanding, mostly. Nobody's dead."

She didn't say anything for a few seconds, then looked up at me. "I feel like I just took my clothes off in front of a stranger."

"I won't tell anyone, I promise."

"I told you, lots of people know. I guess I figured you did, too. It just feels funny since you didn't—almost as if I was bragging. I wouldn't brag about a thing like this."

"It's *okay.*" I looked at her feet. She had on penny loafers and ankle socks with tiny hearts on them.

"You know the worst thing? I mean, back then, when it first happened? I was sure everyone was staring at me, thinking, There's that girl whose mother was so unhappy she killed herself. I felt like I'd been outlined with a Magic Marker."

"Wasn't the worst part missing her?" I glanced over at the place where Judith's mother's life had slowly flickered away. Outside, the wind swept rain against the garage door.

"No, not really. We didn't have the best relationship. Can I ask *you* something? Do you think I've changed? I mean, since you've known me." She paused, looked suddenly embarrassed. "Never mind." She bit her lip. "I won't always be this way. Unattractive, that is. I'm going to grow out of it. My mother was beautiful and when she was my age, you'd never have guessed."

I wanted to give her a hug. But when I reached out to put my arms around her, she jumped.

"Don't."

"Please," I said.

"All right. But it doesn't mean anything."

She sort of slumped forward and put her face on my shoulder, and I held her. Her body wasn't soft at all, as I'd expected, but lean and hard and no-nonsense. I wasn't sure, but I thought she'd begun to cry. The door to the house creaked open and Toby padded out to join us. When we didn't pay him any attention, he sighed, turned a few circles, and settled down onto the concrete floor a few feet away.

I spent a lot of time wandering around downtown, smoking cigarettes, examining my reflection in shop windows. Sometimes I'd go into our town's one music store, Eastern Sounds, and try out instruments. The place was owned by the Ricci family, and if the son, Philip, was working, he'd let you try anything. His mother was tougher—she had no patience for browsers, and if you said, "Can I see that Fender?" she'd ask, icily, "Are you planning to buy, or just look?" I still had much of the cash my dad had left me. I'd been spending it at a steady rate all winter, mostly on small things. I wasn't sure what he'd expected me to do with it. It was hardly a college fund, but there was slightly over seven hundred dollars, which I kept tucked inside an old basketball sneaker in my closet. I'd been considering guitar lessons, but I didn't know who to take from, and I knew that I didn't want to be a "schooled" player. The people I most respected, from Nicky and my dad to the musicians I read about in *Guitar Player*, were the self-taught ones. After what had happened to Nicky's SG, I had an idea.

"I'll buy you another," I said to him. "You pick. All I want is lessons. Show me licks, whatever you want. Maybe like a couple days a week or something."

"You're going to buy me a guitar?" he said. We were across from school at Whitey's Garage, next door to Flight Three, examining the wreck of a car that had lurched in front of a commuter train a few days earlier. There was dried blood all over the upholstery, dashboard, and doors. The safety glass of the windshield, fractured in a thousand places, was greenish-white and folded up on itself. The whole left side of the car had crumpled like a piece of butcher paper and the steering wheel was so turned around that it now faced out.

"It'll be mine, but you take care of it. In return, you work with me. I want to be good, I mean really good."

The way he looked at me, I understood I was asking for the impossible. He'd have to cut me open, rewire me from the toes up. He stamped his feet and breathed on his hands, then went around to the other side of the wreck to peer in the window.

"Dead," he said. "Just like that."

"They say she hit the accelerator instead of the brake."

He continued circling the wreck, fascinated. I thought about how there were places in the world where it was like a hole got punched through time. Standing here, we were connected directly to the very last seconds of her life. There were things she'd wanted, too. I almost felt I could sense them, those unrealized hopes, still hanging in the air.

"What she hit," Nicky said, "was a train."

A *few days later*, in the cafeteria, he came to me with an alternative plan. "How much you got?"

"Five, six hundred dollars."

"Dwight can get us a half-pound of 'lumbo for that." He held out a tiny glassine envelope with a few resiny specks of pot the color of maple sugar in it.

"Jesus," I said, "put that away. Someone might be watching."

"We could sell it, double your money."

"Are you serious? You're going to trust Dwight?"

"He's cool. That other time was a coincidence."

"Nicky, this really wasn't what I had in mind."

"You're just giving your money to the capitalists like a fool. Eastern pays three hundred for a guitar, sells it to you for six. If you do what I'm saying, you got six hundred extra. It's like getting the guitar for free."

I didn't like the idea, and I didn't trust Dwight at all, but I understood Nicky well enough to know that if I didn't go along, he wouldn't forget about it. I could buy the nicest guitar in the world and to him it would always be a symbol of how we'd been taken. Probably, he wouldn't even touch the thing.

"What do I do?" I said.

Dwight called me at home two nights later. My mother was cleaning up from dinner and Hal was upstairs changing clothes for his weekly squash game. I took the phone into the TV room and tried not to sound too suspicious, since I was still within her earshot.

"It's about that thing," Dwight said. "That thing you wanted."

"Right," I said. "What's the story?"

"I can do it for you, but it will have to be a frontage situation.

It will have to be immediate, too. There's a shortage of product happening."

"So, what are you saying?"

"I'll need six and a quarter. Can I stop by this evening?"

There was no way I wanted my mother seeing Dwight. But I wasn't supposed to go out, either. I had a crucial math test in the morning that it was understood I'd be studying for. Fronting money was stupid, but short of going along with him, which probably wasn't an option anyway, I didn't see that I had a choice. A couple of people at school had already placed orders with me and I was going to look bad if I didn't come up with something to sell. "That's no good," I said.

"Then what do you want me to do? You want to do a drop-off? This has to happen tonight, my friend."

"The wreck," I whispered. "Whitey's Garage."

"Too close to home. Ever heard the expression 'Don't shit where you eat'?"

I thought some more. "In the park, behind the shopping center? There's some playground equipment. There's this rocket ship thing you can climb on. Under that."

There was silence for a moment. I wondered where he was calling from. "Okay, that'll work. The other thing will be there by one A.M. I gotta go nearly to Philly for it."

I made an excuse about needing to borrow some notes, put $625 in a brown paper bag, and rode my bike to the park. I placed it carefully under the rocket, anchoring the corners with two small rocks, then walked around in circles a few times to see how visible it was. You'd have to actually be looking for something to see it, I decided. I checked my watch—it was nearly eight. I pedaled home.

It was difficult to study. I kept staring at the clock, picking up my book, putting it back down again. I was still doing poorly in school, but my mother left me alone about it for the most part these days. Neither she nor my dad had gone to college, and I knew it was what she wanted for me in a big way. From time to time, I'd buckle down and work, and when I did this, my grades picked up, which gave me a certain amount of confidence. I wasn't stupid. On the other hand, an argument could be made that I lacked common sense, considering how much money I'd just left out in a public park.

Around eleven, I slipped out the door, rode back to the shopping center, and checked under the rocket. The money was gone. It was cold out and I lit a cigarette to keep warm, turned up the collar of my Army jacket, which was lined and had pockets everywhere. I kept something in each one: matches, candy, cigarettes, rolling papers, spare change, a pen, my Swiss Army knife, Kleenex for my allergies, guitar picks, a pocket Bible some guy had given me on the street one day downtown, two airline-sized bottles of Smirnoff, a condom. I liked the idea of myself as portable and self-contained. After a while, I lay down on a picnic table and stared up at the sky.

I must have fallen asleep. When I opened my eyes, I was looking right into the face of a deer. We stared at each other for three or four seconds before it pulled backward, turned, and went bouncing off into the night. I checked my watch and saw that it was past twelve. To get my blood moving, I decided to walk a bit. I did a circle of the entire shopping center, smoking as I went, my sneakers scuffing softly along the blacktop. The Dairy Queen was closed now for the winter, but there were still a few cars parked out in front of it, engines grumbling. I gave them a wide berth and went back into the park.

I checked under the rocket again, checked under other pieces of playground equipment, the swings, the spinning platform that, when I was little, I used to ride until I was dizzy. I took another walk.

By one-thirty, my fingers and toes completely numb, the true extent of my foolishness began to come clear to me. Even so, I stayed in the park until nearly three, smoking half a pack of Old Golds, before finally giving up and going home.

* * *

33

I failed the test the next morning. I could barely keep my eyes open for it. Afterward, I found Nicky in one of the music practice rooms staring at a cello. He rarely went to his classes anymore, but had figured out a way to slip the lock on the band room door and get instruments out of storage. When I told him what had happened, he rocked his head sadly from side to side. He put the cello back in its case and the two of us went up to Flight Three.

Dwight was in his office. "Guys," he said, as if he couldn't be happier to see anyone. "Come on in."

He was tall, with graying hair and a turquoise pendant he wore on a leather strap around his neck. There were three Frisbees hanging on the wall behind him, and in the corner by the window a pile of softball stuff, some mitts, two or three aluminum bats. The state of New Jersey paid this man some kind of salary to play games with teenagers, supposedly to keep them out of trouble. A coffee mug on his desk read, *Take as needed.*

"Where's my money?" I said.

He shook his head to indicate it wasn't cool to discuss this so loudly. "I should be asking you."

I could feel myself trembling, not just with anger at him, but with humiliation. Until this moment, I'd been hoping there was some other explanation—he'd had a flat tire, the guy wasn't home, something. But what this was going to boil down to, now and forever, was my gullibility.

"Sit down, man," he said. "Have some coffee, if you like. Chill a little. This has got you upset and I can understand that, but you've got to focus. I went to the place you said, but there was nothing there."

"Bullshit." I picked up a pencil holder off his desk and threw it at the wall. It was plastic and didn't break, but pencils scattered all over the floor.

"I really hope we're not going to have to have a scene here," he said, rising.

Nicky put a hand on my arm. "Come on, let's go."

"I don't even believe this," I said. I shook Nicky off and he moved over to the window, where he peered out and down toward the street.

"If you don't leave, I'm going to have to call the cops," said Dwight.

"Again?"

"Get over it." His voice was suddenly harsher. "Stop acting like a child. You want to run with the big boys, learn to play by their rules. I don't know what happened to your cash, but hey—maybe you've learned a lesson here, what do you think?"

Nicky picked up one of the softball bats, turned, and swung it, catching Dwight across the stomach, as well as part of his left arm. It was one fluid movement—grasp, turn, and swing—and it surprised me as much as it did Dwight, who crumpled to the floor, taking his coffee mug with him. For a second there was absolute silence in the room, as if all of us were holding our breath. Then I heard him begin to vomit. At least Nicky hadn't killed him.

"Let's go," Nicky said, his voice emotionless. For a moment I considered taking things, Dwight's wallet, or the house stereo (a piece of crap, but that wasn't really the point). Instead, I just followed him back into the front room, then down the stairs. This time, we walked out the front door.

Downtown, Nicky got this guy he knew, Oliver, a drunk who washed dishes at the A&J Luncheonette, to buy him a bottle of Heaven Hill. I didn't feel like drinking.

"Aren't you worried?" I asked. The whole way up from Flight Three, I'd been nervously scanning around for the police. Since Nicky was already on probation, an assault charge could probably put him away for some real time.

"Dwight won't mess with me. I could get him in too much trouble." He took out a bandanna and blew his nose loudly into it, folded it back up. "You think I hurt him bad?"

"Are you kidding?" I saw him swinging the bat into Dwight's midsection. "You probably broke a rib or two, anyway." With the exception of the war games he played with his G.I. Joes, I'd never seen Nicky do anything remotely violent before.

"Dude had it coming," he said.

I believed this, too, though I still felt fairly miserable about the whole thing, losing all that money. Nicky's expression was distant, his voice flat, almost as if he were being spoken *through*. I admired him for having such a simple vision of how justice ought to operate in the world. At the same time, I knew it would be a hard way for him to go through life.

I left Nicky near the bus station and walked in the direction of my dad's old apartment. I wasn't in the mood to return to school, and I'd been thinking about the place recently. A couple of college kids had moved in almost immediately after he'd left, but a few days earlier I'd noticed a bunch of stuff, including some of his furniture, out on the sidewalk, and I figured they were gone.

A girl on a bicycle, dressed entirely in green and pedaling along the sidewalk, very nearly ran me over. "Watch it," I shouted. It was Judith.

"I'm *so* sorry," she said, getting her balance again. We hadn't spoken since the day in her garage. She had on an oversized green T-shirt and green tights, her face covered in green paint. "I wasn't paying attention."

"What are you doing?"

"My work study. I student teach at Davis Elementary. They're doing a play about life in a pond, and I'm the frog. Once I got this stuff on, though, I discovered I couldn't get it off." She was riding an old Robin Hood and she gestured to a white pharmacy bag in the handlebar basket. "I was just picking up some cold cream. What are you doing?"

"My dad used to live here."

"Can I come up with you?"

"I doubt we'll be able to get in."

She was already off her bike, locking it to a streetlight. "If it's okay, I'll use the bathroom. I really want to get this junk off me."

The strip of masking tape with his name had long ago been

taken off the bell. I pushed the button, waited, and when there was no answer, we went in. At the top of the stairs, we paused in front of the door, which was metal, painted with primer, a Grateful Dead insignia stuck in the middle of it. I knocked, then tried the knob and found it turned.

The apartment was completely empty. No furniture, nothing on the walls. You could see places where the last tenants had nailed things up, the gouged plaster and holes. Over by the wall against which he'd kept his sofa, there were a couple of cans of paint and some spackle, and I guessed that the landlord was getting ready to fix things up. I wasn't surprised, but I was a bit disappointed. Part of me had hoped to open the door and find everything as it had been: newspapers piled up on the floor, guitars leaning against the furniture. I thought about the rust-colored easy chair that was always my seat. It had such big, wide armrests you could put a peanut butter sandwich and a glass of milk side by side on one of them while you watched television and not have to worry about them falling.

I walked into the back bedroom, which was equally vacant. Someone had stubbed out a cigarette on the windowsill. In the bathroom I noted a crack in the medicine cabinet mirror that hadn't been there. There was an almost used-up roll of toilet paper, a sliver of greenish soap in the dish. Judith followed me in and took out her cold cream.

"Ribit," she said. "Excuse me."

I went back out into the kitchen area, which was just a corner of the living room, and began looking through drawers. In one of the cabinets over the sink, I found a bicentennial water glass, one of a set of six he'd received free with an oil change. They were cheap, and the others had all broken over the years— I'd been responsible for breaking a few myself. This was the last one, and you could still make out the picture of Benjamin Franklin on one side, the American flag on the other. I took it down and gave it a rinse, letting the water spill over until it ran cold. Then I took a swallow.

"No towels," said Judith, coming in to join me. Her face was dripping wet. She used the tail of her T-shirt, then waved her hands back and forth in the air to dry them. "Did you ever live here?"

"Not exactly."

"It's an okay place. Small, but homey. What was here?"

"One of those fold-out sofas, a wooden coffee table. This big easy chair I liked to sit in. Let's see, a little Zenith portable TV, a cheapo stereo system. A few albums." Describing it, I was suddenly struck by the meager nature of what he'd had. As if he'd known all along he wouldn't be staying.

"Only a few?"

"Well, he actually had a couple hundred, but when they first decided to get divorced, he stored them in my mom's basement. A few months after he moved out, they got flooded. He said she did it deliberately, but I don't think so. We eventually just drove them to the dump." I remembered holding my breath against the stink, watching my mother heave the cardboard boxes over into the huge bin.

"Can I?" she asked, gesturing to the glass. I handed it to her and she took a swallow. She was tall, almost as tall as me. I liked the way the line of her dark hair bounced around against her white neck when she tilted back her head. "You don't know where he is, do you?" she asked, returning the glass.

"No."

We stared at each other for a moment. "I've got about seventy-five bucks," I said, finally. "Money he gave me. There was more, but I did something stupid with the rest and this is what I've got left."

"Something stupid?"

"Very."

"I'm going to assume that I don't want to know the details of this. But you know what I think? I think you need to spend the rest of that money. Make a clean sweep, you know? Clear out the old mental closet."

It made sense to me.

We went back down and got her bike, then walked to Eastern Sounds. They only had a few instruments in my price range. I settled on a cherry-red Hondo, made in Korea, a Les Paul copy with one black pickup in the center. It was used, and the action was a little high, but it wasn't bad. There was no case.

"It's pretty," said Judith as we stood outside the shop, our reflections shining off the big window full of colorful instruments, sheet music, and effects boxes. The instrument was of less interest to her than the fact that I'd bought it. As I stood with it resting on my foot, in all its gleaming, cheap promise, it seemed a kind of physical proof that the two of us came from utterly different worlds, no matter how much we might want to pretend otherwise. She checked her watch. "I've got to get back to class. Eighth-period econ, if you can believe it. Yuck. But I need an A so I can go to the best college, so I can get into the best law school, so I can get a high-paying job and be incredibly unhappy with it." She smiled. "No time to fool around."

I watched her wobble off down the sidewalk, very nearly picking off another pedestrian before angling onto the street and beginning to pedal more vigorously. I kept watching until she was just a distant spot of green, and then she was gone. Tucking the guitar under one arm, I went off to find Nicky.

Part Two

3

D ear Sirs,
   I am presently an inmate at a penal institution here in Illinois doing fifteen to twenty for armed robbery. One of the guys in my cellblock got a flyer from you with "Prices Too Good to Believe." I am a rock musician and it is my only goal that when I get out I will make it BIG. So I sent you $60 for one of your Gopher Fuzzes, which you say Jimi Hendrix used to use. As you can imagine, that's a lot of money for me, since they only pay us fifty cents an hour here in the prison electronics shop. I still haven't got the box. Could you check it out for me? When I am a big SUCCESS, I will be happy to endorse your company, which I know to be the best in the business, and very honorable.

   Yours Faithfully,
   Furry Couch #C-563-2798

Dear Mr. Couch,
   Thank you for your letter. How are things in Illinois? Here in New York it is very hot. So hot, in fact, that when our air-conditioning went out a couple of weeks ago, we had to close down production for a little while. This led to a small backlog of orders which we are now endeavoring to fill. Gophers are

43

at this very moment being assembled, and should be going out within the next week to ten days. If you haven't gotten your order by then, please don't hesitate to get back in touch with us.

Sincerely,
Spencer Markus
Customer Service Rep.
Mutronics, Inc.

Dear Mutronics, Inc.,

I have one of your original Gophers, and I've had it since the early seventies, and I love it. But when it broke on me about six months ago, I couldn't get anyone to repair the sucker. So I mailed it to you along with a ten-dollar bill. I have a regular gig here at the Holiday Inn in Durango, and my leads sound lousy without it. Also, I think it is probably a collector's item, and I want it back. Could you please check around? Mine is the one with red glitter pasted all over it. Incidentally, you guys are the balls, even if you are a little slow.

Sounding bad in Colorado,
Duke Davin

Dear Duke,

Thanks for your letter. I am sorry to report that we have no record of having received your unit. As you know, the U.S. Post Office is not all that selective as to whom they hire, and sometimes sending cash through them is not the best idea. I'm not saying this is what happened, I only present it as a possibility. However, we'll keep our eyes open, and if a vintage Gopher with red glitter on it turns up, you'll be hearing from us. In the meantime, I'm enclosing one of our current price lists for your convenience (though please note: the Iguana listed is not currently available). Good luck down there at the Holiday Inn.

Sincerely,
Spencer Markus
Customer Service Rep.
Mutronics, Inc.

To Whom It May Concern,
 I am writing on behalf of one of our readers, Mr. Curtis Pomerleau of Gray. Mr. Pomerleau, it seems, has written you on numerous occasions regarding the order he placed with your company for a "Chameleon" guitar synthesizer. In the past I have found that the companies I contact are more than eager to clear up what is usually a simple matter of a misunderstanding. However, in the unusual case that nothing is done, we will print the company name in our paper, along with a caveat. I'm sure you'll want to take care of this matter at your earliest convenience.

Barb Pressman
Action Line
Augusta Times
Augusta, Maine

Dear Ms. Pressman,
 Thanks for your letter. It seems you and I are in the same line of work. Let me tell you, problem solver to problem solver, just exactly what's going on.
 Mr. Pomerleau wisely chose our product, the only guitar synthesizer I am aware of on the market that costs less than $500. Right now, however, we are making some design changes on the Chameleon, incorporating new technology we picked up from the Japanese. Rather than send him one of our old models, which tended to screech and whine, we thought it in his best interest to hold the order temporarily until a new production

run on the unit. Let me assure you that when we do send his order out (and I'm told it will be very soon), Mr. Pomerleau will be more than satisfied. I've enclosed some promotional material on our company, just so that you'll know we are a legitimate concern. The man in the Captain America outfit is Jerry Perry, our founder and president. In reading it over, I hope you'll see that we have nothing but the highest respect for our customers.

Sincerely,
Spencer Markus
Customer Service Rep.
Mutronics, Inc.

4

A *union began* trying to organize us. They hung around the entrance on Twenty-third Street with yellow cards, offering five dollars if we signed. We were under strict orders from Jerry not to. He stormed around the offices as if his shoes were on fire. This was not what he needed, not with the company already teetering. The union people had a violent look to them; it was obvious they were planning something. After a few days they stopped trying to get us to sign the cards, but didn't go away. Instead, they leaned up against the building drinking sodas, talked quietly in small groups, smoked cigarettes.

"Some guy was asking me about you," said Randy, our product tester, as the two of us walked to lunch. A heavy black woman of about forty who wore overalls most of the time, she kept her short hair pomaded straight back and loved rock and roll, particularly anything with loud, distorted guitar. She'd been at Mutronics almost since Jerry had founded the company, and she was one of the few people I talked to at all. I liked her. Randy didn't seem, like many of the other senior employees, to have something she was trying to prove in terms of how cool she was. She was just herself, a fierce, independent continent of flesh in a black leather vest. The beginnings of a tiny beard curled unabashedly from the corners of her chin.

"What do you mean, asking about me?"

"I don't know. He asked me do I know a Spencer Markus. I

told him to fuck off. Union slobs. They ought to leave a person alone, let him do his job."

I didn't like the idea that they knew my name. It occurred to me that now might be an excellent time to quit and find something else to do. Already I was beginning to have uneasy dreams in which various customers from around the country who had been screwed one way or another by Mutronics came to New York with the specific purpose of tracking me down and punching me in the nose.

"Which one was it?" I asked. Some of their faces had grown familiar. There was, for instance, a small man with a yellow sports coat, mirrored sunglasses, and blue-black hair who seemed to be in charge. I tried to imagine fighting him. He was small, but he'd probably be well-prepared. Brass knuckles, maybe even a blackjack hidden in his sock.

"I don't know," said Randy. "Big guy in a cheap suit." She took out a toothpick and worked it around her upper incisors. She had fine, white teeth, the front two edged in gold. "I'm just glad no one knows *my* name. Being the front man isn't always the best deal."

After lunch I went to Jerry's office. "Give me something else to do," I said. "I don't want to be the scapegoat around here."

"Scapegoat?" Jerry planted a dead cigar butt firmly between his teeth and chewed it for a moment. A thick, broad-shouldered man with iron-gray hair that stuck out in a different place every day, he scared me a little. He looked like a former professional wrestler. We had almost no communication. When he passed me in the hall, he either ignored me entirely or eyed me with such suspicion it was as if he'd never seen me before in his life, or perhaps suspected me of spying for the competition.

"Since I sign the letters, I'm afraid that everyone will blame me for what's going on."

He grunted. "What else can you do, Markus? Run an oscilloscope? Design products? Track down a bad transistor?" He stared at me, his face a great moon of indifference. Then he broke into a big smile, the one he probably used on loan officers at the bank. "Hang in there, buddy," he said. "You're doing an excellent job. We're about to turn the corner here."

Behind him, electronic light sculptures made up of red, green, and blue LEDs set against a background of black velvet blinked on and off like carnival rides at night. I recognized them from one of the older catalogs as Disco Light Art, another product of his that had died an early death.

"All right," I said. "I just thought I'd ask."

"Don't worry, you're completely safe here as long as you stick with me. We're all going to weather this thing together." He handed me a fresh stack of mail, and I retreated to my desk.

I'd been working at Mutronics since June, when I'd answered a classified ad in the *Village Voice* that read, simply, "Rock and Roll Customer Service." I knew about them vaguely. For years they'd been running the same small ad in the back of guitar magazines, a pen-and-ink drawing of a screaming head, hair sticking out in all directions (I now suspected this cartoon was modeled on Jerry), and underneath it a product list with prices. The day of my interview, I spent twenty minutes in the reception area with a crew of applicants that included a guy with a purple Mohawk and someone with a spiderweb tattooed over one half of his face. The fact that I'd worn a jacket and tie seemed to help, because although I'd been the last to arrive, I was the first one called.

My interviewer, a tall guy with a big nose and a white chemise Lacoste with the collar up, introduced himself as Lenny De-Marino and led me to a tiny room way in the back of the factory. "Okay," he said, handing me a guitar. "Play something."

"Like what?"

"I don't care." He looked bored. "Jerry wants someone who can play the guitar. It's not part of the job, he just wants to know that you can."

I tried to guess what Lenny DeMarino might want to hear, but all I could think of was Billy Joel, since Lenny looked and sounded like he was from Long Island. I'd muddled my way through four years of college doing almost nothing but music: I'd bashed out punk versions of Beatles songs with the Blue Meanies, space-jammed with Astral Tape-Head, even strummed bluegrass for two guys who were learning banjo and who called themselves the Sons of Scruggs. But I did not know any Billy Joel.

For a while, junior year, I'd taken jazz lessons, and I'd been practicing a Charlie Parker tune, "Donna Lee," ever since. It was like a speech I'd learned by rote in a foreign language; I didn't understand it at all, but on a good day I could make it sound convincing. When I got to the end I always stopped dead, as if I'd just sprinted a quarter mile.

The strings on the guitar were at least two years old and smelled like rust. I shot through the opening bars, watching proudly as my left hand seemed to move of its own accord. I couldn't imagine any of the other applicants would show them something like this. They'd probably give me my own office. Then I had the strange feeling that I was repeating myself. Was I really? Had I forgotten something? I faltered, trying to re-member, told myself to stay calm, not to think so hard. It was too late. My fingers jammed up and I froze, lost.

"Um," I said, staring helplessly at the neck.

"A jazz guy." Lenny gave me a patronizing look. "We're more of a meat-and-potatoes, rock-and-roll crowd around here."

"I like pretty much everything," I said, conscious of how lame this sounded.

He wasn't interested. He took the instrument from me and leaned it up against the edge of the table. "I assume you can type?"

I became official apologist for the company. Well before the union showed up, it was apparent that things were not going well. Lenny needed someone to help him answer the mail that was flooding in. I soon understood he had no intention of answering *any* mail himself, now that he had an assistant. Every morning I'd squeeze myself onto the F train, take it to West Twenty-third Street, hike a block and a half, and ascend in the graffiti-covered elevator to the factory on the fifth and sixth floors of a gray, turn-of-the-century building. After sweeping the mouse droppings off my small steel desk, I'd settle down to work. I tapped out letters to people named Roy in Oklahoma City, Tony in Green Bay, even a number of inmates at various prisons. I apologized for orders paid for but never received, also repairs that had somehow disappeared into the systemless chaos, then just as mysteriously reappeared a year later and been shipped back, still broken. I apologized on triplicate forms to Better Business Bureaus, nationwide. Though at first I tried to treat each problem that came up as if it were unusual, a small mistake that might easily be righted, I soon realized that this was not the case. Mutronics was a ship with a rotten hull, and while the rest of the crew sat on the deck getting suntans, I'd been sent below with an IBM Selectric to bail.

The company was an anachronism, a little piece of the early seventies that had broken loose and was still spinning in place. There was a big dusty poster of Jimi Hendrix in the main hallway, its edges curling up, its lower left corner stained with what looked like coffee. Jerry kept an old claw-foot bathtub in the hallway outside his office and had a Hammond organ set up along one side of his desk. With the exception of the actual workforce, who were mostly Hispanic and Asian and confined to the huge production area in the back, the staff were longhaired guys in their early forties, weathered and tired from the strain of trying to be both businessmen *and* subscribers to a worldview that required total disdain for people like themselves. None of them noticed me or even said hello. I was virtually transparent to everyone but Lenny DeMarino, and he spent most of the day in his office, reading automobile magazines.

When Randy went on break, I'd often go back to her room

and plug in. Getting out of sight of my typewriter was liberating, and I passed quickly through the stale air of the factory like an escapee. I'd hook together three or four effects boxes and be amazed at how the company guitar came alive in my hands. Sometimes I'd rock out, hoping that Lenny would pass by and hear me, but if he did, he never mentioned it. More often, though, I'd experiment. With all that processing between me and the amp, I could conjure up church bells, a B-52 with engine trouble, a crowd of violins. I'd stay back there as long as I could, happy just to be away from Lenny and his endless supply of letters.

My *girlfriend, Sally,* and I sat together on the sofa watching "M*A*S*H." She was doing her best to ignite the end of a tiny roach that wouldn't cooperate. Rick, our other roommate, was in the kitchen cooking one of his private meals, seemingly random mixtures that filled a frying pan and usually involved chopped vegetables, Hamburger Helper, and a fried egg. We'd been living together, the three of us, for nearly five months now, in an apartment in Brooklyn Rick had inherited from one of his sisters who'd gone off to join the Peace Corps.

"Listen," she said. On the television, Hawkeye and Trapper John were alone in their tent. Laughter swelled around them, then died quickly, like noise from a passing car. "Tune out the dialogue and just listen to the background. It's like thousands of invisible people."

"You just notice more on this show because all the operating-room scenes don't have a laugh track. It's really obvious when it suddenly kicks in."

"Imagine, though, just for a second. Maybe that's death. Maybe, when we die, we go live forever in old sitcoms."

"People do that already. You don't have to die."

She sat quietly, staring at a spot just over the television. She had a round face with small features, an insistent, shapely body she did her best to hide in loose-fitting T-shirts and jeans. Sally had wanted to be an actress in college, but never got cast in anything but minor roles because there was always someone prettier, or with more "personality." When I'd met her, she was dealing pot for an old boyfriend, Steven, who rode his motorcycle up every fourth weekend or so to bring her another half pound. It was a relationship she didn't know how to get out of, but when she'd finally gotten up the nerve to tell him about us, he admitted that he had someone new himself, a fifteen-year-old. Which, she'd pointed out to me coolly, was exactly how old Sally had been when she started going out with him.

" 'Life is what happens while you're waiting for life to begin,' " she said. "I saw it spray-painted on the back of an exterminator's truck today." She dropped the roach onto the table, stood up, and walked out through the hall, into the unoccupied room that was over the bedroom we shared. When she didn't come back, I got to my feet and went to join her.

She was examining one of her pinecones, running a finger along its wide-spread seed pods. The spare room had a bookcase in it, and she'd been filling its shelves with things she found in the park: interesting-looking rocks, chestnuts, green-rinded, brainlike Osage oranges. At the beginning of summer, Sally had applied and been accepted for a job as a ranger. It was a real job, a city job, with benefits, and we were both sort of amazed. It fit her, though. She didn't actually know much about about the specifics of plants and trees and birds, but she did have a general enthusiasm for nature. In college, she'd decorated her room with posters of solitary mountain climbers, waterfalls, and tree frogs.

"I want to move up here." Her lips tensed the way they always did when she'd made up her mind about something.

"What's the matter?"

"I need more room. Since this one's available, I think I ought to use it."

"Room for what?"

"*Room.* Just to be."

I glanced out the window. The woman who lived across the

street had no shades on her windows and often walked around her apartment naked. Lately, I'd been coming in at night and standing in the dark, watching her, even though the distance was far enough that you couldn't see much. She was walking back and forth now, clothed, talking on the phone. She looked straight back at me for the first time, then turned abruptly and passed out of my sight.

"What are you staring at?" asked Sally, in a more gentle tone. "Look at me. I'm not breaking up with you. I just want to feel a little less crowded. I pay the same amount of rent, I think I should have my own room."

"No problem," I said, though I sensed the opposite. "I'll sneak up, you'll sneak down. It'll be fun."

She stared at me. "Why don't you just quit?" she said. "We'll go to Europe. I'm sure if I asked, my dad would loan me enough for the both of us. Think about it—Switzerland, the Alps, Italy, all that art. Or we could go someplace wilder, like India."

I shook my head. "It's not the right time."

"It's the perfect time, Spencer. It's autumn. The tourists are going home, prices are coming down."

"I mean for me. I can't afford it, and I don't want to go into debt to your dad. He doesn't even like me. I couldn't stand it."

"Well, I can't stand this," she said, kicking at a loose floor-board. The house wasn't in very good shape. The second night we'd all stayed there a forty-pound chunk of stone had broken away from under the third-floor window, waking all of us when it hit the dirt with an impressive wallop. Still, I sort of liked it. I liked the gas lantern out next to the stoop, the way the windows sagged from years of gravity, like an old person's eyes.

"I'll definitely go someplace with you," I said. "Just not right now."

She had a top-quality backpack and tent that an outdoorsy uncle had given her for graduation, a sturdy set of hiking boots she marched about the park in for practice. Every Sunday, she spread out the travel section of the paper and checked airfares. She was just waiting for me.

"What the hell is so great about what you're doing?"

"It's the music industry," I said. "I've got a foot in the door."

"You're a clerk, Spencer. I mean, I don't want to be discouraging, but face up to it. You're a clerk and you get paid to lie to people. And not even very well."

"I lie very well. I'm a champion liar."

She rolled her eyes. "I meant your pay. You're not saving anything. You're just wearing a little path in the dirt between here and lower Manhattan, back and forth every day like all the other moles in this city, and pretty soon it will be so deep you won't be able to see over the top anymore."

"You better ask Rick," I said. "It's his place."

We went back into the living room where he was eating, a comic book propped open in front of him. Sally told him what she wanted to do.

He swallowed and wiped his mouth on a piece of paper towel. Rick was big and good-looking in a pale, Nordic way, with delicate skin and almost no beard. When he listened to you, there was something almost calculatedly thoughtful about his expression, like a judge considering a case, and I often wondered if he'd practiced this to make up for the fact that when he smiled, his face transformed into that of an enthusiastic child.

"I was thinking of making that into a darkroom. Or a study. But now that I'm writing, I can't see that I'll need it for anything." Although he'd recently taken a job, Rick was living primarily off a trust fund, experimenting with careers. At first it was photography, but his camera had been snatched in Battery Park while he tried to convince a balloon seller to let him take his picture. His latest project was a screenplay. He wouldn't say what it was about, but we could hear him at it late at night, typing one or two words, then silence for minutes, then three more keys striking, then more silence. At the rate he was going, we joked, completion date would be sometime in the next century. Still, I envied him. He didn't actually need money. Everything he did, he did because he felt like it.

"She needs a place to *be*," I said.

55

We stayed in the living room while she moved her things. September had arrived feeling very much like the middle of July, and although there were fans going in every room, all they did was blow around the heat. Even the cockroaches who shared our kitchen seemed to trudge these days instead of scamper.

After Sally had finished and shut the door, Rick flicked a bottle cap that hit me in the forehead. "Let's go bowling," he said. He'd been sitting with his feet out the window and drinking the same beer for nearly a half hour. I was staring at last Sunday's crossword from the *Times*, wondering whether, in light of the fact that unhappy customers were now apparently showing up in person and asking for me by name, it might be worth it to take Sally's suggestion.

"I don't want to bowl."

"It'll relax you, change your mood." He poked my arm. "It'll be air-conditioned."

"Bowling makes me nervous. It's a stupid sport. It's stupid to even call it a sport."

"More people bowl on any given weekend," he said, "than attend professional football games in an entire season. Think about that." He put his beer down and wiped his mouth with the back of his hand. "Anyway, we don't have to bowl. I'm just thinking we could go out. Cheer you up." He pulled his chair closer. "If you're worried, I can tell you what to do. Get away from her. Pay less attention. She'll come back at you like a spicy enchilada. Women *like* to be treated badly."

"That's ridiculous. And I'm not worried."

"It's the truth. Just nobody wants to admit it."

I didn't have a lot of respect for Rick's theories, but I did admire his love life. On weekends, a succession of different women, some from our school, some he'd just met at clubs, came and camped in his bedroom. I usually ran into them on my way to or from the shower, and I'd introduce myself. They always appeared slightly amused, as if I were a weird cousin of Rick's he'd warned them about in advance. Sally gave them hard, silent looks. His current girlfriend was named Susu (Sally called her "So-So"), and she sometimes wore chokers, black velvet ones like the women in the whiskey ads. She had another boyfriend, who was some kind of artist out in Santa Fe, and was only in New York earning money so she could go out and join him. It sounded odd to me, this split loyalty, but Rick didn't appear to have a problem with it.

"Come on," he said. "We'll go have some fun."

I knocked, opened the door, and told Sally we were going out. She was writing something, and she looked up from her pad in surprise.

"Guy stuff," I said. "We're going to have a few beers, talk sports, you know."

"Why can't I come?" She picked up a rubber band and stretched it back and forth. "What are you really going to do?"

"I won't be back late."

"I get it. Bonding." She shot the rubber band up at the light fixture. "I'll be fine here."

We drove into the city in Rick's Vega, crossing over the Brooklyn Bridge, then veering down to the FDR Drive, snaking up along the East Side. The car had a hole in its muffler, and every time he accelerated, it sounded like a work crew drilling concrete.

Rick and I had been roommates for four years at a small college in upstate New York that was known for its hockey team and not much else. In our senior year we'd moved into a rundown apartment across from the river and the railroad tracks. It probably wasn't the healthiest situation, being together so long, and we'd had our share of shouting matches, even one episode where, drunk and full of self-importance over some perceived insult, I'd tried to wrestle him, only to find myself facedown in the snow, his knee pressed into the base of my spine. But basically we still got along. Rick was a minister's son and a military school graduate from the Midwest who believed in God, Clint Eastwood movies, and the Chicago Cubs, more or less in that order. In that last apartment, a tiny house, really, with crumbling plaster and warped fake paneling that bulged out from the walls like a funhouse mirror, his room had been upstairs, mine down. We were a mile downstream from a paper mill, and the air was constantly thick with the sulfur smell of the pulper. Sally lived on campus, but often spent the night with me on the secondhand mattress I'd bought and laid out on the floor. At seven o'clock each morning, a freight train would pass by, setting the whole house rocking, and if there was sun, since my window faced east, it would suddenly start strobing as its rays were broken up by the passing cars. It was like waking up inside a film projector.

Bowling was never an issue. We got a six-pack, cruised around, and looked at hookers. I drove, with Rick calling directions. Somehow, he knew where all of them were. Not just the cheap kind that shouted at you outside the Port Authority, but the classy ones, standing on Park Avenue wearing fancy outfits, looking like they were really just waiting for a friend. I would have never known, but Rick did, and it made me wonder how much else I didn't know about him and the life he was leading. He made me pull over next to one particularly beautiful woman, blond, in a white skirt and jacket, even though I insisted he was wrong. She stuck her head in our window. Underneath the jacket I could see she had on a low-cut black bra.

"No way," she said when she saw us both. "I don't do twosomes. I'll go with one of you, but that's it."

"Come on," said Rick. "We're harmless."

"You couldn't afford it anyway. What are you guys, in college?"

"We work for the city," I said. "Traffic light detail. We check and make sure all the lights are synchronized properly."

"Go on," she said. "Get lost."

She turned and walked away, taking up a position a bit further down the block, where she checked her watch with impatience, looking for all the world like a woman waiting for a limo. Which, I thought, she probably was.

"Forget it," Rick said. "I've got someplace else for us to go."

We changed places and he drove. He raced cabs and dodged pedestrians, heading crosstown and then up Twelfth Avenue, onto the West Side Highway, past warehouses and the skeletons of abandoned piers. Across the river, I could see the lights of New Jersey, hovering in the dark. I was too busy holding on to the door to ask where we were going, and it was nearly impossible to talk over the engine noise, anyway. At Ninety-sixth, he got off and drove up a few more blocks before finding a parking space on Riverside.

"What now?" I asked.

"Follow me."

We walked to an apartment building a few blocks away. The doorman, who was at a desk reading a copy of the *Post* through half-glasses, looked up, seemed to recognize Rick, and waved us past.

We rode the elevator to the sixth floor, then tapped on the door of apartment 6-F. It was opened by a pasty-faced little man with his hair parted in the middle, wearing a blue smoking jacket. "Come in, come in!" he said.

"Desmond," Rick said, "this is my buddy Spencer. Desmond is an actor. This is his apartment."

I shook his hand, which was both soft and bony, and the two of us followed him into the living room. Susu was there, on the sofa, next to a guy in a white T-shirt and jeans with curly, dark hair and a great tan. He had an almost pretty face. On the glass coffee table in front of them there was a large square of tinfoil, partly open. Three thick lines of coke were drawn out next to it, ready to go, along with a rolled twenty-dollar bill.

"You guys are just in time," she said. "They can have some, can't they, Pete?"

The guy shrugged as if to say anything could happen as far as he was concerned.

"That be okay with you, then, Pete?" Rick asked, sitting down in a chair opposite them. His face was flushed around the cheeks and neck. Picking up the bill, he proceeded to take in two of the lines. "Spencer?"

"Oh, I don't know." I tried to read his expression.

"Go on," said Pete, with no real enthusiasm. "Feel free."

I inhaled the other one. Immediately, the back of my throat turned numb and my mouth tasted like I'd sucked on a piece of tin.

Desmond came back from the kitchen with bottles of beer, and I happily took one from him. There was a long, tangible silence in the room, distinctly uncomfortable. From one of the back bedrooms, I could hear a television playing.

"What kind of acting do you do?" I asked Desmond. I felt like somebody ought to say *something*.

"Well, right now I'm not doing any. I've done regional theater in the past, some industrials. Next week, I'm having my teeth bonded, and after that I plan to really hit the auditions." He smiled at me, tapped one of his front teeth. "Too many cigarettes, too much coffee. With whiter teeth, I'll be turning down work. What do you do?"

"Customer service representative," I said.

"Get out there and service those customers, do you?"

Susu stood up suddenly. "Is it hot in here? God, I just feel like I could melt."

"It's hot everywhere," said Desmond.

"You want to go for a walk?" Rick said. "Come on, Spencer, let's take her out for some air."

Pete's eyebrows went up, just for a moment, then he slid back into his persona of total impenetrability, took a swallow from his beer, and pulled a cigarette out of the pocket of a jeans jacket that was draped over the arm of the sofa beside him.

I didn't particularly feel like being alone with Pete and Desmond, even if it would allow Rick to sort out whatever it was he wanted to sort out with Susu, so I followed them to the elevator.

"What's the deal?" he said to her.

"He's just some guy Desmond knows. Don't be so suspicious."

"Suspicious? Me?" The elevator arrived and we all got on. "Spencer? What do you think?"

"I have no opinion on this," I said, watching the scoured brass doors shut us in.

"Do you think she might have slept with that guy?"

Susu shook her head in disbelief. "Come off it, will you? I barely know him."

"You told me you were going to be working tonight."

"Only after you said you didn't want to do anything. I just got my schedule mixed up." She put her arms around him and gave him a kiss on the lips. "And then Desmond said his friend Pete was coming around with some good blow, and I didn't want to miss that, did I?"

We walked through the lobby and out into the street.

"Where to now?" Susu asked.

"You're the one who wanted air," said Rick. "Let's go into the park."

We found a bench from which we could look out onto the water and smoked a joint that Rick produced from a cigarette case. "It's okay, you know," he said. "I just don't like the sneakiness, that's all. Go ahead and see other people. Just don't lie to me."

"Like you care at all. Like you're aware of anything about me."

"Come on. You know that's not true."

She didn't say anything. She was a thin girl with big eyes and a smallish nose, pretty enough, but in a calculated way. I tried to picture what her mother might look like and saw an older, tougher version of her with a lot of ugly jewelry and two or three face-lifts, one for each husband. Susu had a way of not meeting your eyes when she spoke, as if you might notice something in them she didn't want you to.

"You want to go back up now?" said Rick.

She shook her head. "I want to stay with you. Why don't we go do something?"

"Like what?"

"I don't know. Go to a bar, find some music. It doesn't matter."

A large sailboat was passing by, its contours lit all along by tiny golden lights. I thought I could just hear music coming from it, and I imagined what must be going on aboard, the tinkling of champagne glasses, people eating expensive hors d'oeuvres, important people, rich people.

Rick sucked the last of the joint, the ember glowing up between his lips, then tossed it and exhaled. "Spencer and I are having a boys' night out tonight. You go back to Pete and Desmond."

"I told you, I don't want to. I'd rather stay with you."

"Too late. Maybe you should have thought about that earlier." He was up already, walking back out toward the street.

Susu and I stood looking at each other. "It's my birthday," she said. It might have been something she'd just remembered.

"Happy birthday. How old are you?"

"Twenty-three." She leaned forward and gave me a kiss, brushing my lips lightly with her tongue. "There."

"What was that for?"

"Good luck."

"Yours or mine?"

"Both."

I walked her back to the building, then caught up with Rick. In the car, he apologized. "She's been seeing that guy for weeks, at least I'm pretty sure she has," he said. "Not that I really care. Now we've both been dissed by our women, let's go have some real fun, what do you say?"

He piloted us down to the Lower East Side, where he parked and led me to a smallish building with a yellow sign outside that read MICHIKO. After being buzzed in, we climbed a flight of stairs and were greeted by a middle-aged woman in a kimono who took seventy dollars from Rick for the two of us. She led us into a parlor and seated us on a plastic-lined sofa. There was another sofa across from us, empty. After about a minute, seven younger Asian women paraded in and sat opposite us.

"You've got to be kidding," I said.

"Not at all. See anything that looks good?"

All of them were pretty in one way or another, but not stunning, or even particularly trashy. Just normal-looking. Chatting among themselves, they might have been a group of eighth-graders in a school gymnasium, waiting for a boy to come along and ask them to dance.

"What happens?" I said.

"You pick one, then we get baths."

"You pick one."

"You're the guest."

I ran my eyes along the line, avoiding meeting any of their eyes, trying hard not to seem to be appraising them. They wore silk robes, some open suggestively to reveal a little cleavage.

"I don't know."

"Aw, hell," said Rick. He stood and went over to the woman seated on the far end and whispered something to her. Then he spoke to the one next to her. That one, taller than the first, in a yellow robe with a green sash, came over and took my hand.

"Okay?" she said.

We were led to a locker area, where we undressed and hung our clothes. The girls gave us each a little black bag with a drawstring to put our valuables in. I didn't have much, just my wallet, house key, and a fake Rolex watch I'd bought on the street. The little crown emblem had broken free and roamed the inside of the crystal, every now and then jamming the hands.

Towels around our waists, we followed the girls to the sauna. "You do this a lot?" I asked Rick, once we were alone. I noticed that there was no knob or latch on the inside of the wooden door. If you were forgotten in here, I thought, you'd pucker and dry up like an apple in an oven.

"A few times." He opened up his bag and took out his wallet. "Here." He handed me a credit card. "For the tip. Don't spend more than a hundred bucks."

63

"Tip?"

"You don't get anything without a tip. Just a massage."

"I can't spend your money like that."

"Sure you can. Don't make a big deal out of it, or I might change my mind. Imagine you're in Vietnam. The kids I went to high school with? Some of them, that's all they talked about, how they would have loved to have been there. I said it, too, but not because I had any interest in killing gooks or walking point through some snake-infested jungle. I would have been at the bordellos. We had one instructor who'd been, and the stories he told us—man." He wiped a trickle of sweat off his temple with the back of his hand. "I guess this is as close as I'll ever get. Most of these girls are Korean, not Japanese. Not that it makes any difference—it's all just a big game of make-believe, anyway."

"Tonight was Susu's birthday."

He squeezed his eyes shut and smacked his forehead. "Damn. I knew that. But how did you?"

"She told me in the park." I thought about how she'd kissed me. That one moment had been more exciting than this entire bathhouse visit, so far. I couldn't even remember what the woman Rick had chosen for me looked like. The notion of "tipping" her seemed abstract in the extreme.

"The girl loves cocaine too much for her own good. Still, I guess I was a jerk back there, considering."

"How serious are you about her?" It felt funny to be sitting here like this, practically naked. His arms had been expanding from daily sessions with weights. I wondered, if I started working out tomorrow, how long it would take to have arms like that.

He shrugged. "Not serious at all, really. We have a kind of understanding. She's got this guy out in New Mexico, which, to tell you the honest truth, is one of the things I like best about her. Whenever I get pissed off or see her do something stupid, I just take a deep breath and remind myself that in the long run, she's someone else's problem."

"That works?"

"Most of the time."

"But you must feel something for her."

"Sure. More than something." He smiled. "I know what you're after. I won't end up marrying her or anything. I'll end up marrying some Donna Reed type—there's no real way out of it. It's what I was brought up to do."

Just when I thought I could stand the heat no longer, the women came and took us to a room with metal gurney beds to wash us. After that, we dried off and were led to seats. Apparently, all the bedrooms upstairs, where the massage part was to take place, were in use. Rick's woman came and got him.

"Don't leave my buddy waiting long," he said to her.

"Just two minute," she said, and then to me, smiling, "Very busy night."

"Meet you back down here," said Rick. "Enjoy."

"I might just go." I was thinking about Sally.

He looked disappointed. "Don't worry about the money. It's my treat. You've got a birthday coming up yourself, don't you?"

"Sure, in about five months."

"Early present, then." When he saw that I was still hesitating, he shrugged. "Suit yourself."

"Okay," I said. "I'll stay."

I sat for a while when he was gone, thinking about it more. I could see into the front room, where a rowdy group of drunken men in suits had just arrived. One of them was wearing a rubber Rambo mask and kept asking, "Yo, where the white women at?" It made me want to disappear, hearing them, imagining the matron's tight smile as she rang up their admission on the register. Then my woman appeared and took my hand gently. I went upstairs.

Sally was sitting at the kitchen table, drinking tea. It was after two. Rick had abandoned me and headed straight for his room when we came in. I told her we'd gone to Susu's.

"Where does she live?"

"Upper West Side."

"Nice place?"

"So-so."

"Very funny." She clinked a spoon around the inside of her mug. "Your father called."

"What?"

"Your father. Around midnight."

On the spur of the moment once, when we were all drinking and trashing our respective families, I'd told her my father lived in Florida. I'd been into John D. McDonald novels, and I claimed my dad, like Travis McGee, lived on a houseboat.

"He said he'd call back tomorrow. Or today, I guess. He wasn't very talkative. You smell like soap."

I sniffed my sleeve. "I used this stuff in the bathroom there. Very fancy. I think her roommate is gay. Strange guy, totally hung up about his teeth." I tried to kiss her, but she turned her head away. I was tired. In five hours I had to be back at Mutronics.

She yawned. "I'm going to bed."

"I didn't have a very good time," I said.

"Well, I'm sorry to hear that."

"I mean, I missed you."

"You don't have to apologize for going off by yourself. You don't even have to claim you had a bad time. Really, I don't mind that much." She took her cup back into the kitchen, then shut the light and moved past me into her room.

I wandered around for a while, looked in the refrigerator, stared out the window into the backyard, turned the TV on, then immediately off again. Finally, I went down to my room.

The house was full of tiny noises. The fan by my bed hissed and sighed as it nodded its head one way, then the other. Above me the floor creaked as Sally moved around.

I couldn't sleep either. In the darkness I paced back and forth, stopping every now and then to peer out my window, which faced east, looking for the beginnings of light.

"Hey," I said out loud to the darkness. My voice sounded nasal and forced, as if I were hearing it back on a tape recording.

I went into the bathroom for some toilet paper to blow my nose. As I came back out, the phone chirped and I picked it up. It was nearly five.

"Hello?" I said.

I couldn't tell if someone was there or not. The sound was distorted, a kind of crackling, windy sweep, with strange electronic noises mixed in the background, like someone whistling in an electric storm.

"What?" I said, louder. "Say something."

It might have been him, then again it might not. There was nothing to indicate that anyone was on the other end. Just sounds, indistinct and otherworldly.

Rick stuck his head out. "Who is it?"

"Some other galaxy."

"Have them call back." He looked pissed off and tired. "It's the middle of the night."

I replaced the receiver and went back in my room, climbed under the covers, and tried to will myself to sleep. Though the steaks had continued to come to my mother's each year, I had not heard a thing otherwise, had long ago given up hoping to. Now I could not stop the parade of images that meandered through my mind—cartoon figures of my father in which he was dressed variously as a plumber, a policeman, an army lieutenant, a Bowery bum. I saw him with his hair cut short and military like Rick's, then with it halfway down his back the way it had been when I was a kid. I dreamed him up a hundred ways, but on none of them, for some reason, was I able to put a face.

5

Dear Mutronics, Inc:
Let me try a term out on you. Mail Fraud. Ever hear of it? That's when unscrupulous businesspeople use the U.S. Mails to bilk unsuspecting customers out of their money. Sound familiar?

Attached are copies of the other five letters I sent to your company, none of which you replied to. This will be my last. The next one goes to the State Attorney General's Office, who will I'm sure be interested to know what you guys are up to there in good old New York City. A copy of my check to you, dated over a year ago, is also enclosed. Please note the endorsement on the back, which reads "Payroll." Just what the hell is going on there?

I don't want the products anymore, just my money back. Let's see some action here, or we will be talking lawsuit.

> Sincerely,
> Bernard Lewis
> San Diego, California

Dear Mr. Lewis,
First of all, let me say that I can understand your concern. There has been a slight turnover here in the Customer Service Department, and as a result, some cases got overlooked. Please

be assured that I am now giving this my personal attention. More than likely, you are unaware of the situation here at Mutronics. A local division of the Meatpackers Union has set up picket lines outside our building, making it impossible for us to ship anything at all (UPS won't cross the lines). I've checked, and your order is packed and ready to go (I'm not sure what the original delay was). If you'll just hang in there a week or two, you should be getting your equipment.

> Thanks for your patience,
> Spencer Markus
> Customer Service Rep.
> Mutronics, Inc.

Dear Sirs,
   I saw your ad in Guitar Universe. Could you please send me a catalog?

> Thank you.
> Kate Noonan
> Dubuque, Iowa

Dear Kate,
   Enclosed is our special price list. We're out of catalogs right now, but we're working on some new products we're quite happy about, and we'll keep you posted. These are exciting times at Mutronics. We'll look forward to your order.

> Sincerely,
> Spencer Markus
> Customer Service Rep.
> Mutronics, Inc.

Dear Mr. Markus,
   I checked with UPS, and they have traced the package I sent to you. It was signed for and everything (the guy's name was Fi-

delito something-or-other). As I mentioned before, this is a special box for me, and I wouldn't know where to begin looking for another. Please find it. If you can't fix it, send it back to me and I'll get someone who can. I don't care about the ten bucks, I just want my Gopher.

Getting a little worried here in Durango,
Duke Davin

Dear Duke,

Good to hear from you. Right now I have two of my assistants combing the building looking for your unit. To my knowledge, we have never lost a repair, a record we are extremely proud of. Rest assured, we will find it. Things are a little tough here right now, though, as we are the target of an organizing effort by unscrupulous members of a local union. We expect to have the matter resolved within the week, at which point we can resume business as usual.

Thanks for your patience,
Spencer Markus
Customer Service Rep.
Mutronics Inc.

Dear Mr. Markus,

Well, I waited the two weeks that you said. Still no PEDEL. I'm sorry if it is hot there, but tell me about it. Illinois is no refrigerator, as I'm sure you know. Some of the GUYS here told me to ask for my money back on you, but I said No, this is an honorable company. You have always sold good products at a fair price and you know what the spirit of ROCK AND ROLL is all about, as I do. So HURRY UP and get me my PEDEL to me. My career awaits.

Sincerely,
Furry Couch #C-563-2798

6

The *union people* gathered in an angry circle around the building entrance, some of them carrying signs, all of them shouting. I pushed through, ignoring the names they called me, and pulled open the heavy door. An egg struck it from the outside and dripped slowly down the glass.

Jerry was running around barking orders at people, the ones who'd been brave enough to come in. Many of the foreign workers hadn't. When he saw me he stopped and checked his watch. I was late. I'd slept less than four hours and my eyes hurt, my mouth tasted bad. I felt as if I'd been dragged behind a bus.

"I need you to help with production today," he said. "Everyone's gotta pitch in here. Go upstairs and see Carmen, she'll tell you what to do." He was wearing a black Mutronics T-shirt with his own face on it that was too tight and rode up slightly on his belly. "Oh, yeah," he said. "There's someone here to see you. A store owner. He's back in testing."

As I worked my way through the empty factory, back to the time clock to insert my card for its daily chomping, I tried to remember the most outrageous thing I'd told a music store recently. We'd done a mailing to individual customers promising prices roughly the same as our dealers got from us, and a lot of them had been calling in, angry. I would promise to get them an extra discount, which usually worked. I had no authority to do this, but it got them off the phone. I figured by the time they found out, I'd be gone anyway. Maybe the whole company would.

My dad was at the testing table, underneath Randy's shrine to Eddie Van Halen, a collage of cutout posters from teen fan magazines. He had on a suit coat and jeans and a skinny tie with piano keys along one side. When he saw me, he stood up and stuck his hands into his pockets. "They told me I could wait back here. Supposedly, I'm checking out this new digital delay."

I took a step forward, then stopped. He didn't look that different, just older. He walked over and stuck out his hand, so I took it. "It's good to see you," he said. A prototype of our latest product, the "Elephant" (for its sixteen-second memory), was out on the table, and I saw that the amp was turned on. He'd been playing the company guitar. "Listen to this," he said. He turned and hit the button with his fist and "Stars and Stripes Forever!" began cascading out of the amp.

"Very nice."

"Makes you want to stand up and salute, doesn't it? You can have the Bo Diddley beat, I'll take march time anytime. I could show you that, if you want—it isn't hard. Maybe later. I love the box, incidentally. Best thing this company's done in years. What do you say, want to take a walk?"

"I'm supposed to go upstairs."

"Let your old man buy you breakfast."

We were both silent for a moment. "It'll be all right," he said. "I guarantee it."

We rode the elevator back down. There was no one to see me leave since everyone was on the sixth floor, with the exception of Jerry, who had shut the door to his office. We walked out through the crowd of demonstrators. They called us names and cursed in Spanish. I didn't know where to look, so I watched my dad's shoes, pointy-toed cowboy boots with metal tips. They made a nice solid sound when they hit the pavement.

There was a coffee shop around the corner, and it was cool inside. We got a table and stared at our menus for a while, then both ordered French toast.

"What's with all the picketers?" he asked. "You guys do something wrong?"

"We do everything wrong. That's not why they're here. They just want us to join their union."

He sipped his coffee. "I never had any use for it. If you're in the union, at least as a musician, you spend half your time lying about it so you can work the nonunion gigs, which is to say most of them. I'll bet you're wondering how I figured out where you were."

"I don't know," I said. I was studying him while trying to appear not to be. "Did you call Mom?"

"Nope." He dug a folded piece of paper out of his pocket and handed it to me. It was a form letter from me, promising a repair turnaround time of four to six weeks. I'd photocopied a stack for Fidelito in Receiving. "I sent in a pedal I had for repair and got this in the mail. 'Spencer Markus, Customer Service Representative.' You major in business at college?"

"English."

"I'm still real proud of you." He folded the letter up and returned it to his pocket.

"You never used Mutronics stuff," I pointed out. "You always said it was unreliable."

"I was right, wasn't I? I figured this was a sign—time to go and visit. Finally. Look at you." He reached over and placed his hand on my shoulder. Then he took it away, poured more syrup onto his French toast, put down the server, and licked a drop off his finger.

"So, where have you been?"

"Augusta, Maine, most recently. Canada before that. You know about me and letters. I'm not even sure what a stamp costs these days." He wiped his mouth with a napkin. "How were the steaks?"

"Fine," I said. "Great."

"Look, this is hard for me, too. But we're both adults. What's past is past." He looked at me for a few moments in silence. There were more lines in his face than I remembered. If he felt awkward at all, he was doing a good job covering it. "Hey," he said, suddenly, "check it out." He pulled his hair back off his ear and showed me an earring in the shape of a tiny guitar. "Solid gold. Designed it myself. I've got a friend, she makes jewelry. Lots of craftspeople up in Maine. It's a very artistic place. You should come up and visit."

Part of me wanted to hug him. Another part wanted to kick him. I asked where he was staying.

"Flea-bag hotel. Crack vials on the bathroom floor and hookers in the lobby. It's an experience, but at least it's a cheap one. The music business isn't real high-profit, not my end of it, anyway. I do my own act now, or I plan to. I'm through depending on other people. Too much damn trouble. Self-reliance, you know? That's the ticket. I told your boss I was a store owner to get in. I wanted to surprise you."

"Surprise me? You tried to call me."

"I did?"

"Last night. My girlfriend took a message."

He nodded. "Yeah, that's right, I did." He smiled. It was as if there were some other being in him over which he had little control, a playful sprite that sometimes got up in the middle of the night and made phone calls. "Girlfriend, huh?"

"I was still surprised, though. Look, why don't you come over to my place this evening? We can sit around and talk then. We've got an extra room. You can stay there."

"Out of the question. Really, I don't mind the hotel."

"You have to come stay with me. End of discussion." It was something he always used to say to my mother, and I was a little surprised to hear it from myself.

"All right," he said, "if you're sure." I had the feeling that he'd been waiting for this invitation all along. "I'll get my stuff and come back around five to meet you."

We got up to leave. He took out his wallet, the same black one he'd had years ago. It was falling apart, the leather cracked and broken. I also noticed that he seemed to have no credit cards, just cash.

"I want to hear everything," I said. "I'll bet you've got stories."

"You'd be surprised how few," he said. "Hey, so what did you think when they told you there was someone here to see you?"

"Truthfully?"

"Yeah."

"I thought it was someone come to kick my ass."

He laughed and took two toothpicks out of the holder by the register and gave me one. "That's a hell of a way to live," he said.

I put the toothpick in my mouth, and the two of us went back out into the bright sunlight, desperados moving unnoticed among the citizenry.

All of us sat around a long workbench in the dim cathedral of the sixth floor. It was where the real grunt work went on, and I'd only seen the place a couple of times. Randy said you needed a visa to go up there, but now all of us were lined up along the table and assigned little tasks, even Lenny DeMarino. I was given a box of nine-volt Mutronics batteries to test. They were from Malaysia, and about every other one was useless. I'd unwrap the cellophane from around them, then touch them to a tiny meter. I was having trouble concentrating, and every time I looked up at the clock, it seemed not to have moved at all. Next to me, Randy fumbled with printed circuit boards into which she was supposed to insert two tiny lime-green capacitors. Individually, they looked like Chiclets with legs, but all piled together they were insects, trying to climb over each other to get on top.

"I've been working here ten years," she said. "I never had to do anything this stupid." Giving up on one of the capacitors, she flicked it across the floor. Carmen, a matronly woman with a solid, six-foot frame, and a noticeable mustache, raised her eyebrows at her from where she stood at the far end of the table, overseeing us.

"What do they want, anyway?" I asked.

"The union? Better wages I guess, health benefits, all that

good stuff." She shrugged. "They won't get far with Jerry. These people love him. He takes them on picnics, talks Spanish to them. Once, about nine years ago, he hired a topless dancer to come in and boogie around the assembly table. A couple of the girls turned in their soldering irons, but other than that, he's never had any popularity problem. He actually *is* taking advantage of them left, down, and sideways." Randy grinned and wiped a line of sweat from the side of her face with her shoulder. "They just don't realize it. Compared to where they come from, this is a great deal—a forty-hour workweek, half an hour for lunch, four bucks an hour." She tapped the side of her head. "It's only oppression if you think about it that way."

I threw another battery into the discard pile. The intercom crackled and the sound of Jerry's organ came pumping through it, first a few trial chords, then a slow, bluesy riff that moved down the keyboard, ending up so low it dissolved into a breathy, barely audible murk.

"If you're getting bored," said Randy, "there's another way to test those." She picked up one of my batteries and unwrapped it. "Cheap shit stuff. Last about a week if you're lucky." She put the end in front of her mouth and touched her tongue to the terminals. "No good," she said, tossing it in with the discards. "Your turn."

I picked up one and did the same. A jolt of current stabbed my tongue.

"That one's a keeper," said Randy, laughing at my expression. My tongue had an awful, metallic taste on it.

"You," I said.

She nodded, and with great formality unwrapped the next battery, then held it up in a toast and said, "Time to catch a buzz." She put it to her tongue, held it there for a second, then took it off.

"Nothing?"

"Not much."

I didn't like the way this was going, and I didn't want another shock. But the odds should have been in my favor, or at least fifty-fifty. I chose another battery. Over the intercom, Jerry began to sing, a song he was apparently making up as he went along, his voice an imitation of growling, Delta-style blues, most of the words unintelligible. The phrase "Socialist gangsters" kept coming through loud and clear, though.

"I got a feeling this is going to turn into a holy war," said Randy. "And I'm not sure I want to stick around to see how it comes out."

I put the battery terminals to my tongue and got the same shock as before. "Damn."

Randy bent the legs off a capacitor. "The worst part about it," she said, "is the uncertainty—not knowing what is going to happen."

"Bullshit," I told her. "The worst part is the pain."

I found my dad waiting at the front desk a little before five. "Jimi," he said. He was standing with Randy, who'd been excused from her capacitors about an hour earlier to go down and test a rack of fuzzboxes.

"Said he wanted to see you." Randy had her bag over her shoulder and was ready to go. She took me aside and whispered that this was the guy she'd been telling me about the other day. "I told him we were about to close."

"It's okay. I know him."

"You do?"

Randy studied me as if this were particularly unlikely, then she looked again at my dad and clapped her hands. "You guys are related, right? I should have seen it before. Older brother?"

"You got it." My dad came over and held out his hand, appearing, just for a moment, to lose his balance, then catching himself. "I'm Spider."

"Spider?" I said.

"That's right." He winked at me. "Time to head down and face the mob?"

I tried to decide how drunk he was, but it was hard to say. I wondered if this was what he was like all the time now.

"You didn't get hassled on the way in?" Randy asked.

"I can take care of myself." His eyes were pink and his clothes smelled sour and smoky. It was the way I remembered him smelling when, as a kid, I'd waited up for him to come home from gigs. My room had a view of the driveway, and I woke up with each pair of passing headlights, waiting for the ones that would turn in our drive. He'd stick his face up against the window as he passed by and if I waved, he'd come in and tell me good night.

"You ignore these guys, nothing will happen," he said as we got on the elevator. "They're all talk."

The three of us made our way out through the front entrance. It should have been a simple matter to pass through the remaining union people and walk the block and a half to the subway. Except that despite what he'd said, he seemed to be taking the whole thing personally. With each insult hurled at us, he spun and stared at the source. He was showing off. Randy and I tried to keep our gazes fixed on nothing, just straight-ahead, no-nonsense walking at a good clip.

"Be cool, folks," said Randy, nervously. "We don't need to be no heroes."

But he kept twisting from side to side, looking like he wanted nothing more than a good fight. "Where'd you say they were from?" he asked, loudly.

"Meat packers," said Randy. "Read the signs."

"I saw that. I just don't get it."

"Tell me about it. My guess is they took a look at a product list and saw all those Gophers and Possums. We'll probably have the USDA down here next trying to figure out what we're *doing* with all this roadkill."

The picketers were thickest around the entrance, perhaps twenty-five of them. From there they formed a sort of ragged corridor that dwindled away over the next twenty yards until it became hard to tell them from the passing throngs of people on their way home from work. We went by the last obvious union people, both women, who spat in tandem on the concrete.

"*Puta!*" said my dad. He knew about three words of Spanish, and this was one of them.

I let go of his arm, which I had been holding for fear he might do something stupid. We seemed to be in the clear. Almost at the same time, there was a loud smack next to my ear and Randy stumbled. For a moment I thought the oozing yellow substance on her temple had somehow come from inside her head. I realized it was egg about the same time another one came sailing and hit me directly in the chest. It was surprisingly painful, like getting hit with a rock. Another smacked against my shoulder. They were coming from my left, near the curb, and the person throwing them had the arm of a good, accurate out-fielder.

The next thing I knew, my dad had made his way between two parked cars, and had his hands around the neck of a short, broad woman with bright red hair and a shopping bag in her hand. She howled obscenities in Spanish and English, did her best to kick him between the legs. Randy still looked confused. Yellow slime trailed down her neck and collar, flecks of eggshell clung white against the black of her shirt.

As I started to move toward him, so did a knot of union men, about six of them. Someone kicked Randy from behind and she spun around and tried to kick back, but missed and fell to the sidewalk. Considering her size, I was amazed that she'd reacted so quickly. For my own part, I was so charged up with adrena-line and fear, I wasn't sure what to do.

My dad let the woman go and came over to me, his hands clenched into fists, but down at his sides. The woman resumed her egg-throwing, now at point-blank range, striking both of us with alternating shots.

"Let's go," said a man to me. He was about six-foot, with a remarkably square head, wearing a white short-sleeve shirt. His hands were up, ready to box. He had hairy knuckles and a shiny gold watch.

"We don't want to fight," I said, taking a step backward. "We've got no problem with you."

"Motherfucker!" screamed the fat woman. "You hit a lady."

My dad shook his head in disgust. "I didn't hit you." One of the union men came over and pushed him in the chest. He pushed back, saying, "Fuck off me, Pancho."

Something traveled toward me at a high rate of speed, in an upward arc. Before I could move, it caught me dead on the lip, jolting my head backward, and I went sprawling to the sidewalk, my mind momentarily a night sky.

I was conscious again in what seemed no time at all, but things looked very different. The person who had hit me was gone, as was the fat woman. Randy and my father each had me under one arm and were helping me to my feet.

"Cold-cocked," my dad was saying, shaking his head. "Like a punching bag." His voice sounded like it was at the end of a long tunnel.

"You okay?" asked Randy. "You know what day it is?"

Looking at her, I saw there was a cut just over her eye, and it had begun to swell. "Who hit me?"

"That little fucker, the one with the mustache? Hit you and ran. They all ran when you went down like that."

The world was still spinning. There was a pressure in my head, a pounding like someone playing timpani.

"Remember me?" Randy said, with concern. "I work with you."

I tried to laugh, but it was as if the blow had rearranged my wiring, and instead what came were tears.

"Let me see," said my dad. He leaned close, examining my face, probing at my upper lip with his finger. I smelled the beer on his breath, saw up close the graying stubble of his beard line. "Open your mouth."

I obeyed and he peered inside. "Looks like they're all there. Any of them feel loose?"

I shook my head. Tasting blood, I turned and spat some of it into the street. Already my lip was inflating like a balloon.

He chucked me on the back. "I think you're all right."

"We'll get 'em," said Randy. "Don't you worry about it. One way or another, they'll pay."

"Come on," said my dad. He seemed dead sober. "Let's go back to your place. Where do we go? That subway entrance over there?"

Before we could get to it, a cab pulled alongside the curb. Jerry was in the front seat. "Get in," he said, waving his hands with great energy.

"I'm walking," said Randy. She looked determined, didn't even slow down. "I'll see you all later."

We climbed in the back and Jerry told the driver to go around the block. "I saw what happened," he said. "What happened?"

"I thought you saw," I said.

"Well, I kind of saw. Not everything."

"I got punched. It's no big deal. I'm all right."

"You want to go to the cops, fill out a complaint? Maybe that would be a good idea. How about we take you over to the precinct house?"

"I think I just want to go home. I'm tired." I was impressed by Jerry's seeming ability to be everywhere at once.

"Whatever you feel like, that's what I want you to do. Of course, if you make a complaint, it could help us in the long run, you know, in case there's legal action." He cranked his head around and stared at my dad, as if noticing him for the first time. "Who's this guy?"

He stuck a hand over the back of the seat. "Spider Markus. We met earlier."

"You told me you ran a music store."

"Well, that's true, I do. Or I did, at any rate. I'm Spencer's father."

"His father? No shit? Well, that's good, then. You can take care of him, make sure he's okay." He looked at his watch, an oversized chrome thing with three or four dials on it. "You want me to drop you off someplace?"

We'd made almost an entire circuit of the block. "The subway will be fine," I said. I looked back down the street to where I'd been punched. There was no evidence at all that anything had happened. Just the usual hordes of people getting off work, hustling along, ignoring one another. I'd been part of a momentary disruption, like a rock tossed into a fast-moving stream.

Sally made us dinner. My dad sat at one end of the table, helping himself to cheap burgundy. It was Rick's writing wine, and he bought it in heavy-duty jug sizes. Rick sat next to him, matching him glass for glass while forking down tremendous quantities of spaghetti heaped with Italian Combination grated cheese product. Sally kept looking back and forth between the two of us. I'd explained to her that, at least for a little while, she'd have to move back into my room, and she'd seemed agreeable. I was still dizzy, and my lip felt like a small peach had been stapled to it.

"I was in Toronto for a while," he said, not looking at me. "Did a bunch of things. Bartended, drove a newspaper delivery truck, collected money at the door of a strip bar. Good music scene in that town. For a while, I backed up this guy, 'Jumbo' Goins. Three hundred pounds of Mississippi truck-driver who played bass and sang like Albert King. But it was just too much trouble. He couldn't tune his instrument, for one thing. And he had this thing about hiring extra guys to play gigs without ever rehearsing them, so it was always a big mess on stage and no one made any money. Anyway, I missed the States, and after about a year I came back. I had my guitars with me, of course, though I ended up selling them off one at a time, until finally it was just the Tele left—I wasn't going to part with that. Then I got this job working in a music store in Augusta. Loved it. I was sales manager within a month. But I quit to get back to playing."

He downed the better part of a glass of wine and touched a napkin to his lips. "The guy I worked for went out of business. He had a real old-time music store, one of those places that specializes in sheet music and accordions and clarinet reeds. He didn't know anything about electronics except what his distributors told him, and he didn't want to learn. You can't do that and survive. These days, electronics is music."

"The medium is the message," said Rick.

"Exactly."

"Was this before or after the houseboat?" asked Sally.

"Houseboat?"

"Spencer said you lived on a houseboat," said Rick. "He said you worked for the FBI."

He tipped his head to one side and looked at me. "Did you say that?"

I shrugged. "I might have."

"I can neither confirm nor deny any rumors," he said. "For your own safety, the less you know, the better." He put a hand on my shoulder and squeezed. "How's your mom?"

"Great."

"And old what's-his-face?"

"Hal. Fine, too. Is that it on the wine?"

"Unless you want to get more," said Rick. "Which would be okay by me."

My dad stood up, placing his napkin on the table. "I'll go," he said. "I'm the guest, it's the least I can do."

I walked with him to the liquor store near the subway entrance. It was a humid night, but in contrast to the apartment there was at least a breeze outside. In it, I detected a faint odor of fish, working its way up from the docks.

"That's a very fine-looking woman you've got there."

"Thanks," I said. "I like her." I felt a little odd about this, as if we were discussing a car, or a new guitar. I wasn't sure I wanted his approval.

"I haven't had spaghetti like that in a while."

"It was just store-bought, with peppers and onions chopped into it."

83

"Good, though. Not all women can cook. It's a dying art form. Your mother couldn't even cook frozen food. There was always ice in the middle."

"You're living alone, then?" I said. In the past, I'd been aware of his different girlfriends. They seemed to change from month to month, and I never really got to know any of them. There was a generic quality to the women he found in the bars: nice bodies they weren't afraid to show off, faces they felt less certain about and hid behind a touch too much makeup. Occasionally, if I ran into him someplace with one, he'd look slightly embarrassed, then introduce me and say, "Hey, this is Karen," as if they weren't necessarily together. Sometimes he'd introduce me to the same person three or four times. He seemed to feel for some reason that he should not appear to me to be involved with anyone. So we had always maintained the fiction that these were simply his "friends."

"Same old thing. Just like the old days, except I can't go downstairs and get pizza anytime I want. I miss that. I rent a little house. It's got a little garage, a little microwave, all the comforts."

At the liquor store he bought another bottle of the wine Rick liked, paid for it with a twenty, and stuck the change into his pocket. He caught sight of himself in the mirror behind the counter and seemed disturbed. His eyes were bloodshot, he badly needed a shave, and after his shower he had forgotten to comb his hair. On the way out he leaned over and said, "I don't always look this bad."

"Me, neither."

When we returned, Rick had already disappeared into his room and closed the door. He had his Madonna tape playing softly, and the metallic thumps that resonated from within told me he was lifting weights. We went upstairs where Sally was finishing the dishes.

"I would have done that," he said.

"Oh, no, I really don't mind." She dried her hands on a dishtowel, pushed a stray bit of hair out of her face. "I'm going to sleep, guys."

"Sally gets up early."

"I changed the sheets in there for you. And I tried to clean up a little. Don't mind my things, just make yourself at home."

He looked confused. "I didn't realize I was taking your room."

"It's okay. Spencer and I can share for a while." She eased past us without looking at me and went downstairs.

"I guess you've got some kind of situation here."

"Oh, hell," I said. "I don't know."

We climbed the metal ladder up through the hatch to the roof and passed the jug of wine back and forth in silence for a while. It was a beautiful night; above the dull glow of the rooftops the sky was clear enough to see the stars.

"I'm going to quit Mutronics," I said, after a while. "It's not worth getting killed over."

"Don't do it. Hang in there. When the going gets tough . . ." His voice trailed off as he searched for the words. "You have to get tougher."

I ran my tongue over the salty front of my fat lip. I alternated between believing that this, me and my dad drinking wine together on a Brooklyn rooftop, was perfectly normal, and that I should relax and enjoy it, and the odd feeling that I was somehow part of a clever con-job, that this man was not my dad and never had been. I was being set up. At any moment helicopters would appear over the horizon shining lights on me, and union men would descend carrying AK-47s, dressed in fatigues. My mind, I realized, was drifting in and out of awareness, as if I were nodding off behind the wheel of a car. One moment I seemed to actually see the helicopters, hear their spinning rotors, understand intuitively that there was no escape—the union would get to me. The next I'd shake my head and realize it was only a car passing in the street below. I hadn't slept much at all the night before, my head had been used as a punching bag, and I had drunk eight or nine glasses of wine. I had a hangover already, and I was still drinking.

"Look at that," he said, pointing.

I followed his gaze and locked my eyes on the new curtains the woman across the street had installed. They were pulled partway open, and I could see her standing there, naked, running her hands along the sides of her body, tracing figure-eights over her breasts. I held my breath and squinted, unsure what I was seeing. The image dissolved into a checkerboard of gray and white floaters—if I closed my eyes they were still there, seeming to move on their own.

"Sometimes she dances around in the evenings," I said. "I've seen her."

He turned and looked at me curiously, then started to laugh. I squinted again at the window and realized that although the light was on, the curtains were in fact closed, and what I had seen was only in my imagination. Following my dad's eyes, I saw they were focused on something farther away. I moved over directly behind him, so close that I could smell his hair, my chin touching the side of his head. I put my hands on his shoulders for balance. There, lit up in the distance, just visible between two apartment buildings, was the Statue of Liberty, a sliver of shining green. It seemed an impossibly beautiful gesture to me that amidst all these impersonal buildings, someone had put up a statue of a woman.

"I took you there once," he said. "You remember that?"

When he said it, I realized that I did. What I remembered were stairs, tightly spiraling upward, made of a kind of metal grid you could look through and see straight down hundreds of feet. I remembered nothing else, not the view from the top, not the ferry ride over to the island, which we must have taken, not the hot dogs or ice creams we probably had afterward. I just had an image of my feet balanced on those precarious steps, and the kind of fear that would make a four-year-old boy unable to put one foot in front of the other.

"I had to carry you up," he said. "At least I think I did. But once you were at the top, you didn't want to come down."

For a moment I wanted to tell him that everything I'd ever done, from climbing those stairs, to learning the guitar, to moving in with Sally, all of it had been in one way or another for him. But the person on whose shoulder I now rested my head didn't see that. He perceived two separate realities, one long in the past which he had been a part of, the other my present life, for which he bore no responsibility, and could simply visit, like a Monopoly player passing through one of his properties.

"Hey," he said, digging in his pocket for his wallet. He pulled it out and extracted a business card. I took it and examined it in the thin, spectral light. It read, in bold print, SPIDERMAN DAN, and then underneath, in smaller italics with quotes around them, *"Master of the Telecaster."*

"That's me," he said.

I looked again at the card. This time the letters flickered out of focus and I had to squint. "I don't mean to be difficult, but isn't that Albert Collins?"

"Nope, he's the Master of the Stratocaster. Anyway, I want you to call me Spider from now on."

I was pretty sure he was wrong but didn't really feel like arguing. "You're not serious."

"I am dead serious. It's my stage name, and it's what I go by now. Plus, we can't have you calling me 'Dad.' You're too old."

"Spider," I said, trying it out. I couldn't decide if it fit him or not. "I don't know. It feels funny."

"Don't worry," he said. "You'll get used to it."

7

He *pulled aside* the curtains in my room, allowing sunlight to blast through the old, smudgy windows. The clock showed nearly eleven.

"Relax," he said. "I called in for you. Jerry said to take it easy and rest up."

My head was pounding, my mouth was dry, and my stomach felt like it had been kicked. I groaned and lay back on the bed.

"Just your basic, garden-variety hangover." He held out a glass of orange juice toward me, along with three aspirin. I sat up, took them, drank the juice, then leaned forward and put my face in my hands. "Fight it," he said. "You're stronger than it is."

"I'm not sure about that."

"Get up, get the blood flowing. Losing a battle doesn't mean losing the war, after all."

"It wasn't a battle, it was more like an ambush. I wish I'd had a chance to fight. I would have squashed that little bug."

"There's the spirit," he said. "Who knows? You may get another chance someday."

Upstairs, he'd laid out a whole meal for us: bacon, toast, coffee, and a Danish coffee ring. "No eggs," he pointed out.

I did my best to eat something, but I wasn't really hungry. The bacon was blackened and crumbly. "Maybe I have a concussion."

"Maybe," he agreed, slicing some more Danish. "Treatment's the same as a hangover—aspirin and bed rest. I've had them before. Stepped backward off a drum platform once in this little club in Toronto, hit my head against the side of a speaker column. It hurt for a week. Took to wearing dark glasses, even." He pushed his chair back and crossed one leg over the other. "Where does your roommate work? Rick."

"Adult book and video store on Forty-second Street. It's called PlayWorld, I think, something like that. He doesn't need the money, but he's writing a screenplay, and he claims it's a good way to gather material."

"Material about what?"

"I don't know," I admitted. "He won't talk about it." I squinted, rubbed some sand from my eyes. "We could go visit him if you want. I've never been, but I keep thinking I ought to."

"Whatever you want, that's what I want to do."

I thought about it. I looked and felt like I'd been mugged. I couldn't see going anywhere.

"And your girlfriend's one of those Smokey-the-Bears?"

"That's right."

"Interesting. Cops and crooks. Where do you fit in?"

"Comic relief," I said.

He read the paper, then I read it. We made more coffee and watched part of a talk show on television, featuring transsexuals of both genders talking about their problems of adjustment. We played cards. It wasn't that different from when he used to write me notes for school so I could spend the day hanging out with him, except for the awkwardness. We weren't sure what to say to each other, or how to act. The apartment seemed unusually small. We kept running into each other, flashing fake smiles, pretending everything was normal.

He got out my guitar, the same one he'd given me. I hadn't been using it much lately. "Lot of gunk on these strings," he said. "You got a rag or something?"

I found him one and watched as he rubbed each string down, examining the marks they left with obvious distaste. When he finally put the rag aside and began to play, I watched his hands. They were strong, yet at the same time somehow delicate, with enlarged knuckles that looked as if they'd been bashed around a bit. When he wasn't playing, he often seemed unsure what to do with them. He'd stick them deep into his pockets, or play with them, cracking his knuckles unconsciously one at a time, sometimes pressing his fingers together into a bridge under his nose, as if he were praying.

After a while he stopped and held it out to me by the neck. "Go on," he said, "let's hear something."

"I don't feel like it."

"Don't be embarrassed. You must be smoking by now. I'll bet you are. Show off a little. You're not shy, are you?"

"No, I just don't feel all that well."

"Because I'd sure like to hear you."

I told him maybe later.

Around two, Randy called from work.

"Be happy you stayed home," she said. "There's about forty of them down there. I got egged again on the way in this morning. There's police now, though, and barricades. Jerry says the TV news are coming later to do a story."

I told her I was okay, and that I'd be back tomorrow. I realized that I missed the excitement. I had a certain personal investment in Mutronics. If nothing else, I wanted to stick around to see how things turned out.

We went to the park with a Frisbee. I thought the fresh air might do me some good. It was cooler out, finally, with a hint that fall might actually be coming. The long meadow was empty, except for some Jamaicans at the far end playing soccer. I winged one high and long and he backpedaled but couldn't quite get under it.

"Hey, Spider," I shouted, "you're getting old." Calling him that didn't feel as strange as I'd thought it might. After all, I hadn't called him anything for years.

"The hell I am." He picked up the Frisbee and shot it back at me hard, his long arms coiled around, giving his delivery a whiplike follow-through. The wind caught it and I had to chase it down, which I did, leaping high in the air to make the catch. Immediately, my head started to beat as if something inside were trying to smash its way out. I had to sit down.

He ran over and examined my eyes. I was too sick to get up, but I knew if I waited it would pass, and when I sat with my head against my knees for a while, it did.

"Do you think we should take you to a doctor?" he asked.

"I don't know." As the pain in my head subsided, I realized I was sitting on some sort of root. I shifted slightly, but even that small movement set the pain back to throbbing. I'd never had anything seriously wrong with me before, just the normal things, the occasional sprains and fevers that any kid goes through. Growing up, these had always been the province of my mother, who kept a list of emergency numbers typed alphabetically and taped to the wall by our phone.

He stared at me, weighing the situation, the sudden recipient of responsibility he had in no way wanted. "I think we should get you looked at," he said. "This might be serious. Who's your doctor?"

I told him I didn't have one.

"Why not?" He seemed surprised.

"Do you?"

"There's nothing wrong with me."

I got up on my knees, took a deep breath. "There's a hospital about a half mile from here."

"Can you walk?" He helped me up, I took a step or two and decided that I could, as long as we moved slowly.

We sat two hours in the emergency room before a nurse led me to an examination area. My headache had subsided, but any sudden movements brought it right back. A young, redheaded doctor with a mustache looked in my eyes, had me close them and touch my fingers to my nose. He made me walk a straight line, turn, and walk some more. Pushing at my inflated lip with his forefinger, he turned it up and peered underneath. He stuck a flashlight under my nostrils and looked up them.

"So," he said, finally. "Your head hurts?"

I didn't smile. I just wasn't in the mood.

"Don't tell me, you walked into a door."

"I was punched."

He nodded. "That was my next guess. Most likely, you have a mild concussion. There's nothing you can do, really, just take it easy, don't look at bright lights. You ought to feel better soon."

The throbbing had diminished to a small pinpoint, but I pictured it as a malicious presence gathering strength, preparing for another, even more painful assault.

"I'll give you some pills," he went on. "You'll float through the next couple of days like a great big cloud, and by then it should be fine. Don't operate any heavy machinery, as they say." He handed me the prescription. "I want you to see a neurologist, too, just to be sure. Set up an appointment on your way out." He wrote a name on a sheet of paper. "And, Cowboy, try and stay out of fights for a while."

Spider was waiting, reading a copy of *Redbook*. I told him I was okay. "A concussion," I said. "Just like you said."

"What now?"

"I'm supposed to make another appointment. And I go get these pills." I waved the prescription form. Just having it in my hand seemed to make me feel better, and I decided to forgo the other appointment. I knew about the medical establishment— once they got their hooks into you they squeezed you for everything they could get. And I was worried about where the money would come from, since I had no health insurance.

At the drugstore I got two different kinds of painkillers— medium-sized green-and-white Fiorinal capsules that had a slightly fishy odor to them, and Tylenol with codeine. I took one of each.

The next day passed in a kind of warm fog. I went back to work and found that the piles of letters had multiplied overnight. I spent the morning picking up one and then another, unable to bring myself to answer any of them. In my prescription haze, it seemed that all was essentially right with the world, or at least right enough that no interference on my part was called for. So I just sorted through them, pulling some out to read, ignoring others entirely. Many of the letters were barely legible. I had already invented what I thought of as the typical Mutronics customer, a rock-and-roll patchwork doll pieced together from the impressions made by literally hundreds of letters. He was a small-town kid from the Midwest, saving his money to buy the gleaming distortion-booster in the local music store window. He and his friends had a band they called Nightshift, or Lynx. They watched MTV and hung out in record stores and stole cash from their parents when they weren't looking. With a Mutronics effect, the tinny truth of just how bad a player he really was could be obscured, because he had discovered that the secret to fooling everybody is to put up a wall of sound between you and the world. Enough distortion and delay, and the mistakes disappear. We could do that for him, at a price he could afford, at least until the product broke down, which ours did with regularity. It was funny to look around at all the dust, mouse shit, and disembodied electronics that covered every available inch of space, and realize that what we were really in the business of producing was dreams.

After lunch the power went out. Through listening to the conversations of the various sales reps passing by in the hallway, I gathered that Con Ed had been threatening this for some time. Apparently, Jerry hadn't been paying the bills. Carmen, working with grim determination, a flashlight, and a ladder, hooked up a lengthy series of extension cords from the back of the factory all the way out to a hallway lighting fixture by the elevator, the nearest source that wasn't on our meter. I understood then why Jerry found her so indispensable.

I attempted to write a little by hand, but it was dark, and the strain on my eyes made my head throb even more. So I sat at my desk and pretended to be working, instead listening to the scratch and rustle of the mice in the filing cabinet behind me, eating their way through years of invoices.

The next morning I stopped at a grocery around the corner and bought three *yahrzeit* candles. I put them on my desk where they flickered in their little jars, casting small, yellow circles of light over the mail. I understood they were supposed to be candles for the dead, but they were the cheapest ones I could find, and I allowed myself to believe I was lighting them for someone, somewhere, even if I didn't know who.

We fell into a pattern. Spider would ride in with me each morning, get off with me at my stop, then take off walking north up Sixth Avenue, his black jacket flapping in the breeze. "I like it," he said, when I asked him why he bothered. "I'm very interested in this whole commuting lifestyle. And I've never had much chance to spend time in New York."

Lunchtimes, he'd come back and meet me in Madison Square Park across from the Flatiron Building, where we'd eat the bologna and mustard sandwiches he'd made us that morning. He claimed to be just walking around the city. He went to Forty-eighth Street to look at guitars and talk to the salesmen. He bought a fedora at a secondhand shop, which made him look like a film noir gangster. We sat on the benches, watched people, made cynical comments.

I kept him up on what was going on at the factory, which was basically a waiting game. A diminished, less-enthusiastic group of picketers still showed up each day with their signs, but the eggs had stopped. Police were on hand at eight-thirty and again at five o'clock to make sure there was no violence. UPS still would not pick up or deliver, and I had a growing sense that the company was not going to last much longer, at least not unless the picketing ended immediately. But at least I wasn't having to work that hard. Sitting outside with Spider, eating our sandwiches in the air and sun, broke up the day nicely, made things seem somehow less grim. The Fiorinal and codeine helped, too. Both of us kept our eyes open for the guy who'd hit me, and we devised gruesome, medieval tortures for him. I proposed feeding him eggs until he gagged on them, swallowed his own puke, and died. Spider approved of this, but had his own variation. He wanted us to hang him by his ankles off the side of the Verrazano Bridge after he ate the eggs. "It'll be ugly," he promised. But we never saw him, and where for the first few days I'd carried my anger like an open knife in my pocket, it gradually grew less focused as the event itself translated into a series of images: the upward arc of his fist coming at me, my dad's concerned expression when I opened my eyes, Jerry's almost magical appearance in his cab. They might have been from some movie I'd seen.

Lenny DeMarino had been absent since the day Jerry made him work up on the sixth floor—the day I'd been punched. I asked the Mrs. Hong who handled payroll (there were two others on the staff) what was up. Was he taking vacation?

"No work here anymore," she said. She had short, dark hair, round, black-framed glasses. "Gone. Many people, gone."

Of course, I knew this. The receptionist, Julie, was gone, as was Hector, who'd been in charge of international sales. Frank, the quiet little man with a cluttered office near the mail room, who I understood to have been one of the real brains behind R&D for Jerry, had moved on, too. Still, in a small way, it felt like an accomplishment to have outlasted Lenny. I wondered if this meant I'd effectively been promoted.

"Do you think I could have his office?" I said.

"I don't know, you ask Jerry. Anything you want, you ask Jerry. I don't know. Maybe. You ask."

After thinking it over, I decided not to. My office was in a large room located about midway through the building, to the left off the main corridor. Originally, I'd shared it with a couple of higher-level technicians, Lee and Kim, but both of them had quit, too, and I now had the entire space to myself. Moving to Lenny's paneled office up front seemed somehow out of keeping with my image of myself in relation to the rest of the employees. Technically, I was management—I was white, had a college degree, and dealt with the public. But I felt more like one of the workers, and certainly, I spent more time in back with them than I did up front. I figured I'd stay where I was.

The Mutronics sales force, the ones who had stuck around, couldn't sell any products because of the UPS embargo, and so, having little else to do, made regular trips up the fire escape to the roof to get high. I began tagging along. They were wary of me at first, and I guessed they suspected me of being Jerry's spy, since Lenny DeMarino almost certainly had been. Cat had long dark hair he wore in a ponytail and dressed in tight jeans and black silk shirts open nearly to the navel. He claimed to have once played on tour with Bob Marley, but I'd heard him fooling around with a guitar one day in the back, and he was so awful it couldn't have been true. Handing me a joint the size and shape of a small burrito, he asked me whether I was looking for work.

"Not yet," I said, between puffs. "Are you?"

Dan, another salesman, started to laugh. He was a short guy who rode a motorcycle to work and compensated for his height by always wearing black leather boots with big heels. I didn't care for him much—he was just too full of himself—but Jerry loved him. Dan had been Mutronics' most successful salesman the past two years running. "I would if I were you," he said.

"I just got me an offer yesterday," said Cat. "Selling electronics up at Sam Ash."

"My wife and I are looking at moving to the West Coast," said Pete, our computer man. "Silicon Valley."

"You're really all leaving?" I asked. I was amazed. These people had been with Jerry for years.

"Wait until you see your paycheck this week," said Dan.

"What about it?"

"Fifty bucks." Cat took the joint and shook some of its huge ash off with an expert flick of his forefinger.

"Fifty bucks?"

"That's it, and you can expect it to go down from there. Jerry's out of money. The payroll account is dry."

"Which is where I cut out," said Dan. "No tickee, no laundry."

Cat nodded in vigorous agreement. "When you're out of Schlitz, baby, you're out of beer."

"*I want my* room back," Sally said. "It's been over two weeks." I had just climbed into bed, and I was surprised she was awake. She'd been going to bed earlier and earlier, and as a result she now woke up at four A.M., went up to the living room, and sat drinking coffee and doing bong hits until it was time to leave. I barely saw her anymore, only the burned matches she left on the coffee table.

"I'll talk to him about it tomorrow." I planted a kiss between her shoulder blades, then rolled onto my back and clenched my teeth against the wave of pain the movement brought about.

"I found a photo in his room," she said. "A woman holding a baby."

"Excuse me?"

"A baby, Spencer."

"What were you doing in his room?"

"My room, remember? It's where my things are."

I lay quietly, staring up at the dark screen of my ceiling. Sally rolled over to look at me, then touched my cheek.

"I think he's done the same thing again."

I could feel the pounding in my head, closed my eyes against it.

She leaned up on one elbow. "Spencer?"

"What?"

"Did he or did he not run out on your mother and you?"

"It's more complicated."

"It's not complicated, it's simple. Did he or didn't he?"

"I don't feel like explaining right now. My skull is about to explode, all right?"

She was quiet for what seemed a very long time. Then she said, "Would you ever do anything like that to me?"

"Of course not."

"But you have cheated on me. There was Rachel Hightower."

"I never did anything with Rachel Hightower."

"Oh, come on. At the cast party after *Superstar?* You two were all over each other."

I'd been in the pit band for our college production, pretending to read the sheet music, instead memorizing my parts off the album. At the party, Rachel and I had made out in a back bedroom for a while, then the next day pretended neither of us remembered. Still, word had gotten back to Sally, and we'd almost broken up over it at the time. "A drunken grope. We've been through this before. Nothing happened. Why are you dragging all this up, anyway?"

"I don't know." She sat all the way up. "I'm just trying to figure it out. It's one thing when you're nineteen, but it's different when you're, well, whatever he is. It's a poor excuse for a person who'd walk out on a wife and baby."

"You don't know that," I said. "You're making assumptions."

"What's the matter?" She looked at me with sudden concern. "I'm sorry—I didn't mean to upset you." She put a finger to my cheek, then traced a line there. "I'm just confused—about us, about everything."

"Then what do you want?"

"I don't know. Sometimes, though, I just feel as if I can't even breathe."

* * *

In the morning, the pain was so bad I could not get out of bed. I sat up, closed my eyes against the throbbing. It ran back and forth between my temples, pressed over my eyes, blinded me. I lay back down and moaned.

For the next three hours I stayed flat on my back, hurting too much to move and far too much to fall back asleep. I was convinced that at any moment my skull might split wide open. In fact, a part of me longed for it—it would have been a relief. There was no one to help me. Sally had gone to work and Spider was apparently still asleep upstairs, too far away to hear my quiet moans. I sat up a number of times, but the space from my bed to the door might as well have been the Grand Canyon.

Ultimately, a need for the bathroom got me to my feet. Each step sent a shock wave shuddering up me like the weight on a carnival strength-meter, registering loudly on the bell that was my brain. Squinting against the sunlight, I shuffled out into the hall, then to the bathroom. With one hand I braced myself against the wall and reassured myself that at least part of my body still functioned. The kidneys then, as well as the bladder, must be doing fine. It was comforting to think of them humming away at their jobs without any supervision—dependable employees still showing up for work, even if upper management was in serious trouble. Still in my underwear, I flushed—a thundering of tsunamic proportions—staggered back out into the hallway, and pointed my face upward.

"Help," I said. The stairway seemed to have become a full-sized version of the Escher print Sally had thumbtacked to the wall of the landing, overwhelmingly steep and logically impossible. I eased back into bed and cried a little, then fell mercifully asleep.

Spider came downstairs about noon, the sound of his feet on the stairs slow, as if each step downward were another decision. The steps creaked and groaned under his weight. He stopped outside my door, paused, then gave it a push. He had his suit jacket on, and his fedora. His bag was in his hand. I wondered if Sally had said something to him. More likely, he'd sensed that he was overstaying his welcome. I was lying on my back with both forearms covering my eyes, a position I'd found that didn't hurt so much.

"You're here," he said, surprised. He put down the bag, came over and put a hand to the side of my head. "You got a fever?"

I turned sideways, my arms now crossed in front of my chest. Even that small amount of movement set off a whole new wave of pounding in my skull. I didn't think I could even speak.

"Where's your pills?" He hunted around my dresser and came up with one of the bottles, shook two out, and brought them to me. While I swallowed, he went back into the hall to phone a car service.

"I'm okay," I managed to say. "Don't worry about it."

As I listened to the soft sounds of his voice from beyond the door, I thought of the long, low conversations he and my mom used to have when I was little, late at night, after they assumed I'd already fallen asleep. I'd be convinced they were planning some surprise for me. The next day, I lived in expectation of what it would be—a tray of brownies maybe, or a trip to the drive-in. I would watch them for signs, certain that they were just teasing me, prolonging the wait. And though I should have learned by repetition that in fact the long talks had nothing to do with me, that it was their own lives they were discussing and whether they ought to go on trying to live them together, I didn't. I was always working myself up into a state of anticipation, then getting disappointed, never willing to admit that I wasn't the constant center of their universe.

"I want to speak to Dr. Arlen," he said, mentioning the name of the neurologist the emergency room doctor had written down for me. I was surprised he remembered. He was put on hold for a long time. Finally, someone else came back on, and after a brief exchange, he got louder.

"Look, this is serious. My son has a head injury. You people saw him once and sent him home without any kind of test or anything. I'm a lawyer and I'd hate to have to sue, but that's how this is shaping up. I don't care how high the demand is for the equipment. All right, I'll wait." And then, after another few minutes of silence, "Hello, Dr. Arlen? Daniel Markus here. It's about my boy."

The cab arrived and we rode into the city, to a hospital on the Upper East Side where Dr. Arlen apparently had connections and had gotten me scheduled in as a favor. After an hour's wait, I was ushered into a big white room. A male nurse shot contrast dye into my arm and I lay flat on my back, my head inside the enormous CAT scanner. It made a loud, rumbling noise, like a washing machine changing cycles. I closed my eyes and tried to make my mind a blank. I didn't care what they found, just so long as they found something. Behind the glass panel of the control booth, I was aware of ghostly shapes moving about, working the controls, monitoring me.

Afterward, I rejoined Spider in the waiting area. I was actually feeling a little better.

"How was it?" he asked.

"Fine," I said. "I have dye in my veins."

He kept moving his hands around, drumming his fingers on his knee, intertwining them, then putting them awkwardly in his lap. I knew what he was thinking: that he'd done this to me.

We had to go upstairs for the diagnosis. Dr. Arlen had called in the order for the CAT scan, but now we met with someone else, a tall, young doctor with sandy-blond hair who wore a bow tie and had on running shoes. He shook both our hands and introduced himself as Dr. Lutz.

"Please walk across the room," he told me. I did it, pretty well, I thought. Still, he seemed to see something worthy of note, and scribbled on his clipboard. Then he withdrew a set of transparencies from an envelope and put them out for us to look at, photos of my brain. At the top, center, a small line wandered downward, then took a sharp right turn and disappeared. Other than that, I thought it looked okay.

"What exactly happened to you?"

"Punch in the mouth," said Spider.

"That's it? You didn't hit your head at all?"

"I don't think so."

The doctor's expression said he didn't quite believe us. "You've got a subdural hematoma. It's essentially a bruise inside your skull. Boxers get them sometimes—your head is jarred violently and the brain gets a bump. It swells like any normal bruise, only in this case there is no place for it to go. Your skull is not elastic." He said this as if it were somehow my fault, then pointed to the photos, indicating a small black space. "Here is the bruise. As you can see, the left hemisphere of your brain has been displaced quite dramatically. In fact, it's remarkable that you can still use your right leg and arm at all."

The pain behind my eyes seemed directly connected to my stomach. I felt sick. "My brain?" I said.

"What we do is drill two small holes to relieve the pressure."

"Drill?" said Spider.

"It's one of the oldest operations there is. Craniotomies, of a sort, have been performed for thousands of years."

"How could that be?" I tried to appear interested in this from a detached, anthropologic point of view. My hands were trembling, though, and I could hear a distinct note of hysteria in my own voice.

"Well, the survival rate wasn't very high back then. We do much better now." I tried to laugh, but what came out was more of a snort. He made some more notes on his clipboard. "We need to get you admitted immediately so that the operation can be performed in the morning. The swelling is very pronounced."

At the admissions desk, when I said I had no insurance, the woman peered at me over a pair of steel-rimmed glasses and said, "Perhaps you ought to try another hospital."

"He was injured on the job," said Spider. "You just charge it to workmen's comp."

She ignored him and tapped her pen against the desk twice. "How were you injured, sir?"

"I was leaving work, and these people jumped me. It's definitely job-related."

Her steady gaze said she doubted it. "If you were leaving work, you weren't *at* work."

"It was part of being at work. I mean, I was *there*. I had to leave sometime, right?"

"It's not the same."

"I think it is."

"There are other hospitals."

"We like this one," said Spider.

"We can attempt to file a claim, but I'm afraid I cannot admit you on that basis. We'll need a minimum deposit of two thousand dollars against costs."

Spider sighed, then, to my surprise, produced a maroon checkbook and wrote out a check for the amount. "Hell of a system," he said.

The woman took it and looked it over. "I'm afraid we'll need something local."

"I'm afraid this is all you're going to get. Go ahead and do something unusual for a change. I don't live here."

She took the check, put it aside on her desk, and gave me a clipboard with a bunch of forms to fill out. It was the end of the day; apparently, she was feeling charitable.

Within an hour I was gowned and in a bed. My roommates were a group of older men, all unconscious except for one, a Mr. Lipton, who was so out of it that he kept attempting to drink from the urinal on his night table. An orderly came in from time to time to check on him. I could not understand why he didn't simply empty the urinal, or take it away. There was a pitcher of water on the table as well, but Mr. Lipton wasn't interested.

One of the other two men was hooked up to a machine that monitored some aspect of him, perhaps his heart. It blinked a green light every few seconds.

They wouldn't feed me anything, and the hunger pangs made my head ache even more. Spider and I sat in the room discussing what I could have for my first meal after the surgery.

"Red meat," he said. "That's what I'd do. Something to get the blood going again."

"It'll probably be Cream of Wheat."

He shook his head. "No, sir. You can get anything you want. I happen to know that the chef here was trained in Paris."

"Okay, then," I said. "Steak. With baked potatoes, fresh peas, and a good French wine."

"And for dessert," he said, rubbing his chin as if deliberating over a highly complex menu, "Baked Alaska."

When I was little, on the rare nights we all ate together, he used to like to say the same thing, putting on a bad imitation of a French waiter's accent. He'd always thought of Baked Alaska as the epitome of high-class desserts, something so extravagant as to be almost absurd. I'm sure he had no idea what a Baked Alaska actually was, but that didn't matter, it was just the sound of it. I hadn't known either, until I spied it on a menu the previous spring, at a birthday dinner Sally treated me to. When it arrived, I was disappointed. I didn't know what I'd imagined exactly, but this wasn't it. I'd wanted something huge, like the state of Alaska itself, something that would make everyone in the restaurant turn and look in awe.

"Maybe just a burger," I said. "With fries, onion rings, coleslaw, and a big, nasty pickle."

"There you go," he said. "God bless America."

At nine they made him leave. "You can stay on," I told him. "You don't have to go. Use my room." I wondered if this was going to be it for another seven years. I'd gotten along fine without him before, I could do it again. Still, feelings I'd long ago dug a deep hole for were busting their way out of the ground like corpses in a grade-B horror flick that just wouldn't stay buried.

"Don't worry, I'll be back to watch you eat that meal. Here, I almost forgot." He reached into a bag and brought out copies of *Playboy*, *Time*, and *Downbeat*, with B. B. King on the cover. " 'Babes of the Big Ten.' That ought to keep you going. Good articles in there, too, of course."

"Thanks," I said, somewhat embarrassed. I put the magazines facedown on the night table. I figured I had to ask. "Is there anything you want to tell me?"

"No," he said. "Not that I can think of."

I barely slept. One of my roommates began to snore around midnight, a horrible, rasping noise like a metal rake being dragged across asphalt. The other one lay still, but the blinking of his machine was like a malevolent cat's eye opening and shutting. Also, though I lay on my back staring up, I was sure that Mr. Lipton was watching me. When I tried to look across the room at him, all I could see were shadows, one of which was certainly his form, but whether or not he was actually sitting up and staring, I could not tell. At times I thought I might be asleep, but then I thought that if I was capable of thinking that, I must be awake, at which point whether or not I had actually been asleep became irrelevant, because the mental gymnastics posed by the problem of deciding became enough to truly wake me. I would put a hand to my eyes, be reminded again of the pressure in my head, and remember quite clearly where I was and what was happening.

In the morning they put me on a cart and wheeled me from one testing area to another. They did my heart, my blood, my urine. I was starving and it made my head hurt even more. After each test I was returned to my room. Five minutes later another orderly would show up to take me someplace else. None of them told me anything, and each time they came, I assumed it was for the operation itself. It was an odd form of torture. I'd read about Dostoyevsky being placed before a firing squad, then getting a last-second reprieve. They said it was only after that moment that his real genius clicked in. Since at any moment holes were going to be drilled into my skull, I thought I should try and get the most out of the experience. I made little deals with myself. If I managed to live through it, I decided, I would become a religious person. I would eat only rice and organic vegetables, move to a mountainous region, and live a life of contemplation. Either that, or go the other way, take up a profession. Law, for instance. I could dedicate myself to helping the little guys, exploited workers like the ones at Mutronics. I could ask Sally to marry me, apply to law school, make some real money. By noon, I had convinced myself that this operation was going to be one of the best things that had ever happened to me. When that Puerto Rican guy clocked me, he'd actually caused me to take a step back and reexamine myself. He'd literally knocked some sense into me.

Finally, around four, they came to get me for real and things happened very quickly. I was wheeled into an elevator, then out, then around some corners. Flat on my back, I tracked our progress by watching the ceiling. It occurred to me someone had really missed an opportunity in leaving it blank. Thousands of people were rolled along these corridors in just my position, eyes upward, and all they ever got to see were white squares with little holes in them. Why not advertising? Sell space to aspirin companies, insurance companies, personal injury lawyers. Or maybe just some nice, nerve-calming artwork to look at. Something abstract and hypnotic, with soft colors that lulled you and suggested reassuring things, open spaces, sunlight, comfort. Images to take with you into the operating room.

A young man in a green gown bent into my field of vision and grinned at me. I smiled back, sure that this was someone I knew, maybe a high school friend who now had a job helping out in the hospital. Moments later, as they transferred me to a steel table in the operating room, I saw that he was the man in charge of putting me under. He slid a needle attached to a tube into the underside of my arm, then removed it. He tried again. After the third try I heard him say "Shit." He grinned again at me and we switched arms. The anesthetic just wouldn't flow right. I was growing nauseated from all the stabbing. Closing my eyes, I willed my veins to open, tried to create a vacuum in my body. I could tell that it was working because he stopped muttering to himself. My eyes became heavy steel doors like the ones that used to slam shut during the opening credits of "Get Smart," which I suddenly remembered watching with my dad, hanging around his apartment afternoons, making cheese-melts in the toaster oven during the breaks between reruns of television shows that were black and white, even if the commercials were in color. I thought this was how my mouth tasted, black and white, or gray, rather, like my saliva had turned to paint, and then I was briefly in a cartoon of my own directing, a fist coming at me again in stop-motion photography, Mr. Lipton sitting up in bed and noticing me (what was he doing in my cartoon, anyway?), a jet airplane starting up its engines, which may or may not have been the drill (though wouldn't they have had to cut me first?). The questions came at me like drumrolls as the world accelerated. Then a fast shift to black and a kind of sleep that only the heavily narcotized know—sinking under three feet of warm mud and feeling glad about it.

8

A *supermarket version* of "Hey, Joe" banged away at my consciousness like a fly against a closed window. The notes whirred around on top of one another, vaguely recognizable, suggesting the lyrics with syrupy violins. *Hey, Joe, where you going with that gun in your hand?* I thought about this—not about Joe, whoever he was, but about the person asking. In the middle of a crime of passion, here was this guy conducting an interview. Getting straightforward answers, too. *Going out to shoot my old lady.*

Then it was no longer "Hey, Joe," it was "Love Story." I decided it had been that all along, though it struck me as odd that I hadn't been able to tell the difference. I also decided I was not in a supermarket. The source seemed tiny and far away, but I could not drive it from my ears. I was in a hospital. The understanding came to me the way a drowning person hears an urgent message from the deepest recesses of his mind, shouting "Water! You are under water!" when sleep seems more attractive than air. I swam thickly to the surface, opened my eyes, and asked, "Could we listen to something else?"

A nurse with frizzed blond hair shushed me. "It's four in the morning. The music is to relax you. How do you feel?"

"Okay, but if I die right here, it will be your fault for not changing the station." Even flat on my back in the recovery room, I could still be cute.

"Would you like some water?"

I figured I was still asleep, only imagining that I was saying things to her. In fact, she was herself probably something conjured by my subconscious. She seemed about my age, had a beautifully shaped body filling out her nurse's uniform, which was white as a sail. Big brown eyes, too. A definite mirage.

"I'd like a hamburger, french fries, coleslaw, onion rings, chocolate milkshake, and a big, nasty pickle. Extra ketchup."

"I'll get you some water."

I spotted where the music was coming from, a big, old-fashioned radio on her desk. As I tried to sit up she stopped me.

"You can't move," she said. "I'm very serious. Listen. You have to remain exactly in that position for the next couple of days. You're still draining. You've got two drains in the back of your head."

I saw with alarm that something else was running into my arm.

"The IV is just an antibiotic, in case of infection. Here." She put a straw in the water and held it up for me to sip, which I did. Immediately, I had to pee, and I told her this.

"Go ahead."

I asked her what she meant.

"You have a catheter. Just relax and go."

Now I was definitely awake. It was all I could think about. My whole body tensed, as if subjected to an electric current. "Could you take it out?"

She looked doubtful. "I suppose. I wouldn't recommend it, though. Much easier this way. Otherwise you're going to need help every time."

"Please." I was starting to feel dizzy.

Quickly, efficiently, she reached under the sheets, untaped something from my leg, then gave a little yank. I winced, but it seemed a first step toward freedom. At least I was no longer a filter in an elaborate plumbing setup.

She held me while I peed into a stainless-steel pitcher, which she then took away and labeled for analysis. Her face indicated no sort of reaction one way or another. Just another penis to her, no particular star qualities.

"About the music." It occurred to me that for the first time in over two weeks, my head didn't hurt.

"This is the recovery room. I'm trying to create a good atmosphere."

I was too tired to argue. Maybe she was a frustrated deejay. There were others in her audience, but I could not see them, only hear their breathing, the occasional blip of a monitoring machine. A warm fatigue began to tug at me, and I surrendered. Already my nurse was fading into a religious mist in front of me, her features dissolving among the fluorescent lights, the antiseptic air.

"I love you." I was unlikely ever to see her again, but there was a part of me that had never meant anything so sincerely.

"And I love you, too," she said. Or at least I thought she said it, though it was entirely possible she said something else, like "I'm nothing to you," or "Oh, sure you do." Still, I fell back comfortably into my dreams, clutching at the words like a warm blanket, pulling them over me, diving down deep.

When I awoke next, I was alone in a completely different place. It was daytime and all I could think of was that I had nothing to do. I could hear people walking around outside my room, an occasional laugh, a set of directions. These people had plenty to keep them occupied—if you worked in a hospital you were never bored. But I could see that being a patient was going to be torture. I imagined the pile of letters on my desk at work growing higher and higher. Who was going to take care of them? Randy? In spite of the fact that I felt generally dishonest when I did my job, the thought of Randy trying to deal with customers made me edgy. I was the one who knew the right things to say, how to pacify them. I was important, not her. Oddly enough, it seemed I actually took some pride in my work, even if it was work done for someone else. I'd always thought of this as a false, made-for-TV emotion, reserved for steel-workers at closing time, on their way out of the mill and over to the nearest beer commercial. Of course, there was the business with the paychecks. Perhaps Randy wasn't even there any longer. Maybe no one was. Even so, I wanted to *know*.

For a while, I kept my mind occupied by plotting my escape. I could knock out one of the orderlies, take his uniform, and walk out the front door. Or remove a few ceiling tiles and go for a long crawl through the heating vents. I could hide in a laundry hamper—that always worked in the movies. But there was still a big problem: I had drains in my head. What did that mean? If I stood up, would my brains leak out? I held up my left arm, the one that was not hooked up to the IV, and saw that the inside center was one enormous purple-black bruise, as if I'd been hit with a sledgehammer. All that jabbing, trying to find a vein. It didn't hurt, though, and ugly as it was, I felt removed from it. My body, I decided, was one thing, my mind something completely different. Instead of escape, I resolved to develop my mental abilities. I would learn astral projection, and with my spiritual self unbound, move around the hospital at will, slipping unnoticed into the operating rooms, the cafeteria, the nurses' lockers.

I fell asleep again.

I'd never slept so much. It seemed every time I opened my eyes, I was ready to close them. I dreamed a mixed-up jumble of things, but the one constant factor, the thing that made me wake up each time, was the memory of my headache, the pounding, ice-pick throbbing behind my eyes. It would bring me lurching to consciousness only to find, to my astonishment, that there was no pain at all.

I asked Dr. Lutz about this when he finally appeared, still sporting his bow tie, carrying a clipboard. He had the kind of smile you can only learn in medical school bolted to his face, wide as a car grille.

"Not unusual," he said. "Phantom pain, the same thing amputees sometimes feel. You know, the foot hurts even after it's been removed. In your case, you are so used to having a headache, you're remembering what it felt like. It should stop happening in a day or so." He made some marks on the clipboard. "Trust me, I got it all out of there. There was quite a bit of fluid, in fact."

"Does that mean something?"

"Not a thing. It all came out nicely on its own." He adjusted his tie. "Oh, and you've got visitors," he said on his way out.

Sally and Rick had come together. Sally carried home-baked chocolate chip cookies, Rick a selection of Sgt. Rock comic books. He was smiling, but his face was pale, as if he hadn't slept much lately. Sally wore new glasses, round ones that made her look intellectual.

"Wow," she said, taking in all the equipment.

Rick put the comics on my night table. "When do you think you'll be getting out of here?"

"Around ten days. That's what they told me at first. I guess it depends."

Sally put her hand on mine. "Do you feel better, at least?"

I told her I did. "But I'm having memory pain—when I fall asleep, I dream that my head hurts and I wake up."

"Ouch."

"Then when I wake up it's gone."

"I'm going to find the guy who hit you," said Rick. "I got you the number of a lawyer, too." He put a card down on top of the comics. "This is a top man, Kravitch. He got some people I know from work off on a drug charge. Very tough—I already talked to him and he says for you to call."

"What about my dad?"

"The Spiderman?" said Rick. "The Master of the Stratocaster?"

"Telecaster. Gone, right?"

Sally squeezed my hand. "When I came home from work there was just a bottle of wine on the table, no note or anything."

I wasn't surprised. Still, I'd thought he might at least stick around to see how I turned out.

"What is this stuff?" said Rick, poking at one of the hoses running into my arm. "Looks like Tennessee corn whiskey."

"Antibiotics. Glucose. Hospital lunch."

Sally didn't think it was funny. "You had no right to get hurt like this," she said. "You scared the shit out of me."

"I'm going to leave you two alone for a while," Rick said. "Just hang in there and relax—I'm on the case. And if there's anything you need, you know, vibrator, love-doll, edible underwear, just give a holler."

"Please." Sally put her hands on her hips.

"Sorry, can't help talking shop. I'll be out in the hall."

"I don't believe I live with that person," she said when he was gone.

"Rick's all right. He's just going through a phase."

"I'm sorry about your dad. I hope I didn't drive him off."

"He's not half that sensitive, don't worry about it. It's no big deal. I'm just glad you came down to see me." The effort of even this short amount of conversation was taking its toll, and my eyes began to close on their own.

"I miss you."

"You do?" I struggled to remain awake, remembering vaguely the plans and promises I'd made to myself on my way in to the operating room. "Look, let's get married," I said.

"And have kids?"

"Yeah, kids and a dog and a station wagon and a yard."

"Boys or girls or both?"

"Either. All three." I was fading fast, but still I clutched to consciousness; this was important. "I'm serious. What do you say?"

She kissed my forehead. "It's a lovely idea," she said. "But you don't mean it."

I got my first real meal that evening, turkey and mashed potatoes and peas, Jell-O and milk. It was fed to me by a big Jamaican woman who was in an enormous hurry. No sooner had she placed one forkful in my mouth than she had the next one poised, waiting for me to reopen. I chomped furiously, trying my best to enjoy and at the same time inhale the meal. I was starving.

"Come, child," the nurse said, "I ain't got all night."

In my weakened state, chewing took a great effort, but the taste of real food, even hospital variety, was so wonderful that I wanted the meal to last forever. Some mashed potatoes had slipped off the fork on their way to being crammed into my mouth, and lay cool and wet by my cheek. My nurse shook her head.

"Look at this mess you makin'. I ain't cleaning this up, no sir."

I tried to lick the offending potatoes up with my tongue, but it would not reach. She put a huge oblong of Jell-O in my mouth and removed the tray, which still had plenty of dinner on it.

"It's a crying shame the food you wasting," she said, shaking her head. I swallowed the Jell-O, but by then she was gone.

During the evening a patient was brought in against his will—I could hear him struggling in the hall. A nurse hurried by to help the orderlies and gave the man a shot of something. I used the phone by my bed and called Sally, who was watching television. There was one over me, peering down like a big, colorful eye, so I found her channel and we watched together, a detective show. All the villains had either a mustache or bad skin. We didn't talk much, just an occasional comment about a character, or a guess at what was going to happen next, but it was comforting to have her by my ear. After a while I heard her calling my name repeatedly.

"What?" I asked. "What's the matter?"

"Spencer, hang up the phone," she said. "You're asleep."

I continued to wake up and nod out with very little clue as to how much time had passed. I knew it was night because it was dark out, but the rest was guesswork. At one point, I heard a commotion outside as the patient who'd been causing trouble earlier got loose again and began wandering the halls. This time they needed security guards to subdue him. I could only make out a sliver of the action through my partially open door, but I could hear most of it. When all was quiet I fell asleep again.

I dreamed about Spider slipping into the hospital after visiting hours, grabbing a white orderlies' jacket from a supply closet, and taking the elevator up to the eleventh floor, to see me. He carried a bucket and mop, just for added effect, and when he came in he stood over the bed looking down on me with a solemn expression on his face. Though I knew he was there, I refused to open my eyes. I consciously paced my breathing to sound like deep sleep. If I opened them, I was sure, he would vanish into thin air, but as long as I kept them closed he'd stay, and I wanted the company.

As I lay there, though, I gradually became aware that I was in fact awake, and that someone was standing over me. I let my eyes open a crack, just enough to make out a face that was for a moment my father's, but then instantly someone else's. I realized it was the man from down the hall, escaped again. He was broadly built, had white stubble on his face, and a bandage wound at a slight angle across his forehead like a field dressing, in the front of which was a small, irregularly shaped stain. He'd had some kind of blow to the head, too, and it had clearly left him unhinged, or at least further loosened what hinges he had. His blue eyes were smoky and distant. I knew he'd been sedated at least twice already tonight, but here he was, out for another walk.

I tried to remember where the nurse's call button was, but without betraying the fact that I was awake by looking around for it, I was helpless. And it seemed to me that remaining very, very still might be wise.

"Son of a bitch, Jesus Christ," my visitor said. "Matilda."

There was nothing I could do: I was wired in by my arms and skull. I tried practicing my mental communication skills and formed words in my mind to direct him. *Go out in the hall*, I thought as loudly as I could. *This is not your room. No Matilda here.*

But instead, he reached down and touched my face. His hands were so callused it was like having a crab take hold of my nose, which was exactly what he did. He put it between his first two fingers and squeezed.

Hey, Joe, where you gonna run to now?

I'd always had an extremely sensitive nose. I broke it when I was five, tripping over a guitar cord in our living room, and falling face-first against a Fender Reverb. Since then, the slightest bump on it and my whole head started to buzz, my eyes to swim. The process culminated in a colossal, window-rattling sneeze. I knew one of these was coming now.

"Jesus Christ," he muttered again. He let go of me and began wandering the room. He peered into the closet where my clothes were hung, looked out the window, then returned and leaned very close to my face, giving me the benefit of his breath, which smelled like something three or four days dead.

I tightened my jaw, twitched my lip, bit the inside of my cheek. It was no use. I stopped fighting and let it happen.

The sheer force surprised us both. My head came up a few inches from the pillow, then slammed back down with the recoil. It wasn't messy, just loud, the sound originating somewhere deep in my diaphragm and projecting outward in a blast like a steam whistle. It was cathartic and cleansing, and the only really strong statement of which my body was capable. His reaction was slow, but profound. He stood straight up, staring at me in a kind of bewilderment. Then he began to scream. It was like a response, an apelike, primal howl of assertion. Okay, you were pretty loud, he seemed to be saying, but I can be louder. I closed my eyes against the sound. After about ten seconds he stopped. "Motherfuck," he said, as if in awe of himself. Then he advanced toward me.

The noise had brought a whole platoon of orderlies running to my room. There was a scuffle. He managed to bloody one of their noses and to grab hold of the nurse's hair who was trying, once again, to get a needle into his behind. As it entered him he howled again, this time with pain. He did not go under, but his body kind of froze up, and he was put into a chair with straps for his arms and feet to keep him from moving.

"Matilda," he said, softly.

"Try and get some rest now," the night nurse told me as they wheeled him out of my room. But I could not. I kept thinking of how he'd looked, strapped into that chair, his eyes on me the whole time.

My mother and Hal came up from New Jersey the next day. I'd called her the first night and left a message on her machine. There was a ridiculous greeting on it about "the essence of communication being intent," and how if it was the caller's intent to communicate something, they should wait for the tone. It was language she'd certainly picked up from one of the personal growth workshops she'd been taking lately. What I thought now, though, as I looked up at their concerned, worried faces, was simply how nice they looked together. Hal was as thin as ever, sporting a neatly trimmed beard. He was younger than my mom, whom he called Janice. Her whole life she'd never been anything but Jan. It seemed oddly formal, but that was the way Hal communicated with the world, seriously, as if at any moment he might be asked to make a policy decision or negotiate between warring countries. My mother's hair was cut fairly short and I could tell she'd been playing a lot of tennis lately. Her skin glowed against the white of her shirt. They'd been away for a few days at the shore, she explained. That was why she hadn't come up immediately.

"When you get out, I want you to come home. We can fix up the guest room for you. You're going to need a lot of time to rest and recover."

"We'll see." I wasn't ready to make any commitments.

"We saw your company on the news the other night," said Hal. "NBC—you know, that talk show thing they do before the real news? They had this guy on dressed in a Captain America outfit. I mean it, the whole thing—cape, leotard, bright red boots. He was shouting about communists, unions, the American way, industrial sabotage, you name it. Quite a performance."

"How could you let yourself get involved in something like this?" said my mother. "You're not a fighter. Since when do you get in fights?"

"It was a sucker punch. A sneak attack."

"A sucker punch? Listen to you."

"That's what you call it. He hit me when I wasn't looking and I dropped like a sack of potatoes. It's what happens."

"Your father had something to do with it, didn't he?"

"What do you mean?"

"He called me." She bit a little of her top lip under her lower teeth, a nervous habit of hers. She had a permanent dent there.

"He called you?" I was impressed—it didn't seem like something he'd do. "What did he say?"

"Just that you were here. Which, of course, I knew."

"What did *you* say?"

"I said thanks. What do you think I said? I was worried about you, not him."

"He's been in Canada," I said. "And in Maine. He calls himself 'Spiderman Dan.' "

"That's wonderful, Spencer. Maybe someday you, too, can run out on your child and all your responsibilities and take up a new life under an assumed name. I just want to know, did he somehow cause this?"

I thought about the redheaded woman, how he'd shaken her, his long fingers spread out around her shoulders. "It would have happened with him there or not," I assured her. "It was just one of those things."

She obviously didn't believe me. "If I had it all to do over," she said to no one in particular, "I'd ask for a daughter. I'd take her to ballet and horseback riding lessons, and if she stayed out past curfew, I'd ground her for a month."

"All part of the new conservatism," I said to Hal, who was paging through my issue of *Time*.

"I know." He put the magazine aside. "Don't worry, she gets like this sometimes. It'll pass."

"Here," my mother said, absently, "I brought you these." From her purse she withdrew a bag full of expensive chocolate chip cookies. "They have macadamia nuts."

"Thanks," I said, "I love macadamia nuts."

She put them down next to the bag that Sally had left.

"So, what do you do around here for fun?" asked Hal.

"Last night I had a lunatic come into my room and scream for a while."

My mother looked alarmed. "What are you talking about? Who came into your room?"

I was sorry I'd said anything. She already saw me as a lightning rod for disaster, and it didn't make sense to have her worry even more.

"No one. It was just a bad dream. I do a lot of sleeping."

She reached down and touched my cheek. "You shouldn't be all alone in this room," she said. "I'll talk to them."

"Mom, don't. I like it here."

"You just concentrate on getting better. That's your only job now." She took Hal's arm. "We're going to go to the museum. Is there anything we can get you?"

I shook my head. I was on the verge of falling asleep again. I waved good-bye to them through what seemed like a dull ocean mist, as if one of us was departing on a voyage.

The next morning, the doctor was by again to check on me and rewrap my head with a fresh bandage. I fell asleep, and when I awoke I was in a different room, though whether this was the result of some intervention by my mother was unclear. Officially, my room was supposed to be semiprivate anyway, I'd just been lucky those first two days. I looked around as best I could and took stock of my new roommates. I seemed to have two. One I could not really see. The other was an old man who had his television turned up full blast. He was on the telephone discussing his bowel movements with someone.

"Didn't make no doody this morning," he said.

I picked up my own phone and dialed the operator to get the area code for Augusta, Maine. Then I called long-distance information and gave them my father's name. He was listed. I had nothing to write the number down with, so I repeated it over and over in my mind for the next few minutes, trying to decide whether or not to do this.

"I don't know what they'll have for lunch," said my roommate. "I hope something with fiber. Fruit would be nice."

I picked up the phone and dialed, my head only half-turned since I still had the drains in. On the other end there was a distant ringing, muffled, like a cat's purr. Then a woman answered. "Hello?" she said.

"Hello," I said back.

There was a brief pause. "Dan?" she said. "Is that you?"

I hung up the phone.

9

Dear Mutronics, Inc.,
This is the third time I've written to you. Please locate my repair (a deluxe Gopher) and return it to me at once. I'd rather have the thing broken and in my possession than sitting at your offices gathering dust. I'm extremely unhappy with the service I've received, and have already informed the Better Business Bureau here in Cincinnati that you are not a reliable company. Apparently they'd already received complaints, so I'm not alone.

I look forward to seeing my pedal back here within the next ten days.

Sincerely,
Dave Salton
Cincinnati, Ohio

Dear Mr. Markus,
I represent Mr. Bernard Lewis of San Diego. Mr. Lewis sent you a check last September in the amount of $814.95 along with an order for a number of your products. A photocopy of that order as well as the canceled check are enclosed.

We now ask that a full and prompt refund be made of Mr. Lewis' money. If payment is not forthcoming, we will be taking legal action against you and your company.

Thank you for your cooperation.

Sincerely,
Susan Harding
Hubble and Fitch, P.C.
Attorneys at Law
San Diego, California

Dear Mr. Markus,

I have tried to keep the FAITH. I know it's hot there, and I know there's a strike. But please think of ME. I sodder things for 50 cents an hour which barely buys cigarettes. My guitar is my LIFE. I have an original Buster Booster from way back and it still works GREAT. So I know you are a good company. So why are you giving me such a HARD TIME?

I know you'll send me my Gopher soon.

Yours,
Furry Couch #C-563-2798

10

I *left the hospital,* my head still wrapped in bandages, my inner arms a mass of purplish-blue bruises, carrying two unread novels, a stack of read and reread Sgt. Rocks, and a Bruce Springsteen coffee mug that the night nurse had given me. In passing some time together the subject had come up, and it turned out she was a major fan. She had a bunch of the mugs, each with a bad likeness of the Boss in red and black on the front, and a big American flag on the other side, which she'd picked up cheap from a souvenir place that was going out of business. The caption read BORN IN THE USA, but the bottom of the mug announced its actual birthplace as Indonesia.

I took the subway. Slightly dizzy, but grateful to be outside in the real world, I walked very gingerly toward the entrance, then down the steps. I'd only been in the hospital nine days, but the outside world seemed a foreign country. Gentle scoops were worn into the concrete, and I found myself wondering about the actual rate of deterioration. How many footsteps did it take to wear down a millimeter of cement? Were sneakers less abrasive than, say, wing tips? There was water everywhere, making spooky, cavelike dripping noises. I noticed the smallest things: the smooth yet uneven texture of the railing I held on to, which I calculated must have been painted over forty or fifty times. They never cleaned it, they just slapped on a fresh coat of paint over the soot. Years from now, archaeologists could make excellent judgments of air quality from cross-sections of that railing. They'd read like rings in a tree trunk.

On the platform, people kept their distance. My response to having all my hair shaved off had been to let my beard grow, and I sported a scraggly darkness around my jaw that itched like hell. A woman with a baby in a carry-sack kept staring at me, but looked away when I tried to smile back. When the train arrived I caught a glimpse of myself in its window, and understood. I didn't smell bad, but I looked like something fresh from the crypt.

Once seated, I stared at the posters, pleased that I was able to puzzle out the Spanish text of a toilet paper ad, not to mention one for a school for deaf children. Everything amazed me. The train rocketed between stations, jolting backward and forward, slamming our bodies around. I didn't mind. I had a good dose of phenobarbital in me, a prophylactic measure, the doctor said, since as my brain settled back into position, there was some chance of seizures. A fat guy in a security guard uniform ate Chinese food from a little white carton. The smell was pleasant, cheap, warm, and friendly. I closed my eyes and let it carry me away into the kind of semi-sleep I was so used to by now.

When I opened my eyes a few minutes later, it was just in time to change trains. My comic books were crushed where I'd been holding on to them so tightly, my novels had been stolen, and in my Bruce Springsteen coffee mug, someone had deposited a quarter, two dimes, and a penny.

That night Sally unwrapped my head at my request and took a look. It was not a pretty sight. My shaved scalp, just beginning to bristle with new growth, had been painted before the operation with various colored chemicals. It was yellow, mostly, with some green and red mixed in.

"They do that to sterilize the area," she said, adjusting the floor lamp so that more light would spill onto my bareheadedness. With a sponge she daubed lightly at the dyes, which came off easily. She brought two mirrors and gave me one to hold so I could get a look, too. The incisions were huge, and resembled railroad tracks.

"You're good to hang by me through all this," I said. She'd moved back into her own room while I was in the hospital.

"Don't be ridiculous."

The distance between us felt enormous. "How's work?" I asked.

She sniffed. "Yesterday there was this carload of Hispanic guys parked down by the lake? They had a case of beer, and they were playing their radio real loud. Every time one of them finished a bottle, he'd hurl it out into the water. I called the cops on them, but it didn't make me feel much better. It's the attitude that I just don't get, you know? Seeing the world as one big garbage can. I'm afraid I'm starting to hate people."

"You mean particular people."

"Nope, people in general. Every now and then you find someone worthwhile, but the vast majority out there aren't worth the time of day. Now, hold still." She began applying a fresh bandage.

After a week of lying around the house watching television, sleeping heavily and unexpectedly, and taking short walks to the Spanish market on the corner for cans of soup, I got Rick to take a day off from work. Together, we went to the Midtown offices of the lawyer he'd found. It was a cool October day, and the bright sunlight seemed to dance off the edges of buildings and parked cars, throwing the whole city into sharp relief. I wore a blue watch-cap to cover my stitches. I still hadn't shaved. The secretary who greeted us seemed extremely dubious about our appointment, but motioned us to seats and offered coffee. They were new offices, and I didn't know if that was a good sign or not. At intervals, from somewhere in back, a power saw complained loudly.

Kravitch came out and shook our hands. A little guy in an

impeccably tailored suit, he had a thick mustache that looked ridiculous on his small face, like something he'd glued on. Obviously, he was trying to appear older, but mostly he looked silly, and he didn't inspire my confidence.

"Markus?" he said, looking at both of us.

"That's him," said Rick, pointing.

We went into a small room which was equipped with a microwave, coffeemaker, and a sink. Kravitch motioned us to chairs, then hopped up on the counter. "Sorry," he said. "Right now I don't have an office, not until some of the other rooms are ready. You got coffee?"

We held up our cups.

"Okay, then, maybe you ought to just start from the beginning and tell me what happened."

I did my best, starting with the first day the organizers had appeared, finishing with the operation. Kravitch took occasional notes on a legal pad. Finally, he looked up.

"You didn't see the guy who hit you?"

"Not exactly. I told you, I was looking the other way. I saw him out of the corner of my eye. But I know who he is—he was one of the regular guys they had there. I could recognize him easily enough."

"Did anyone else see him?"

"Sure," I said. "A woman I work with, Randy, and also my father."

"Your father?"

"He was in town, visiting for a few days."

"This Randy. What's her last name?"

I thought for a second. "I don't know. She's just Randy. I could find out."

"Okay," said Kravitch. "We're going to need signed statements from both of them. I can take your case, but I want you to understand from the outset that it doesn't look all that good. We don't know who this guy was, and we probably never will. I'm just being honest with you. He could be anywhere. Not only do we need to connect him up with the union, but we then have to show that he was acting on behalf of the union when he punched you. Because, you see, he could have punched you for all kinds of reasons. Maybe you and he had an argument about something."

"I never met him before. I doubt he even speaks English."

"Yes, but the law is tricky here. Suppose I'm driving an egg truck for Jones's Dairy, and I happen to have some private beef with you. It doesn't matter what. I see you crossing the street and I veer out of the way and run you over. Assuming that you live, you don't have a case against Jones's Dairy, you only have a case against me. It doesn't matter that I was working for them at the time, it wasn't part of my job to run you over, so they are in the clear. You follow me?"

"I follow you," I said.

"This guy that hit you doesn't have any money, that's certain. If you can't connect him to the union, you're wasting your time. Basically, we've got to show that the union said 'Punch that guy's lights out.' "

"Who's going to believe that?"

"You and me, for a start. We believe it." He sounded like a coach trying to fire up his team. I already had a bad feeling about this.

"The signed statements might be a problem," I said.

Kravitch shook his head. "You must get them. They're practically all you've got right now. I would also like to encourage you to hire a private investigator to find out who this person is. And while I can do all this on a contingency basis, meaning one-third of whatever we get is my fee, I'll still need a retainer from you of five hundred dollars."

Rick poked me with his elbow and nodded that I shouldn't worry. I was a little stunned—it hadn't occurred to me that this might *cost* me money.

"Call me in a week," said Kravitch. "And get those statements ready."

On the elevator Rick told me he'd pay the five hundred, and I could reimburse him when I got my million, which was the least I ought to expect. "And as for the private investigator, just relax. I'll take care of that too."

"You know one?"

He shook his head. "I'm going to do it."

"Are you serious? These are dangerous people. I don't think it's a good idea."

"I *want* to. This is interesting to me. It's drama, with a bad guy and an evil organization behind him. It's an opportunity."

"I'd feel pretty bad if something happened to you on account of me," I said.

"Nothing's going to happen. I'll be very careful. Besides, the real danger is from the things you don't expect. Step out a door and a piano drops on your head, cross the street on a Walk sign and some guy runs you over because he's late to pick his kids up from school or there's a song he really likes on the radio and he isn't paying attention. Those are the things that get you, and there's no way to plan against them." The elevator came to a gentle landing and the doors eased open with a soft breath. "It's a random universe."

"That's supposed to be comforting?"

"Sure," he said.

I went in to Mutronics to talk to Randy, but when I got off the elevator I was faced with a locked door. I pounded on it for a while, stuck my face up against the small Plexiglas window. It was dark inside, though I could just make out the contours of the waiting area furniture, the ratty chairs, the table with ancient copies of music magazines spread out across the top. I'd already given up and pushed the elevator button again when the lock rattled open behind me. I turned and saw Jerry standing there, his large stomach pushing a black T-shirt over the waist of a pair of faded bell-bottom jeans.

"Hey, man," he said, extending a hand. "How are you feeling?"

He'd called me twice while I was still in the hospital, each time to report on various items of Mutronics news he seemed to think I must be dying to hear. The phone calls felt awkward, like being home sick from school and having the principal call just to talk.

"I'm getting those ICs," he said. "Finally." I vaguely remembered him mentioning a shipment of integrated circuits being held up because he owed the company for three back invoices. "And Inez, from Accounts Receivable? She had her baby. A boy. She brought him by the other day to show him off. Good-looking kid."

He brought me into his office and we sat. The factory was dead quiet; it seemed we were the only ones there. A small color television was on by his desk, tuned in to a hospital soap opera. He was trying to make me feel like family.

"The letters are still coming in. The people support us."

"That's good," I said.

"You keeping a diary?"

"No."

"You ought to go out and get yourself a diary. When you sue these bastards, it will help with your case. I've got a diary I've been keeping ever since they first showed up. My lawyers are looking at it now."

"Lawyers?" It hadn't occurred to me that he, too, might have lawyers.

"You bet. I'm suing them for wrecking my company, terrorizing my workers, restraint of trade, slander, libel, you name it." He picked a cigar butt out of the ashtray and put it in his mouth. "Fucking socialist gangsters. I'm filing Chapter Eleven here, so if you got anything in your desk you want, you better go get it. Everything goes at auction next week."

I thought of the enormous pile of unanswered mail by my desk. "You mean that's it? All those customers waiting for their orders?"

He blinked a few times. "I owe a lot of money. The lawyers and accountants will count up what we've got and figure out who gets what. It's out of my hands at this point."

"I need to find Randy," I said.

"You heard what happened to her?"

"What?"

"Punch in the mouth, like you. Knocked out one of her teeth. I tried to get her to go down and file a complaint, but she wouldn't do it. She just took her stuff and split. I haven't seen her since."

He got up and led me back through the dark hallways to the payroll office, which he unlocked. He gave me his lighter to hold over the filing cabinet while he searched for the personnel file. When he found it he read me the address. "Song, Randy. No phone listed here," he said. "I think she might not have one."

"Song?"

"Good name, huh? She's part Korean. Either that or she was married to one, I forget which."

"Listen," I said, "I was just wondering. Did we ever get paychecks?"

"Sorry, the well's dry." He dug into the pocket of his jeans and a number of crumpled bills spilled out and to the floor. "I can give you a few bucks."

"That's all right."

"You sure?" He gathered the fallen notes from the floor, began trying to assemble them into some kind of order. "Here's twenty."

I took the money, walked back to his office with him through the silent halls.

I left Jerry sorting through the mounds of paperwork on his desk, looking considerably humbler than he had in the past. I walked to Randy's apartment, which was in a sad-looking brick building down on Avenue A, its exterior covered in soot and graffiti. When I arrived I pressed the buzzer for number nine. There were no names next to any of the buttons. The front door was reinforced with wire mesh. I pressed again, but nothing happened. Walking away, I was relieved I hadn't had to go inside.

* * *

A couple of days later, I got a phone call from one of Jerry's lawyers attempting to convince me that I should throw my lot in with Jerry and the rest of the company in a class action suit, but when I mentioned this to Kravitch he told me no way, that mine was by far the more valuable suit and I should keep it separate.

A week went by, then two. Rick never seemed to be around, and when I did run into him, he continued to look tired. I told him he should take it easy, but he just smiled and said not to worry. Susu had left town, I knew, and as far as I could tell he hadn't come up with a replacement girlfriend yet. I never heard him typing anymore, though he still lifted a lot of weights. If he was doing any private investigating, he wasn't talking about it. During the days, when both he and Sally were off at work, I felt substanceless, like a ghost, doomed to walk the halls of our apartment. But I could feel myself getting stronger. Though I tried not to think about it, I began to wonder what it would be like to be rich.

The bills started to come in for my operation: three thousand for the surgeon, another four thousand for the hospital and related expenses, including my dad's bounced check. Workmen's comp, bearing out the prediction of the admissions lady at the hospital, had rejected my claim. The justification was that my injury was "not work-related." Over the phone, Kravitch gave me the name of a workmen's comp lawyer a couple of blocks from the World Trade Center.

Al DiGrassi was a white-haired Italian man in his mid-sixties who alternated between nicotine gum and menthol cigarettes. He listened to my story while reading someone else's file.

"Okay," he said. "It's taken care of."

I asked him what I should do with the bills.

"Don't pay them, you're covered." He said this with such authority, he might have been in charge of handing out the checks himself.

"But that's not what the comp people are saying." I didn't mention the fact that I couldn't pay them anyway.

"Take those bills and hold on to them," he said. "Anyone gives you grief, you tell them Al DiGrassi's handling your case."

"You're known around here," I said, watching him put down the file. It was clearly marked "Estevez." I wondered if it would be rude to point this out. Surely, he knew I was not Estevez.

He sniffed. "Forty years, I better be." Then he put the telephone receiver to his ear and that was it, I wasn't there anymore. No thank you, no invitation to call and check on the progress of my case, not even a good-bye. I hadn't seen him write anything down like the studious Kravitch, nor was I convinced that he understood the particulars of what had happened to me. But he was on the phone now, actively ignoring me, so I got up, took one of his business cards from the holder on his desk, and left.

Out in the street among all the men in business suits and striped ties, I felt better, almost as if I belonged. I had two lawyers. Hiring my first had made me a little intimidated. With two working for me I felt empowered, part of the invisible network I was beginning to understand held the world together. The strands and filaments were hidden from all but a select few, but they were there, nonetheless, guiding our actions in ways we barely understood.

I read books, watched television, went for short walks. It rained the first two weeks of November, a cold, grim rain that was never particularly heavy but would not go away. The whole world seemed swollen and depressed. I was feeling much stronger, and going a little stir-crazy.

"How about this?" I said to Sally one evening while she was doing dishes. "Take some time off work. We'll drive to Maine and have a vacation."

She'd cut her own bangs recently, and they made an uneven line across her forehead, as if she'd been in a hurry, or just didn't care.

"And do what?"

"I don't know. Hole up at some country inn, go cross-country skiing. Ice skate."

"You don't know how to do either of those things, and I doubt there's any snow." She squirted detergent onto a sponge and worked it inside a glass.

"I feel fine, and I could use some exercise. We'll borrow my mom's car—she and Hal can share for a little while. What do you say? I know it's not the kind of traveling you really want to do, but it's still a trip. A sort of warm-up. When I get my lawsuit money, we can go wherever we want."

She gave me a half-smile. "This wouldn't have anything to do with your dad, would it?"

"Why do you say that?"

"Well, who else do you know in Maine? I'm not accusing you of anything, I'm just asking."

"This is just about you and me getting away for a while, that's all. I want to go out into the world. I'm tired of sitting around. Do you want to go?"

She turned off the water and dried her hands with the Minnie Mouse towel that hung next to the sink. She'd picked it up at a stoop sale the previous Saturday, along with a plastic lobster she'd hung on the wall behind the sofa that made me jump every time I noticed it. "I want to get out of this town so badly I could scream. Yesterday, I attacked a man in the park."

"What are you talking about?"

"He was hiding in the bushes jerking off. So I picked up this rock and started running toward him, waving it and shouting. I wasn't myself at all, I was this crazed lunatic with a rock over her head, screaming obscenities. I chased him about fifty yards."

"Are you out of your mind? What did you do that for?"

"I just told you, I was pissed. I kind of lost it."

"Do you know how stupid that was? Do you realize?"

"Thank you," she said. "Advice from the man who wrote the book on staying out of trouble."

"I'm sorry. But there are crazy people out there. You have to be careful all the time. You can't expect some dumb uniform to protect you."

"I'm well aware of that. And don't call me stupid. I'm not stupid." She put some water on to boil and brought a box of shortbread cookies out of the cupboard.

"I just don't want anything to happen to you," I said.

We had tea and cookies and talked about the trip. After a while, she even seemed excited about it. We decided we'd leave immediately, or as soon as possible. It was quiet down at the park, perverts notwithstanding, and Sally had vacation time coming. Maybe we couldn't ski, but we could hike at least, finally use Sally's tent. I called my mother to arrange about the car. I knew she'd lend it. She responded deeply to hurt things; over the years any number of injured and abandoned birds had been rehabilitated in a box in our garage. Mail-order charities had a field day with her. As a son recovering from a head injury, I was in a position to ask for whatever I wanted.

When I got off the phone, I went downstairs and knocked on Rick's door. There was no answer, so I let myself in.

He was just sitting on his bed, fingers laced together, flexing them back and forth.

"Hey," I said. "What's going on?"

His room was really trashed: typewriter out, paper everywhere, weights scattered around the floor. He had a stack of pornography next to the bed, stuff he'd taken home from work. I picked one up and read the cover. *Latex Lovers?* Who reads this stuff?"

"You don't read it," said Rick. "You look at the pictures."

I tossed the magazine back onto the pile. "You don't look good."

"I can't sleep," he said, his eyes focused on a patch of floor between his feet. "Haven't for three days. I mean, I sleep for little snatches here and there, but then I wake up with a jolt, like somebody just touched me with a piece of ice."

He was in his red plaid robe. From beneath the hem, his pale, muscular calves descended like two hunks of knotty pine. I asked him if he'd tried a couple of stiff drinks before bed, but he said he had and it didn't do anything. Rick had a metabolism that could burn through a six-pack at the same rate most people process a glass of root beer.

"Dope?"

"Makes me more awake. I'm past the point where drugs have any effect. In fact, I took everything I had and flushed it. I'm afraid I'm going nuts, and I don't trust myself."

"Flushed it?"

"Straight to alligatorland. What do you think? Maybe there really is this whole world of hungry monsters lurking just a few feet below all of us. A big, collective unconscious waiting to get us. We all have bad dreams. Who's to say they don't come from someplace?"

"I don't know about that, but next time, ask before you flush. I mean, really."

"Sorry. It was a spur-of-the-moment thing."

"Maybe you should have your head drilled. It's expensive, but you feel great afterward. Me, I'm the head-drilling poster boy."

"There's a whole tribe of South American Indians who have that operation routinely," he said. "To take the pressure off, let out the bad spirits." He picked up a twenty-five-pound hand weight and began doing curls. "I lie in bed thinking, Okay, now I'm going to get some sleep. I start thinking about it so hard that I end up more awake than before. So I try counting sheep. When that doesn't work, I try counting baseballs. I imagine this pitcher who can't quite put it over the plate, only there's no walk rule—he just keeps on pitching. I counted two thousand pitches last night, before I finally gave up, went back upstairs, and got something to eat."

"Sounds bad."

"I'll get over it, I'm sure." He took a package of photos off the desk and handed them to me. "I bought a used camera and a telephoto lens yesterday. I spent most of today standing around outside union headquarters. Took the film to one of those one-hour photo places."

I hurried through the pictures, examining them. Some were hard to see, blurred or only side angles. About halfway through the second roll, I found him. I was certain of it, the height, the mustache, the eyes set deeply into his face, narrow and dark like Greek olives.

"You're a goddamn genius." I hadn't really believed his sleuthing would come to much. This felt like finding money on the street. "Who is he?"

"You'll have to find that out on your own. At least you've got a picture now." He put the rest of the prints back in their envelope and tossed them onto the desk.

"We're going on a trip. Maine, I think. You'll have the house to yourself. Maybe that will help you get some rest."

"You going to get a statement?"

"Yeah," I said. "But I didn't tell her that. I just said vacation. I think we need it."

"How are you guys getting along?"

"Fine," I said. I wondered what his perception of things was, or if he thought about it at all. "Better than ever."

He nodded, walked over to the window. Then he walked back to the other side of the room. He kept pacing around, making me dizzy. "It's Susu," he said. "She called me last week. She says she's pregnant."

"How did that happen?"

"The usual way, I suppose. She says she's getting an abortion." I waited.

"An *abortion*," he repeated.

"Rick, people do it all the time. I mean, I guess that doesn't make it any less bad, and I understand how you feel, but come on."

"No," he said. "I don't think you do understand how I feel. I don't believe in it."

"No one *believes* in it." I remembered how she'd kissed me for luck. "Sometimes there's no alternative."

He shook his head. Rick had certain, deeply held principles. I'd always known this. Of course he couldn't sleep; for him it would be practically like living under a death sentence himself.

"Give her the money and let her have it. It goes against your conscience, but it's not really your decision."

"The thing is, I'm not even sure she's telling the truth. Or, for that matter, if she is, that it's mine. And, of course, she might just be trying to squeeze some bucks out of me."

"That is a highly cynical view, and one that makes no difference in the long run. You might as well be a gentleman."

"I just can't decide," he said. "And I can't call her. She doesn't have a phone out there. I think they live in a mud hut or something. She called me from a pay phone."

"Decide what? Give her the money."

"I can't do that. What if it's my kid?"

"Okay, you can't do that. Don't give her the money. Forget about the whole thing."

"I can't do that either." He had picked up the weight again, and began pumping it. The veins in his arm stood out thickly under skin. "I mean, she's likely to do it anyway."

"What exactly are you saying?" I wasn't convinced he even knew. Some of his manuscript lay a few feet away from me on the floor, and even at a distance, it looked odd. As far as I could see, there were no spaces between the words. "Hey," I said. "It's going to be all right." I wished I could think of something more, some concrete suggestion to help him cool off. But with the exception of some very brief moments where his guard came down, Rick was basically a closed system. In this sense, I thought, he was like the world that had produced him, the prep schools and country clubs and lacrosse teams and cotillions. The trim, tanned, moneyed people who stood at a distance, as if watching the rest of us scuttle around, attempting to play our own particularly sad game of tennis.

"You doing anything for the holiday?" I asked.

"My parents want me to come visit, but I can't stand the whole scene, so I figure I'll just stay here and work. They tell me sales go up on Thanksgiving. Kind of sad when you think about it, all those lonely men watching videos, a turkey sandwich in one hand, dick in the other."

"You ought to get a real job."

"It is a real job. There's a lot of unfocused desire floating around out there in the world, energy that just builds and builds, kind of like that bruise you had in your head. It's got to go someplace." He pressed his hands together, then drew them quickly apart. "First Law of Thermodynamics."

11

S *ally and I* went down to New Jersey for Thanksgiving with my mother and Hal and another couple, some friends of theirs. My Grandma Jean was there, too, up for the day from MaryCrest, the assisted-living community where she had an apartment about an hour away. I'd always liked her, though lately her grasp on reality was slipping, and she had frequent conversations with her late husband, Albert, that left the rest of us sitting in polite silence. My dad's parents had split up long ago; his father had gone to California before I was born and pretty much disavowed his son entirely. He was a salesman of some sort, when he worked, which I took it wasn't all that often. My grandmother, a beehive-haired woman with pale skin and high cheekbones, whom I remembered fairly well, had smoked herself to death when I was nine. So I was proud of Grandma Jean, my one remaining grandparent, just for being there. When we were getting ready to go, I leaned over her to give her a kiss.

"You take care of my daughter," she said.

"Grandma, this is Sally. She's someone else's daughter."

"Do you think I don't know my own daughter?"

I realized it wasn't Sally she was confused about, it was me. "I'm Spencer," I said. "Your grandson. Your daughter has Hal to take care of her."

She pursed her lips, considering this. "When she was little," she said, "she was very bossy."

"Really?"

"Very bossy. But you're a good boy. You do what you're told." She held up her arms for a hug, which I gave her.

After consulting a few guide books, we'd agreed on Rangeley, Maine. It looked pretty, out of the way, and it seemed a likely place to see a moose, which we'd declared one of our official goals. Sally had borrowed Rick's camera, and for some reason she was intent on photographing every square foot of landscape we passed on the way. She had me pulling over for warehouses, water towers, office parks, and open fields. At a Burger Ranch off I-95, she took twenty minutes to circumnavigate the building, clicking away.

I drove my mother's car with one hand on the steering wheel, the other poised over the radio, switching stations every thirty seconds or so. Sally went whole five-minute stretches looking out her window with the camera to her eye. From the rearview mirror dangled a set of handcuffs, a present from Rick, from his shop. Sally had laughed when I hung them there. I had the key in my pocket.

A little north of Hartford, she shouted for me to stop.

"Why?"

"Quick, just pull over."

I did, and she jumped out. Chill air invaded the space she vacated. Across the highway, a line of phone poles stretched out into the distance. With the sun setting behind them, they looked vaguely religious. Taking up a position a few yards from the car, she lined them up and started shooting. I found another station on the radio, this one playing Hank Williams's "Kaw-Lija." I beat out a two-step on the steering wheel with my fingers.

The two hitchhikers were upon us before I even saw them. College kids, one blond and fairly wispy-looking, the other dark and curly-haired with a full, sloppy beard. They thought we'd stopped for them, a fairly loose interpretation of events since we were a good hundred yards past where they'd been standing.

"All right," said the blond one, breathing heavily from the exertion of jogging to the car. "Thanks."

"We're only taking a few pictures," I said.

"You wouldn't believe how hard it is to get a ride, man. You're saving our lives."

They each had knapsacks. The curly-haired one carried a sign that read simply, NORTH.

Sally came back to the car. "Where do you guys need to get to?"

"Far as you can take us," said the blond one. "I'm Will, and this is Steve."

"Hey," said Steve.

"We're going up to Orono," Will went on. "Maine. It's way up there."

"We're going to Maine, too," said Sally, before I could stop her. "Hop in."

"Do you guys party?" Steve asked as soon as we were back under way.

"Is a bear Catholic?" Sally punched a button on the radio and my Hank Williams turned into something very speedy and loud.

"Hey, leave that," said Will. "I like that." Then he brought out a joint, bit the tip off as if it were a fine cigar, and lit the other end.

"Keep it low," I warned. I had a vision of the four of us in some local jail, Sally off by herself and me stuck in a cell with these two clowns. The joint made its way up to the front seat, where Sally leaned back and drew heavily, then passed it over to me. The inside of the car grew foggy with smoke.

"You guys want to know what just happened to me?" asked Steve. He had a low, serious voice. "These handcuffs remind me."

"This is wild," Will promised.

"I'm sitting at dinner with my family two days ago. Maryland, this is. It's the whole deal, turkey, yams with those little marshmallows on top—I love them—broccoli, a big old salad. Just me, my mom and dad, and my brother T.R. Stands for Thomas Ralston. My father's name is Thomas, too, so we call him T.R. I just cut myself another couple slices of turkey and there's a knock on the door. It's the county sheriff's office, with a warrant for T.R.'s arrest. Seems he'd been breaking into houses in the neighborhood for the past month or so, stealing stuff. At least that's what the sheriff said. My mother said he must have made a mistake. So then we all went upstairs to my brother's room, and there it is, all this stolen stuff, right out in the open. Jewelry, silverware, stereo components. His room looked like a pawnshop."

"Wow," said Sally. "Did you know your brother was doing that?"

"No idea at all," he said. "He's always been a quiet kid, likes to fool around with things. Takes apart radios and stuff like that. Never can get them to go back together right, though."

"I like yams," said Will, after a while.

"What gets me is Thanksgiving, man. Shouldn't that be kind of sacred? It's our national holiday. You shouldn't be able to get busted on Thanksgiving."

I considered ways of getting them out of the car. Will took a harmonica from his shirt pocket and began playing along with a song on the radio, oblivious to the fact that he was in another key. Sally seemed not to mind. She had a crossword puzzle she'd brought along, and now that she was a little stoned, it took up all her attention.

"I need a four-letter word for a 'small, furry animal.' "

"Mouse," said Will, between honks at his harp.

I thought about the mice living around my desk back at Mutronics. I almost wanted to be back there.

"That's five," said Steve. "How about 'bear'?"

"No, it's got to be small."

"Fish," said Will, which was so wrong that it broke them all up for a while. A slight rain had begun to fall, and I began to relish the idea of leaving the two of them standing out in it.

After about a minute's silence, Steve leaned forward. "Vole," he said.

Sally marked it in. "That's right—it fits with the others. Nice work."

"Vole?" asked Will. "What's a vole?"

"A little animal, like a mouse, I think."

Sally put down the magazine. "In French, *voleur* is a thief. Maybe it's the same root."

"Like your brother," said Will. "That little vole."

"Rest stop four miles," I said, reading a green sign that flew past us on the right. "Let's stop for coffee."

The two of them wandered into the coffee shop together while I waited outside the ladies' room for Sally, staring into a vending machine at the plastic combs and miniature tooth-care kits. As soon as she emerged, I hurried her back out toward the parking lot. But at the glass doors, she balked.

"What is going on?" she said.

"They decided to stay. They're going to have a meal."

"I don't believe you. You're sneaking off because you don't like them, but at the same time are too chicken to say it to their faces."

"Let's get in the car."

"I can't believe you're just going to leave them here."

A family of overweight people came through the doors and we had to step to one side. We were making a scene, if a small one.

"I want this to be our vacation," I said. "Not some college road-trip."

"I like those guys. They were fun."

"Would you like to stay, too?"

Shaking her head, she followed me out to the car. Inside, both their knapsacks still lay on the backseat. "Decided to stay, did you say?" she asked. Picking them up, she went back inside the building while I sat with the engine running, watching droplets of rain spatter on the glass.

I half-expected her to return with Will and Steve in tow, but she was alone when she came out, a directed, purposeful figure striding toward me in jeans and running shoes, new glasses fogging over with the moisture.

She got into the car without saying anything, and I pulled back out onto the highway. With Will and Steve gone, the back seat seemed very empty.

"What did you tell them?" I asked, after a while.

"I didn't tell them anything, I just gave them their bags."

"You must have said something, I mean by way of explanation."

She kept her eyes forward on the wet blacktop. "I told them we were having a fight. All right?"

"That's good," I said. "That's a believable, reasonable sort of thing to say. We wouldn't want other people around if we were having a fight."

"Spencer," she said. "It was not quick thinking. It was the truth."

My mother's car was a tightly constructed Japanese sedan, and the welts in the highway made it shiver only slightly.

"I don't see how this is a fight," I said, finally.

I knew roughly where it was, and though a beeline to our destination did not exactly go through Vermont, I'd decided we could cut across the White Mountains in the morning and make the trip that much more scenic. But the Traveller's Rest, which was so easily locatable in my memory, proved more elusive in reality. I kept following roads that seemed right, but then grew darker and more barren until it was obvious they led nowhere. What I was looking for was the sign, that sheep jumping over the two words. It was late. We'd had a greasy dinner at a truck stop, during which Sally had abruptly begun to cry, then refused to tell me why. Now, she drummed her fingers, crossed her legs, and generally indicated her impatience.

"Just what exactly are we looking for?" she asked.

"A motel. A great one, you're going to love it."

"I don't care about a motel. Motels are all the same. They have a bed, a dresser, a TV, and a Bible. Let's just stop somewhere, anywhere, and get out of the car."

"You're going to like this, I guarantee it."

"I don't care," she said. "Anything will do."

It arose from the mist like an Arthurian castle, which was in fact what it had been transformed into. The old sign was still out by the side of the road, but unlit. A new, larger one a few feet away proclaimed the place to be the Cantebury Arms—no *r*. The bulk of it looked the way I remembered, but around the front office there was now a moat and a small drawbridge. There still weren't many cars in the lot.

"We spent two hours looking for this?" asked Sally.

The person behind the desk was Pakistani, and after making an imprint of my mother's credit card, which I'd also borrowed, he handed me a plastic card that would apparently open the door. From behind him I could hear the sound track to an Indian movie, and the warm, spicy smell of curry hung in the air.

"When light comes green," he said, "you push." He gave me back the credit card and disappeared.

It took me about ten tries to get us into our room, and once we were in, going out seemed too much trouble. Sally took off her clothes down to her underwear and hopped up onto the bed. It was a room nearly identical to the one I'd shared with my dad, I was sure of this, but still it seemed smaller. I sat down next to her and put my hand on her thigh. She reminded me of the cover of an old, racy paperback from the 1950s I'd found in our basement once that showed this blond-bombshell type with her slip torn, smoking a cigarette, lounging on a bed.

"Now will you tell me what it is about this motel?"

"Spider and I spent the night here. I was fifteen, and we drank whiskey and then went out to a bar. He sat in with the band, and so did I—it was the first time I ever played in front of people. Then in the morning he took off."

145

"What do you mean?"

"He said we were going to an audition, and I believed him. Then he just left me standing at a bus stop."

The story didn't seem to surprise her, particularly. She shifted her weight. "What's that?"

"What?"

"That sound." Standing, she pulled back the covers, pushed at the sheets with the palm of her hand. "I'm not sleeping on this." She undid a corner of the sheet to reveal a rubber liner that covered the entire mattress.

"I'm sure they didn't used to have those," I said.

We stripped the bed and remade it. Then we lay down side by side and stared up at the ceiling for a while in silence. I put one hand on her leg and stroked it up and back.

She sat up suddenly and rubbed the back of her hand against my beard. "This has been driving me crazy. Come with me."

In the bathroom, I lathered my face, then bent at the knees so she could get behind me and still see in the mirror. She took my razor out of my hand, inspected it, then cleared about an inch along my left cheek.

"Interesting. Tilt your head back."

I did, and she took off another path from under my chin. "Careful," I said. "I'm a bleeder."

"Wait." She brought in a chair from the other room and had me sit in it. Then she climbed into my lap, straddling me, still holding the razor. "That's better. I'm tired of sleeping with a convict. Hold still, or I might have to cut your throat."

When she was finished, she wiped me clean with a towel and put her cheek up against mine. "Smooth as a nectarine."

I picked her up and carried her over to the bed, placed her softly down, and began to kiss her.

"Spencer," she whispered, "don't."

"Is something the matter?"

"No, nothing's the matter. I know this sounds terribly clichéd, but I'm just not in the mood."

"That's okay," I said, figuring I shouldn't press the issue. We'd had by-the-numbers sex a few times since the operation, after which she always seemed in a hurry to get up and do something, as if being with me made her nervous. "This is a vacation. We've got lots of time."

"I suppose." She was silent for a moment, scraping at a cuticle with her thumbnail. "There's something I've got to say."

"Go ahead."

She hesitated. "You're not going to like it."

"That doesn't matter. I *want* you to say what you think."

"All right, then. What I think is that this isn't going anywhere. This trip, us, the whole thing."

I waited, but that seemed to be the extent of it. "Maybe it is and you just don't realize it."

"I'm just not in love with you. I mean, I *am*, just not the right way. Not a way that makes me happy. It's not like there's someone else, so you can't blame it on my judgment being, you know, off. And you've pretty much recovered now—"

"You're not saying you stuck with me just because you felt sorry?"

"No, of course not. But it wouldn't have been very nice to say I wanted to break up while you were still so out of it."

I might have been one of the children she led on nature walks and had to explain something unpleasant to—how that pretty pond they wanted so much to wade in had a bottom jagged with broken glass.

"Why did you even want to come along, then?"

"Because I wasn't sure. And because you wanted it." I could see her lip trembling. "In the morning, I'd like you to drive me to my parents' house."

"You're kidding, right?" I was torn between feeling angry at her and sorry for myself.

"No. It's not so far, and this isn't going to be much of a vacation at this rate, anyway. We can go and argue, and maybe we'll make up, but we'll both know it's only temporary. Eventually, you and I are going to separate. That's been the case all along and I'm tired of pretending I don't know it."

"What about my lawsuit? Stick with me a while longer, you'll be lighting cigars off hundred-dollar bills."

"That's your plan? You're just going to sit around and wait for money to fall out of the sky?"

"Do I have to have a plan? Does everything have to go according to some schedule? Don't you know that when you start trying to make everything run the way you want it to, you're guaranteed disappointment ninety percent of the time?"

"Without a plan you are without goals. And without goals you never achieve anything."

"That's not true. You can live for the moment. Put a couple of million well-lived moments together and you've got a successful life. I don't think you can argue with that."

"Well, I don't want to sit around drinking beer for the next ten years, waiting for some lawsuit to come through, growing fat and old and pasty-faced and poor. I'm just not like you. I'm not happy with moments. Maybe that's a failing on my part, but it's how I am. I feel like I'm wasting my time—I want a regular, normal life."

"In the morning," I said, "you'll feel different."

"In the morning you will drive me to my parents' house. That's how it's going to be."

"We'll see." I wanted us both to be asleep. It seemed to me that she didn't know what she wanted, that with the morning she'd come back to her senses. The two of us sat in silence for a very long time. The crumpled rubber sheet lay in a pile on the desk where we'd thrown it, its dark contours like a mountain range at night.

"I'm sorry," she said, after a while. "I guess this motel isn't the luckiest place for you."

The next day we drove down to Boston. The weather was as dreary as it had been the day before, and the only radio talk show we could find to listen to was a phone-in on capital punishment. To cheer me up, Sally tried to get our own debate going. She said she thought they ought to bring back public hangings, show the people that punishment was a real thing, not some abstract system of courts and appeals and prisons and furloughs. I knew she didn't mean it. Her liberalism was solid as a New England oak.

Her parents were glad to see her, not so glad to see me. I came in for a cup of coffee. We'd met once before, at graduation, when both of them had made it quite clear that they viewed me as merely a passing phase in their daughter's life. Now I saw they'd been right. It didn't make me like them any better.

Mr. Colvin was in a bathrobe and slippers, while Mrs. had on a running suit. They were pale, large people, with more money than taste. We sat around their immense kitchen table. Everything in the kitchen was white or blond wood. It looked like a set for a television cooking show. She gasped when I took off my hat.

"My God," she said. "What happened?"

I sipped at my cup, clinked it back into the saucer. "From the chemotherapy. Very normal to experience hair loss."

"Chemotherapy?" Her expression froze in a polite smile.

"Spencer got bumped on the head," said Sally. "He doesn't have cancer."

"Bumped," I said. "That's right."

"Well, I'm certainly glad to hear that," said Mr. Colvin. "An associate of mine just passed away from cancer last month. He had a tumor removed that was the size of a cantaloupe. Didn't do any good, though. Size of a cantaloupe."

Sally threw her spoon down onto the tablecloth.

"You're not both planning to stay, are you?" continued Mr. Colvin, ignoring my presence entirely. "Because your mother has been under a lot of stress lately, and I don't think it would be good for her to have to play hostess."

"I'm fine, Neil," she said. "They can stay if they want to. There's lots of clean towels in the linen cabinet. Honey, you know where the linen cabinet is?"

"I grew up in this house," said Sally, with her eyes closed. "I know where the linen cabinet is."

"Maybe Spencer would like to wash up. Spencer, would you like to wash up?" The way she was looking at me, she seemed doubtful mere soap and water would do the trick.

"No, thanks," I said. "And you don't need to worry about towels—I won't be staying. I'm on my way up to Maine to visit my father."

"What line of work is your dad in, Spencer?" asked Mr. Colvin.

"Potato farmer."

"Really? Has his own place up there, does he?"

"Not quite. He's a bagger. You know, the potatoes roll down a conveyor belt, and he puts them in those bags. That is, after checking for rotten ones."

"Maine's a beautiful state," said Mr. Colvin.

We excused ourselves and went to get Sally's things from the car.

"If I were you," I said, "I'd get out while I could."

"That's not funny. They're my parents."

"Are you sure? Maybe you got the address mixed up. Maybe these people just look like your parents."

She hoisted her backpack out of the trunk and shouldered it. "You lied to me about going to see your father."

"I just need to get a statement from him, that's all. About how I got punched."

"He was drunk. What kind of a statement can he give you?"

"I've already written one out for him—all he has to do is sign. The point is, there needs to be testimony from a witness."

She stood shaking her head at me. "You're curious, aren't you? You want to meet them."

"I don't want to meet anyone. I thought you and I could have a nice vacation, and in the process I could get his signature. In the long run, it's for us—all of it."

"But the fact remains that you weren't honest with me."

"I'm sorry."

"Say good-bye to Rick for me. Tell him I hope things work out for him and old So-So."

"Just what exactly is going on here? I mean, you'll be coming back, right?"

She scratched at her forearm, where she sometimes got rashes, particularly when she was under stress. "Spencer, you can only follow your nose for so long. Eventually you come to a point where you figure out you really are hopelessly lost. Then the smart thing to do is turn around and go back to where you were when you made the mistake. You cut your losses. That's what I'm doing."

"Cut your losses? I'm glad you can be so emotional about this. What about your friends, your job, all your stuff?"

"I'm tired of my job, and I don't have any friends except for you and Rick, not really. I'll come and get my stuff, or send for it."

There was an oily puddle in her parents' driveway, and I put the toe of my sneaker in it and pulled a streak of wetness back along the asphalt.

"Tell me something to change my mind," she said. "I'm listening. Show me that I'm wrong."

"I just never really thought of us not being together."

"That won't do it. Try something else."

"What are you going to do here anyway?"

She shrugged. "Probably get a job."

"Not travel?"

"Not immediately, no. But soon—maybe in the spring."

"What if I were rich? It could happen, you know."

"I told you what I think of that plan."

We stood looking at each other. A few feet away, two squirrels chased each other around the trunk of a big maple. Hadn't I, like her parents, known this was coming all along? Hadn't a part of me actually been *expecting* it? I had a picture of some old movie in my mind, a short, wizened trainer coaching a young boxer—Victor Mature maybe. "Roll with the punches, babe," he kept saying. "You gotta roll with the punches." I felt as if my face had plasticized; the expression I wore was one of quiet resignation, like finding out that the last ticket to a movie has just been sold to the person in front of you in line.

"Say hi to your dad," said Sally. Adjusting the strap of her pack over her shoulder, she turned and walked away from me, into her house.

12

Dear Mr. Markus,
Once again, let me describe my Gopher. It has glitter all over it. It's red. It is of great sentimental value to me, as I have used it for years. Come on, now. I know it's there, and I really don't understand why you don't simply return it to me.

On top of everything, I just got a mailing from you all with "Prices Too Good to Believe!" at the top. The way you people operate, I'm not sure I'd believe anything about you at this point. Is anybody even there?

> Concerned and getting pissed about this whole thing,
> Duke Davin

To Whom It May Concern,
I am an experimental guitarist and have performed all across the country to excellent notices (see enclosed clippings). My music has been described as "a cross between Robert Fripp and Joey Ramone" (Cal Thomas in the *LA Times*), and another reviewer compared the effect of listening to my piece, "Demonspeed," as "like being woken up by a dump truck at six A.M.— a frightening, disorienting experience that segues into deep anger" (Joe Bolton, *Deep Nation Review*).

Would your company be interested in sponsoring me? In particular, I could use some financial assistance to help me record my current project, "Songs About Food and Suffering," but even just some free equipment would be useful. Be assured that you will receive credit and thanks on all promotional material.

I hope you won't pass on this chance to ally your name with mine. I believe that both of us can benefit substantially in the long run, and your long-standing reputation as a groundbreaking, innovative company fits right in with my vision of a new musical world.

> Sincerely,
> Alan Void
> Void Productions
> East Orange, New Jersey
> (Tape enclosed)

Dear Mr. Markus,

I had my mother call you and here is what she said. She said NO ONE answered. The phone just rang and rang.

What is going ON? I know you must have a Gopher to send me, because it would be like the Nabisco people running out of OREOS if you DIDN'T. I have used other distortion boxes, but I know that yours is the BEST. But I am getting TIRED of waiting.

Here's a good one I just read about. Did you know that Jimi Hendrix was the opening act for THE MONKEES? It's true, but just for a few shows. He was friends with Peter. My guess is they did DRUGS together, which is pretty funny if you think about it, since it was all that marketing and lunchboxes and etc. You just never know about people.

Please don't make me WAIT much longer.

> Your Friend,
> Furry Couch #C-563-2798

13

The house was small, white, with concrete steps that sagged to one side. There were Christmas lights in the front window, a simple strand of green ones. It was after seven, and I'd been driving all day. When I parked, a small stray ran over and peed lengthily on my back tire.

I rang the bell and a hefty man in a tan work shirt with a diet soda in his hand answered the door.

"I'm sorry," I said. "I guess I have the wrong address." I'd gotten this one out of a phone book, but it had been last year's.

The man stared at me. From behind him a woman's voice called out, asking who it was. Then a baby started crying.

"Who are you looking for?" he asked.

"Dan Markus? Spider? I think he used to live here."

He opened the door wider. "I think maybe he did. Cully?"

The woman came forward with the baby held up against her chest. "Who are you?" she asked.

"Just an old friend." I sensed something hostile in the man's expression. He extracted a Winston from a pack in his shirt pocket, keeping his eyes on me all the while.

"He's gone," he said.

Cully stepped in front of him. "Let him in, Brian. It's all right, why don't you come in for some coffee? I've got some made fresh."

She was a good-looking woman in her mid-thirties, with

shoulder-length blond hair, pale, nearly translucent skin, and the beginnings of crow's-feet etched around the corners of her eyes. The baby was in a kind of pink mummy bag that made it seem like a large caterpillar. All I could see was a pair of dark eyes, a little expanse of forehead, and a wisp of delicate hair.

We sat down at a small kitchen table where she poured a cup of weak coffee into which I stirred too much sugar. Brian smoked his cigarette, tapping ashes into a beer cap.

"There's leftover turkey, too, if you'd like a sandwich."

"No, thanks."

"You're Spencer, aren't you?" Cully said without any real surprise in her voice.

I nodded.

"Well, I'm Cully, and this is my brother, Brian." She stood up. "Just let me put the baby away." She disappeared into the back room, leaving me and Brian at the table. It was a small house, more of a bungalow, with no particularly distinguishing features. Some unframed paintings, landscapes, mostly, hung on the wall, with others leaning up against a small component stereo system that was covered in dust. I guessed Cully was the painter, since Brian didn't seem the type. There were also a number of boxes lined up against one wall, cardboard moving cartons.

"Danny's boy?" asked Brian, with amusement.

"That's right," I said.

He began to sing. "The pipes, the pipes are calling—"

"Brian." Cully came back in and resumed her seat. "Have you seen him?"

"I was going to ask you that."

"If you do see him, you tell that son of a bitch he better not show his face around here," said Brian, matter-of-factly. "I'll break his neck."

"Are you his wife?" I asked.

"No, but we've been together four years. Were, I guess you'd say. We were together four years."

"I live in New York. He showed up back in September and stayed with me a couple of weeks."

"He told you about me, then."

"No, he didn't. I sort of figured it out."

"I see." She noticed me looking at the cartons. "I'm going to Italy. I have a small grant, to study painting in Rome."

"What about the baby?"

"Allegra is coming with me."

"Have you got any money?" asked Brian. "Your old man left a few debts."

"Brian." Cully shook her head.

"What? Who's been paying for everything around here? I just figured I'd see if he wanted to help out. Pretty nice car you're driving. I'll bet that cost thirteen or fourteen thousand."

"Leave him alone," said Cully. She took a key out of her purse and tossed it to him. "Here, go get some beer at the Shure-Fine. And pick up some apple juice for me, okay?"

Brian got sullenly to his feet and went to the front door. "Your father's a shit, kid. How about you? Are you as much of a shit as he is?" He shut the door behind him, hard.

"I have to apologize," said Cully. "Brian's been helping me out with the baby and all. He's protective, like any older brother." When she said this, it occurred to me that I, too, was an older brother. Of course, I'd suspected for some time that this might be the case, but it was different actually being here with these people.

"I'm the one that ought to apologize. I really feel bad about this whole thing. I think he expects himself to screw things up, and because of that, it happens that way."

"Oh, I know all about it." Her eyes drifted, just for a moment, as if remembering something. "It's part of what attracted me to him at first. But it's no excuse."

"I'll also make a prediction," I said. "He'll be back, probably sooner than you think." It seemed a safe thing to say, and I thought it might be what she wanted to hear.

"Doesn't matter. I'll be gone. That ought to provide material for a blues song or two." She took her coffee cup over to the sink and rinsed it.

"If I knew where he was—"

"I know where he is. That's easy. He's down in Portland. He sits in all the time with a band at the Iron Horse Tap called the Chili Dogs."

"If you know where he is," I asked, a little confused, "why don't you do something?"

"Like what? Go down there with a rolling pin? Or beg him to come back to me? I've got some pride left, though maybe not a whole lot. He hasn't got any money, so suing wouldn't do me much good. I don't see a lot of options here, do you?"

"You could ask him why he did it."

"Did what, disappear? He did it because he was scared. And I understand that—it's scary. Hell, I'm scared every morning when I open my eyes and it hits me like a hammer that there's someone else in the world who depends on me *utterly*, I mean just to stay alive. It's a scary thing." She shrugged, but it was a feigned indifference—I could see she was upset. "He kept saying how much he was looking forward to this."

"But, I mean, did you have a fight?"

"We didn't have a fight. We had a baby."

We talked a while longer, Cully getting up every few minutes to check on Allegra. I found out a number of things. Spider had been working odd jobs, painting, carpentry, to make his living, not playing music, as he'd told me. For the past year he'd worked for a contractor, fixing up an old house as a summer retreat for a discount-store tycoon.

"Italian marble in the bathrooms, who knows what else—solid gold doorknobs. When it's done it will look more like Versailles than Maine, if you ask me. But it's paying work, or at least it was. I'm sure they've hired someone else. I should have figured out something was going on when he printed up those cards two years ago. 'Spiderman,' " she said, shaking her head. "Jesus."

She invited me to stay the night, but I declined. If I got on the road now, I could make Portland in an hour or so and find the Iron Horse Tap tonight. Before I left, we went together into the bedroom where Allegra lay quietly in a rectangular crib that did not look very criblike.

"Speaker cabinet," Cully whispered. "The speakers were blown, so he took them out, padded the inside, and put the whole thing on legs."

By the front door, Cully gave me a kiss good-bye and an orange to eat in the car. Brian had still not returned, which was all right with me.

"I'd like to help," I said. "I could be a part of this."

She tilted her head to one side. "What are you saying, exactly?"

"Well, I am her half brother. I could try to *be* that."

She wet her lips with her tongue. "I'm not sure it's a great idea. Though I do appreciate the offer. Allegra's not your responsibility, and my plan, at least right now, is to not mention Dan to her at all. I just think that's easier. I imagine the complicated part will roll around soon enough, but for now, anyway, I just want to keep it the two of us."

"Sure," I said, a little embarrassed. "That makes sense."

"But it's really nice of you to ask." She gave me another kiss, lightly, on the cheek.

As I pulled out of the gravel drive, the image of my half sister resting snugly inside an old speaker cabinet remained in my mind. I imagined her floating across the ocean in that thing, bouncing happily along the tops of waves, smiling up at the seabirds and the blue sky.

Near Freeport, I picked up a nail and had to change a tire. The replacement supplied with my mother's car was a temporary that you were not supposed to drive more than fifty on, and it was underinflated. I limped into town, found a cheap motel, and went to L.L. Bean's. It was late, I had nothing else to do, and I didn't feel like being alone. I tried on a blue fisherman's rain suit, complete with hat. I just about disappeared inside the suit, which was oversized, lightweight, and something I would certainly never wear. I'd fished once in my life, when my dad had a gig up in the Hamptons playing a yuppie party. I was twelve, but he'd convinced my mom to let me come along, though when we got to the place it turned out there were no bedrooms for us, as promised. The band played in the living room of this big old house, and when the party finally ended around two A.M., we were on our own to find a place to sleep. I'd curled up in a love seat out on the porch, from which I could smell and hear the ocean. In the morning, he got one of the guys who owned the place to take us out in his boat, even though the weather had turned blowy and overcast. We tried for about an hour, but didn't catch a thing. I was just happy to be out there, but he acted disappointed, as if the outing were the whole reason I'd wanted to come along.

I almost bought the suit, but at the last minute thought better of it and chose a flannel shirt instead, putting it on my mother's credit card. I'd figured on using it for souvenirs for me and Sally, T-shirts, maybe. I was going to take her out for lobster.

The cashier was a Vietnam vet from Bangor, and he wanted to talk. Noticing my hair, he asked if I was in the service, and even though I said no, it was enough to start him off. We drank coffee together from a pot he had going and he told me war stories, full of exotic names, night patrols, buddies being blown to bits by enemy mines. He referred to whole strings of things only by their initials, and I had to guess what he was talking about. I almost disbelieved him because all his stories sounded like clichés. That was the sad part about it—the worst things could happen to you, but later when you told people, they just seemed like a bad movie plot. So I told him my story too, without a bit of fabrication, about being in the hospital, about trying to find my dad to get a statement for the lawsuit, about having seen my half sister for the first time that evening. He listened politely and poured us more coffee. He may have believed me, or maybe not. In either case, I don't think he saw the whole thing as being of much importance, not compared to what he'd seen.

14

The tire was unpatchable and I had to get a new one. Then I drove the rest of the way to Portland, where I had eggs and coffee at a place near the bus station that was full of hookers just getting off work. One caught me staring at her and smiled back pleasantly.

I spent the morning wandering around the Old Port area, looking in gift shops, watching the people hustle around pretending that they lived in a real city and not just a paper-mill town with big ideas. I was tired; I'd only managed a couple hours of fitful sleep. After looking up the Iron Horse Tap in a phone book, I drove there around noon, only to find it closed. I drove around some more and finally parked in front of a laundromat for a few hours and slept in the car, the seat tilted back as far as it would go, my jacket zipped tight and my hands deep in my pockets against the cold.

At seven-thirty, I returned. He was exactly where Cully'd said he'd be, seated at the bar with a bowl of popcorn and a beer. I stood in the doorway looking at him. The air in the place was tart with stale smoke, and in the corner of the room a jukebox pulsed color and shook under the strain of an Aerosmith tune. A woman sat with him, skinny, dark-haired, perhaps thirty, applying polish to her nails. In my pocket I had the statement I'd written. I took a breath and walked over, then placed the paper in front of him.

"Here," I said. "Read this, then sign it."

For a moment, he seemed not to recognize me. He wore jeans and a black jacket over a black shirt. "If you're going to have short hair like that," he said, "you should get your ear pierced."

"I'm in a hurry."

"How did you find me?"

"Cully told me where to look."

"How is she?"

"Leaving the country, with Allegra. Rome, I think she said."

He scanned the typed piece of paper I'd presented him as if it were a summons. "Rome?" he said. "Rome, Italy?"

"Go on. Read it."

From inside his jacket he produced a small pair of half-glasses. "Magnifiers. The eyes start to get a little fuzzy, especially in dark rooms."

It was a short statement, only three paragraphs. It said simply that we had been walking to the subway, that we were pelted with eggs, that we were subsequently surrounded, and that a short man with a mustache had punched me in the mouth. But when he was through, he folded it in half and gave it back to me.

"I can't."

"Why not?"

"I didn't see anything. I was drunk, remember?"

"But you were right there."

"Yes and no. Physically, I was there. But my attention was not on what was happening. One minute you were standing up, the next you were on the ground. I think someone hit you, but I couldn't say for sure."

The woman beside him, obviously bored, screwed the top back on her polish and deposited it in her purse, then took her drink and walked away from us.

"Look," I said, "whether you feel like it or not, you're part of this."

He took a swallow from his beer. "I'm telling you, I can't get involved. But I wish you luck. How much are you suing for?"

Kravitch hadn't sent me any papers yet, and he never talked in specifics, so I didn't know, although I suspected a lot. "It's not the money," I said, "it's the principle."

"Exactly my point. On principle, I can't sign that paper. I'm sorry. Get you a beer?"

"Are you kidding? You're really not going to sign?"

"Really not. How's your head?"

"Don't you think you owe me? Don't you think you could do this one, tiny thing? None of this would have happened if you hadn't charged that redheaded woman like an idiot."

"Jimi, my man, the answer was and is no. Signing your name is serious business. It means you can be held to things. Trust me, you're being used for something here. That's what lawyers do. I don't want to be involved."

I was tired, angry, and after waiting all day for this, suddenly out of patience. I might as well have been a stranger trying to get him to sign a petition. Grabbing him by the lapels, I yanked him off the stool. He went down on one knee, catching himself from falling by grasping the edge of the bar. I let go and he took a step back. Then I tackled him. I was still pretty weak, and he could have easily tossed me off if he'd wanted to, but he didn't. He sunk underneath me, his body lean and bony, the smell of it so familiar I might have been wrestling myself. It was the bouncer who came over and grabbed my arms from behind, lifting me to my feet. A second later I was outside, a sharp knot in my lower back where I'd been kicked.

Spider came out and stood looking at me for a while, his long arms dangling at his sides, a reddish mark on his cheek where it had bumped the edge of the bar.

"Feel better?" he asked.

I turned and began to walk in the direction of my car.

"Hey, don't go away mad." He jogged to catch up. Across the street from us, a man and a woman were arguing loudly about something. They didn't seem to care about people hearing them. I was acutely aware that I'd caused a scene, and I didn't want to cause another one.

"It really is good to see you." There was dirt and sawdust on his coat, and he brushed it off with the back of his hand. "I was going to write you a letter as soon as I got settled. Come in and let me get you a beer."

I kept walking and he hurried to catch up.

"Forget it," I said, my eyes burning. "Just forget it."

"No, really," he pushed. "Come on back."

"You're only interested in yourself."

"What's wrong with that? Okay, I didn't tell you everything. I wanted you to like me, that's all. I figured you might not. Is that so hard to understand?"

I stopped and looked at him. There was no place else I was going.

He explained to the bartender that it was all right, I was just a little upset. It was apparent that Spider had some pull there. He was and always would be at his best inside a bar, I thought. He bought me a beer and ordered us both shots, too. "Old Mr. Boston," he said. "An unpretentious little whiskey."

"I went back to the Traveller's Rest," I said. "Sally and I did."

"That right?"

"You know, that place we stayed?"

He raised his eyebrows. I found it hard to believe he didn't remember.

"It's totally different now. Looks like a castle or something."

"Well, you can't count on things to stay the same. Change is the only thing you can count on. Howard Johnson's, for instance. Those places used to be everywhere. Orange rooftops, that sign with the pie man on it? You probably don't even remember. Just try and find one now. Too bad, too. They made the best fried clams." He drank his shot and I followed suit. "You want a burger? They have great burgers here." He called over to the bartender. "Hey, Phil, give us a couple of menus."

All the sandwiches had cute names. I stared at the menu, trying to get my eyes to focus.

"I like the Willie Dixon. A half-pound burger with mushrooms, onions, green pepper, and salsa. But the Muddy Waters is good, too. That's got barbecue sauce. They all come with fries."

"I didn't know you did carpentry," I said.

"I wouldn't call what I do carpentry. I just whang nails and saw boards."

"You told me you played music for a living."

"I do. In case you hadn't noticed, most artists have to do something else to survive. Come on now, order up. The band's here."

"Sally had you figured out, you know. All along."

"Maybe she thinks she did," he said, tossing his menu onto the bar. "People aren't math problems."

We ate, then he helped them finish setting up. The place began to fill with people, many of whom seemed to know him. I was struck by how easy it seemed for my dad to make friends, how people admired him just for the figure he cut, how he seduced them with those sky-blue eyes.

The Chili Dogs were not a particularly good band, just a bunch of guys who'd gone to college together and played enough parties to gather a following. They played loud and struck poses, and both the guitarists seemed unable to perform without a lit cigarette tucked upright into a tuning peg. Their front man was a guy named Rooster who stood well over six feet and sang like a cross between Louis Armstrong and Tom Waits, a trombone cradled in his arms on which he blew maybe three notes per tune. By the time they started, around nine, the place was packed. The crowd was mostly young and male, white, some in college sweatshirts, a few more dangerous-looking types with heavy-metal T-shirts and eyes glazed over with substance fatigue. They hooted and stomped, and by the end of the first set I could barely see the stage for all the thick necks and blue smoke.

The usual soundman was out sick, so Spider ran the board, and I stood next to him, more or less grateful that the noise level made it impossible to talk. Every now and then he'd make a tiny adjustment to one of the controls.

"What do you think?" he shouted.

"I think they suck."

He grinned at me in a way that made me feel suddenly good. He was in a different league from these people, and this understanding was something we could share. Playing with them was just another compromise in a long line of compromises.

"You know how you tell a good soundman from a hack?" he said. "Watch his hands. A good soundman almost never touches anything. You get your levels right to begin with and leave 'em alone. Any guy who's fucking around with the knobs all the time doesn't know shit. He just wants to feel important."

When he went up, I took over the board. The bass player, who was also tall but not nearly as stretched-out looking and thin as my dad, announced him.

"Ladies and gentlemen," he said. "Our good friend, Spider-man Dan."

As he mounted the stage, it occurred to me that the name reflected the way he thought of himself—someone who spun webs to travel alone and safely, and who, like the comic-book character, could disappear easily into the night. He played his cream-colored Telecaster, standing slightly behind the other players, but towering over them, his head lowered in attention to his instrument.

They did "Nine Below Zero," followed by "Honey Bee" and "I Hear You Knocking." During that one, he dug a slide out of his jacket pocket and began coaxing screams and cries that sounded like some large raptor, wheeling overhead, threatening and hungry. The band played on a different level with him up there. I pushed the volume on his guitar, just a bit, and tried to remember if he'd always been this good. I simply didn't know—it had been so long since I'd heard him. I did know one thing. I resented his appearance of so much depth and soul, when in fact I knew he had neither.

Around two A.M. he collected thirty bucks from the bass player for doing the sound, and we went back to where he was crashing, the apartment of the girl in the bar. It was only a few blocks away. She drove us, though the whole thing seemed like a huge chore to her, and she ignored me almost entirely, beyond saying that her name was Katrina. She was pretty in a sort of emaciated way, with bangs and a bit too much makeup, but I couldn't see that she had anything on Cully. There was a tiny back bedroom and he told me I could sleep there for the night. The roof angled down over a dusty old sofa, and I lay on my back feeling as if I were bunking on a ship. There was no pillow. When I rolled up my jacket to use it, I discovered the handcuffs, which I'd taken down from the rearview mirror and stuffed in my pocket earlier because they drew attention to the car, and because they reminded me of Sally. I put them in my shoe and tried to go to sleep.

Slightly before dawn, I got up and dressed, then went into the next room. Spider was asleep with Katrina, snoring heavily. Somewhere on her desk, which was piled high with magazines and catalogs, a clock ticked. I clipped the cuffs onto both his wrists, then poked him a few times in the chest.

"Come on," I said.

He cracked an eye at me, then attempted to roll over the other way, but the cuffs prevented him from moving his arms. This time both eyes opened. The covers shifted to reveal part of Katrina's long, heart-shaped back.

"What?" he asked.

"Come on." I held a finger to my lips and motioned to her sleeping form. She said something unintelligible, then buried her head deep underneath a pillow.

He'd been sleeping in underwear and a T-shirt, and I helped him on with his jeans and boots, then draped his jacket around his shoulders. I grabbed his wallet and keys and put them in my own pocket. Katrina slept through it all.

We walked to my car, which sat alone now in front of the dark bar. I unlocked the passenger side and he got in. Neither of us said anything. He maintained a kind of bemused expression, as if, even cuffed, he were still in control of this situation.

At a 7-Eleven we stopped to use the bathroom and I got us two cups of coffee, which we drank in the parking lot, the engine running to keep us warm.

It wasn't until we were actually under way that he began to get angry. Facing the nearly empty black ribbon of interstate, still wet in the cold and fog, he seemed suddenly to understand that I really planned to take him with me.

"You'd better pull over right now," he said.

I kept my eyes on the road.

"And take these things off. Enough is enough."

I adjusted the volume on the radio, which was tuned to a classical station.

"You're wrong," he said. "You don't need me, you just think you do." His voice grew quieter, calmer. "What makes you think a statement from me will be worth a damn? I'm your father. Of course I'm going to support your story. That won't convince anyone of anything."

"You're all I have," I told him. "The way I see it, you owe me this. Rick took pictures of the guy. I didn't think to bring them along, but since you're intent on being such a jerk about signing a simple statement, I'm dragging your sorry ass back and making you identify them."

"Don't call your father a jerk," he said. "I raised you better than that."

"Are you serious?"

He shrugged. "Okay. But think hard. If I can't say for sure that you were hit, how can I say for sure who hit you?"

"You *know* for a fact I was hit. You took me to the hospital, remember?"

"I won't get involved in this legal shit," he said. "I won't lie."

"Lie? Are you kidding me? Where did you get this system of values? Have you even seen your daughter lately? Don't you even want to know what she looks like?"

He was staring straight ahead out the windshield. "There's an exit coming up. You can let me off there."

"Big deal. You're afraid to get involved. Me, too. The whole world is like that. No one wants to. It means making choices, and choices have consequences, and that might, just might, lead to responsibility." I realized he was pointing at something.

"Look."

"You're just a big damn child." I slowed way down. Perhaps a hundred yards ahead of us, a great, dark object was moving from left to right across the highway.

"I've never seen one."

The moose stopped and turned to look at us, and I kept the car crawling slowly toward it until we were only about twenty feet away. It was as big as a horse, the scrubby patches of hair on its back and chin like thick, brown moss. It had huge, wide antlers.

"I wonder how many stations he gets with those things," Spider said.

Unconcerned with us, the moose turned and continued on his way, disappearing into the trees.

I took the exit and pulled into a Texaco station. The sun was barely up, and in a way, it seemed as if the whole morning might not really have happened. He got out of the car and walked around to my side, where he stood looking down at me. He was right, of course. Taking him back to New York wasn't going to accomplish anything. I felt slightly foolish. Worse, I realized that, angry as I was, I was also glad for his company. It was going to be a lonely drive.

He held out his wrists, which were still bound together. I passed the key through the window.

"Where'd you get these things, anyway?" he asked me, dangling them in front of his face for a closer examination. " 'Love Cuffs'?"

"Rick gave them to me."

He nodded and tossed them past me onto the backseat. "Wallet?"

I handed it over, as well as his keys, wondering for just a moment what they were the keys to.

He didn't move, only stood there, framed by the dark mouth of one of the station's service bays. "I do want to see her," he said, finally. "I was there the whole first month, changing diapers, all that stuff. She's beautiful, and I'm not proud of anything about this. But I'm just not what she's going to need. I don't figure I'll be doing anyone any favors pretending that I am."

15

I *returned the car* to my mother's. There was no one there, so I just stuck the key in the mailbox and hiked uptown to the bus station, slept much of the way back up to the city. When I finally got back to the apartment, there was a note pinned to Rick's door that read, "Gone to New Mexico. Will be in touch. (This may take a while.)"

I pushed open his door. The room had been tidied. The stack of magazines was gone, and he'd disassembled his weights. The bars now leaned up against the wall in the corner; the weights themselves were stacked alongside in two piles, like cairns. I sat on the edge of his bed. There was a lingering scent in the room of cologne.

I knew how Rick was when he got started on something—enthusiastic, almost manic. I imagined him driving nonstop across the country, his radio turned up all the way so he could hear it over the sound of his rotted muffler. He could have bought himself a better car any time he wanted, but he always said he didn't care, he'd rather have a piece of junk and not have to worry about it so much, which made sense, given our neighborhood. He'd get out there and find a cheap motel, start playing detective, try to figure out where Susu was staying. I had no doubt he'd succeed. I didn't know what he had in mind exactly, though if Susu was pregnant, he'd certainly try to convince her to have the child. And if she wasn't? I turned this one over in my head, but it just didn't make much sense. Possibly it was something her artist friend had put her up to. Rick had money, and for all his attempts at walking the wild side, was basically a responsible guy and an easy touch. Certainly, they would never have counted on his driving across the country to find them.

I stayed three nights in the apartment by myself, but it felt lonely and silent. It didn't help to think of Rick out there, actively doing something about his life, while my own seemed to have gone so completely off course. I read the help-wanted ads in the *Times* and the *Voice*, but as far as I could see, I wasn't qualified for anything.

Finally, I called my mother and told her I was coming down for a visit. I cleaned out the refrigerator of the few things that might rot, took the subway to Port Authority, and hopped a Suburban Transit bus back home.

She had my old room, which she'd redecorated and turned into a guest room the year before, waiting for me, the bed neatly made, a brand-new bathrobe she'd bought hanging in the closet. It was blue terry-cloth, thick and soft, and I put it on immediately. I went up to the kitchen, where she was sitting with a glass of scotch.

"You stay as long as you want," she said. "I'm just glad you're here."

"Me, too." In fact, I felt like a stranger. I walked around the kitchen opening cupboards, pulling out drawers, amazed by the wealth of normal things: silverware and dishes that matched, a refrigerator fully stocked with food. It was not a huge house, but it was a comfortable one, full of conveniences, and most importantly, inhabited.

We had a couple of drinks together. Hal was away on a business trip in Florida. In contrast to Brooklyn, here everything seemed particularly quiet and still. Occasionally, a car swept down the street, but other than that, there was just the humming of the refrigerator, the whisper of heat in the vents.

"Honey," she said, "how do you feel?"

"Not bad at all. The headaches are gone completely."

She stared at me for a few moments, as if verifying that I was indeed her son. "Hal and I are getting married."

"Really?" I said. Then, before I could stop myself, I added, "Why?"

"Well, it just seems to us that after all this time, we might as well. Hal's been pushing for it for years—I'm the one that's held off."

"Because you were afraid of making the commitment?"

She looked surprised. "No, sweetheart, not at all. Because it was so crummy the first time."

I got up and made a peanut butter sandwich to go with my scotch. "If it was so bad before, why do it again?" The idea of her remarrying bothered me, though I wasn't sure exactly why.

"Because I've come to the conclusion that it isn't all convention. There's a reason that people get married, as opposed to just sharing meals and a bed for years. It has to do with getting bigger. This may sound stupid to you, but it's my theory that everything is constantly expanding. That's the state of the universe, after all."

"That's not your theory, it's something you paid for. More vending-machine consciousness."

She shook her head. "Nope, this is all mine. The greatest act of sacrifice you can make is to give yourself up to another person, to decide that the two of you will become one separate unit, together."

"All right, maybe it's yours. But isn't it kind of meaningless? I mean, you're divorced. Half your friends are divorced."

"Because, the first time around I didn't know what I was doing. It's impossible to know when you're just a teenager. And, of course, Dan wasn't the most intelligent decision I've ever made. I'm grown up now, and I can understand the significance." She downed the rest of her glass and put the cap back on the bottle. "How was your trip, anyway?"

"Great. We saw a moose."

She smiled. "Come on."

I left my sandwich and we went outside, moving quietly across the lawn toward her garden, which was way in the back, just at the border of a residual strip of woods that stretched in a thin band all along the edge of the neighborhood. The developers had thoughtfully left the trees to give the impression that the area wasn't total suburbia, which it was.

"Look," she said.

A family of deer were munching contentedly on some vegetables. My mother, I saw, had something in her hand, and as she raised it up in the darkness, for a moment I thought it might be a gun, but it turned out to be an air horn. There was a blast of sound like a ship departing and the deer scattered.

"My God," she said, laughing. "I really love doing that."

That night I had a dream in which I wandered around New York trying to find a pair of shoes. At one store, the salesman went in back to find my size, then simply did not return. I finally went myself and found him lying dead on the floor. I went to another store, and there the doors were locked with a sign hung out saying CLOSED UNTIL FURTHER NOTICE. I went into the subway to buy a token and the person in the booth couldn't see me. I shouted at him, but he just continued what he was doing, which was sorting tokens into piles. Then I looked down and saw that my feet were not touching the ground but floating an inch or two off the cement. I suddenly came to the terrible realization that I was the Angel of Death. I woke in a sweat and went to the guest bathroom, which my mother had recently redone in pastels, where I washed my face with a bonbon-sized piece of soap shaped like a seashell. It took me an hour of sitting up, reading my old comic books, before I could finally get back to sleep.

*   *   *

I spent the next few days walking around town, revisiting the places that held some kind of importance for me: the rack outside the high school from which my bicycle had been stolen, the former candy shop, now a real estate office, where I used to go to buy licorice and jawbreakers. A tunnel ran under the next street over from ours—a concrete sewage pipe, really—that allowed a small creek called Randolph's Brook to pass under the street. The name supposedly dated back to Revolutionary War times. What I remembered was that you had to keep your feet spread wide and hop back and forth if you didn't want to get them wet, and that there was a point right in the center of the thing where, even though you could see light at both ends, you were standing in nearly total darkness. It was a place you wanted to run from as quickly as possible.

To my disappointment, I found that the entrances on both sides had been closed off with chicken wire to make sure no one got in. I also saw that one corner of the fencing showed signs of a lot of bending up and down. Kids were still playing in the tunnel, and that made me feel kind of good, even if the entrance was too small for me to get in.

I ran into Nicky Dormer, shuffling along in front of Woolworth's, wearing five shirts under a fatigue jacket, eating a piece of pizza. From his pocket, he took out another piece and offered it to me. I asked him where he was going.

"U.C.," he said. "You got any money?"

I went into a liquor store and bought him what he wanted, a gallon bottle of sweet vermouth.

Nicky had gone to the local community college for a semester, but had been arrested a couple of times, once for cocaine possession, then later for attempting to steal an upright piano (my mother had sent me a clipping from the police blotter without comment). I thought about him sometimes with a kind of vague regret, because we had been friends, at least for a while, and I didn't think friends should abandon one another.

We walked out to the church, about a two-mile hike, and all the way he said almost nothing. The jeans he wore had a grayish tint to them, and a stale, fermented odor arose from the vicinity of his shoes.

He had a kind of lean-to built underneath a pine tree. From the outside you couldn't see a thing, but underneath there was a natural chamber that was high enough in places to stand. He had a small battery-powered amp there, along with the same red Hondo I'd bought him, wrapped up in a piece of old quilt. There was also a Mutronics phase-shifter. When I saw this, I pointed to it, pleased at the opportunity to show off.

"That's where I've been working."

Nicky looked at me skeptically.

"No, really," I said. "I answer letters for Mutronics, take care of problems, handle repairs. Up in the city."

"Can you get this fixed for me, then?" he asked. "It's messed up."

"This is probably not the best place to store your shit, out here under a tree. Why don't you keep it inside?"

He rubbed at his nose with the corner of his sleeve, and I realized. This wasn't just a place for him to hang out anymore. He was living here. I noticed an old sleeping bag rolled up next to the foot of the tree.

"How much do you think it would cost?"

"To fix?" I picked it up and examined it. I knew nothing about how effects actually worked, but I wanted to at least appear knowledgeable, so I twisted the knobs, shook it to see if it rattled. "Ten bucks, maybe," I said. "I don't know. Right now the company's got some problems. I'd wait on sending it in."

"I got a warranty."

I pictured the cardboard box Lenny DeMarino had shown me on my first day, where we tossed the yellow warranty cards that came in the mail. There had to be thousands, unsorted, the names painstakingly printed on them by their trusting owners. I thought about the piles of dusty boxes on tables, stacked on the floor, waiting for the attention of technicians who had long ago stopped coming in. "Well, that ought to help. But I'd still wait a little while."

"I bought the thing," said Nicky. "It ought to work."

"You actually live out here?" I asked, to change the subject. "I mean, what happened to your mom's house?" Nicky's house had always been an object of fascination for me—mid-sixties tasteless, with a black-and-white color scheme that extended to the furniture and lighting fixtures. The ceiling had tiny stereo speakers built into it, and on the floor of the living room there were oversized fuzzy-dice footstools we used to kick around. African wood carvings decorated the mantel. It wasn't a place you'd ever want to live, but it was fun to visit when she wasn't around.

"Moved to Chicago—she got a new job."

"And you decided to stay?"

"I have to stay. I move, I lose my benefits." He sat down and put the guitar in his lap, but did not play anything, instead staring intently at a smudge on the knee of his jeans.

"Benefits?" I asked.

"From the state."

There was a bit of grass stuck in the back of his hair that had been bothering me for a while. I reached over and pulled it off him, at which motion he flinched, as if I were removing a sliver. It had never occurred to me that things might work out this badly for Nicky. For anyone I knew. I picked up the phase shifter.

"I'll get it fixed, but it might take a little while."

"Whatever," he said. "I got time."

"Nicky," I said, "why do you always wear so many shirts? Most people wear one, or maybe two at the most."

I feared I'd insulted him. When he answered, his face was a mask. "The revolution comes, money won't be worth anything," he said. "Barter economy. The more you got on your back, the better off you'll be."

"You're going to trade your shirts?"

"Maybe. I might just need them to stay warm. Nuclear winter and all."

"If that happens, you'll need more than shirts."

I left him there, eating his second slice of cold pizza. I couldn't decide if this revolution idea was something he'd come up with after the fact in order to justify his own behavior, or if he'd really been planning for it all these years, preparing for the world to come apart around him. Carrying his broken effect in one hand, I trudged out to the street, then turned in the direction of my mother's house.

At the library I saw Judith Horner. True to her prediction, the odd angles of her face had come together into a kind of no-nonsense prettiness, or maybe it was just self-confidence. I hadn't seen her since high school. She was just home for the weekend from NYU Law School, she said. Her father was out of town and she was taking care of Toby. She batted her eyelashes a lot, and it took me a minute before I realized she was wearing contacts.

"You got a haircut," she said. "I'm not sure it suits you."

"Actually, I've had surgery recently."

Her eyes widened in alarm. "On your head? Spencer! What happened?"

"Fight." I was glad for the opportunity to sound tough. "Some guys jumped me."

"That's terrible!"

"I'm all right now. I have two holes in my head, though. Want to feel?"

She hesitated. "I think I'll pass. I'm not very good with things like that. I faint every time I give blood."

The man behind the counter watched us with an expression of mild distaste.

"Listen, would you like to get a drink or something?"

"I can't right now, I've got a dentist appointment in twenty minutes. But we could meet later." She held the book she'd

179

checked out up tight against her chest. "It's a little embarrassing, but I still come back to have my teeth cleaned."

We arranged to get together at a place downtown, The Loft, around eight. As she walked out, I watched the tight way her jeans fit her, the slender, inverted V of her legs.

She was already there when I arrived that evening, sipping a Rusty Nail. I ordered the same. The bar at The Loft was located above the main dining area, and the center of it was cut out so that from where we sat, we could look directly down onto the people eating their meals.

I started telling her about everything that had happened. I made it sound as funny as I could, turning the union people into cartoon characters with humorous accents, doing my best to describe what Mutronics was like now, with its empty workbenches and heaps of equipment and paperwork, lit only by candles and an illegal gasoline generator in the back room. It made a good story. She shook her head in disbelief, hung on each detail. We had three more drinks each. She picked an ice cube out of her empty glass.

"What do you think?" she asked, gesturing with her eyes.

I looked down. Two overly made-up women in similar black outfits with lots of jewelry had just been served a large salad. It sat in the center of the table in its own bowl, while they worked the tiny portions they'd transferred to their plates.

"Do you know them?"

"No, do you?"

"No."

"Good. If I miss, I'm buying. Otherwise, the next one's on you." Her cheeks were flushed, and the ice melting between her upheld fingers sent a glistening track of water down her wrist.

"Go."

She tossed the ice over the edge. Both of us immediately

pulled our heads back and pretended to be deep in discussion. We waited for a reaction from below.

"You weren't even close," I said, finally.

"I don't know, I think it was a pretty good shot. All right, I get to go again. This time, watch more carefully."

One time, in fourth grade, she'd ridden her bike over to my house expressly to tell me a dirty joke she'd learned. I'd always remembered this—not the joke, only the fact that she'd done it. It had seemed so out of character for her. Tonight, she wore a denim shirt that was unbuttoned just far enough to reveal the top of something white and lacy.

"You may get us thrown out."

"I can see it now: 'Legal career ruined over ice incident.' 'She always seemed like such a *nice* girl. But apparently she had these tendencies. She liked to throw ice. Who could have known?' " She slipped another cube out of the glass, looked around to make sure no one was watching us, then tossed it out into space. It landed clearly in the middle of the salad bowl.

"Direct hit," I said.

"You know, that could be me in a few years."

"Not a chance. You're nothing like them."

"That's so nice of you to say." She opened her purse and put some money on the table. "Come on, let's get out of here."

"I owe you a drink."

"I know. I want to collect on it someplace else. I think we've had about as much fun as two people can have here."

On our way out to the parking lot, she told me about Toby. "He's getting old. He has fits fairly regularly. I don't know how much longer my dad is going to be able to handle it."

"Fits?"

"Epileptic ones, I guess. It's really sad when it happens, because he doesn't know what hits him. We give him pills and that helps some." She took my hand and held it, just for a moment. "It must have been awful for you, having such terrible headaches and not knowing what was wrong."

"Actually, a good smack in the head was just what I needed," I said.

Back at her house, Toby greeted us with a couple of happy barks. He was a huge dog—I'd forgotten how huge—with deep brown eyes that gave him a very human range of expressions. I scratched his head and he responded by wagging his tail for me, then hurrying into the kitchen where I heard him begin to eat.

In her childhood bedroom, under the benign attention of a dresser top of stuffed animals and with the radio tuned to a top-forty station, we stood and kissed. We did this for a full five minutes. From out in the hall where we'd banished him, Toby gave an occasional, mournful whine. "Chill out," Judith said to the door, finally, breaking away from me. Then she slipped her hands back around my waist. "Do you want to stay?"

We kissed again, pressed up against each other. I didn't answer.

"Well?" she asked. "Because I'm kind of drunk, and I think we need to decide now."

"You mean the night?"

"No, the month. Of course that's what I mean. You really can be difficult. What's your decision? Because I'm sinking fast."

I told her yes.

"Good," she said. Moving away from me, she lit a candle, turned out the lights, then proceeded to take off all her clothes. "What do you think?" She held her hands out, palms up. She had tiny breasts with small, dark nipples. In the flickering light, her shadow was huge against the wall. A soft thud sounded against the door as Toby settled down outside, resigned to the fact that we weren't going to allow him in. "Poor baby," she said. "He hates to miss anything."

I woke up at three A.M. to another, more violent thump from outside. My mouth was dry and my head hurt a little from all the

Drambuie. For a moment I had no idea where I was, only that I was uncomfortably warm.

"It's Toby," Judith whispered, this time with alarm.

There was a scrabbling sound now, and more thumping, very rhythmic. Judith turned on a small light on the night table and put on a flannel bathrobe, then opened the door. I pulled on my jeans and followed her.

Toby was at the end of the hall, partway into the kitchen. His thick legs spun furiously with each spasm, and his eyes were closed up tight, his mouth open wide as if he were choking on something and trying to cough it out. There was a strange, skunky odor, too.

"I'm sorry about this," she said. "They're getting more and more frequent."

"Is there something we can do?"

"Just wait it out, that's all."

I stepped past the dog and got myself a glass of water. Toby's pills were on the counter next to a Skippy peanut butter jar that had a label taped to the front of it that read *DOG* in Magic Marker. I read the pill label and discovered that Toby and I were taking the same medication.

Judith moved past me and took down a roll of paper towels. Toby had stopped spasming now, and simply lay on his side panting. There was drool all over his face, along with some blood, and the fur around his midsection was wet. The skunky odor had become more intense. Judith got down on her hands and knees and began mopping up around the dog, speaking quietly to him as she did so. I felt suddenly sure that I didn't belong here. The question was how to extricate myself without being too rude.

"I should go."

"You don't have to," said Judith. "I'd like you to stay."

"My mother is going to wonder what happened to me."

"Call her in the morning."

I nodded, stepped back around the dog, and went to her room. I found my shirt and shoes, put them on, then went back out. Toby was up on his feet, appearing very unsteady and confused. Judith looked at me, then tightened the sash on her robe.

"Leaving anyway?"

"It's better if I go now. I'll call you."

"You don't have to. It's all right."

"I'll give you a call tomorrow. Maybe we can have dinner."

"My father is coming back tomorrow. I'm going back up to the city."

"Well, I'll call you there."

"Suit yourself."

I went to kiss her and she kissed back, but without much passion, which made sense, considering the way I was ducking out. I didn't even know *why* I was doing it. "I live with someone," I said, which of course was no longer true.

"Spencer, it's *all right*. I understand. Go."

Moments later I was outside beneath a clear, fall sky, breathing the delicious, cold air. I felt good, better than I had in a long time.

Over the next few days, I watched a lot of television, went for walks, spent more hours at the public library reading magazines. I tried out guitars at Eastern Sounds, noticed with a kind of mixed pride that they had a few Mutronics effects in their display case. A couple of times I almost called Judith, but then I stopped myself, unable to think of what I would say when she answered.

In the local paper I read about one of the bands my dad used to play with called Dugout. They were still around, performing at a place called the Pipe and Bowl on Route One. There was a picture of them in the ad, but I only recognized two of the faces. One guy was nearly bald. The other had grown a full beard, put on about forty pounds, and had the look of a hillbilly mountain man. The other three were young, more my age. All of the members were dressed the same: black shirts open at the top two buttons and white slacks. Seeing the ad had a truly shocking effect on me—New Jersey suddenly seemed an enormous carnivore that ate people and spat them back out wearing silk shirts and shit-eating grins. To his credit, I thought, Spider had seen this long ago. I packed my things and kissed my mother good-bye.

"May first," she said. "Keep it open." She had a copy of *Bridal* magazine in front of her, and was taking notes on a small, pale blue pad.

"Absolutely," I promised.

"What are you going to do now?"

"I don't know," I replied, honestly. "Look for a job, I guess."

She clicked the top back onto her pen. "You take care of yourself. And you can come back anytime. You know that."

She was preoccupied with all the planning, flushed with anticipation. She really did seem happy. Something had been tugging vaguely at the back of my mind for a while, and I decided to come right out and ask.

"You're not pregnant, are you?"

"Good God, no," she said. "I love you, honey, but once was more than enough, thank you very much."

When I got back to the city, it was late. The bus had been caught in traffic, and I was feeling irritable. Then the subway out to Brooklyn ground to a halt underneath the East River for nearly a half-hour, during which time a saxophone player who had a recently-got-out-of-prison look to him, and only three fingers on his left hand, entertained me with repeated choruses of "Body and Soul." We were alone in the car together. I closed my eyes and imagined the sound as an animal lost in the woods, calling for its mate. Shortly after the train started up again, he pushed on to another car without ever asking me for money. It occurred to me that perhaps I'd seen a ghost, a phantom tenor-player who only appeared when the F train was stalled on the riverbed. Maybe he was even the reason we'd stalled.

There was a light on in the apartment, in Sally's room. After the strange train ride, I was already feeling a bit spooked. I'd been gone a week and a half. I stood in the street for a few minutes, watching. Someone passed briefly in front of the window, and though I could not tell who it was, it was certainly not Sally. Rick's car was nowhere in sight, and I thought it unlikely that he'd have returned so quickly. There were piles of garbage out by the curb, and one of them held the remains of some old furniture. I took a hunk of wood that had once been a table leg, kicked a cockroach off the end, and approached my front stairs. As quietly as I could, I slipped the key into the lock, then pushed open the door.

All the way up the stairs, I kept telling myself I was making a mistake. There was nothing tough about me—one punch and I went to the hospital. I would be much better off calling the cops and letting them take care of the intruder. But at the same time, after all I'd been through, I thought it might be sort of nice to clock someone with a table leg.

I stopped on the landing and listened. Whoever it was didn't seem in a particular hurry. There were footsteps, then the sound of running water. Then the television.

I climbed the rest of the stairs. The door to the living room was partway closed, and from beyond it a narrator spoke brightly about the lakes of central Michigan. Instead of kicking open the door, as I'd envisioned myself doing, I simply stuck my head through the opening and, turtlelike, peered around.

Spider was seated on the sofa in a T-shirt and jeans, a beer in his hand, his feet up on the coffee table. "Hey," he said, when he saw me. "Come on in."

There were empty beer bottles everywhere, along with a mass of white carry-out bags that indicated he'd been living for the most part on what you could order at Wendy's and Burger King.

"How'd you get in?" I still had the table leg in my hand. I leaned it up against the side of the television.

"I have a key," he said. "From last time." He took a swallow from his beer and wiped his lips on the back of his hand. "You don't mind, do you?"

"I don't know," I said. "It depends."

"I was beginning to wonder when you'd get back."

"What, exactly, are you doing here?"

"Well, I'll tell you." He took his feet down and sat up. "I got kicked out."

"Kicked out of where?"

"Katrina's place. It was bound to happen. Never tell a woman you're taking advantage of her."

"You said *that?*"

"I was kidding. Mostly. I mean, I *was* taking advantage of her. I was sleeping there rent-free, eating her food. Anyway, she got kind of testy after you showed up and we both disappeared that morning. Made her suddenly think I might not be so dependable." He put down his beer, found a cigarette in the front pocket of his shirt, and lit it, drawing deeply and exhaling. "She asked me why I'd bothered to come back. I said, 'Why would someone in their right mind walk away from such a good thing?' I guess she didn't take it as a compliment. Plus, I never told her about you. I think it made me seem a lot older to her all of a sudden." He gestured toward the table leg. "Planning to smash my head to a bloody pulp?"

"Something like that. So, it's my fault?"

"Not at all. I didn't say that."

"Good. How long have you been here?"

"Four days," he said. "You had a couple calls. One from Sally, another from your lawyer. I'm sorry you guys didn't work it out, she seemed really nice. Oh, yeah, and Jerry called, mostly to see how you were doing. I told him fine. He's got things going down there again, says there's plenty of mail piled up and waiting, anytime you're ready." He smiled at me, the creases around his lips pulling back into friendly parentheses. "I start tomorrow myself."

"Start what?"

"Phones, I guess. Whatever needs doing. I asked him for a job, and he said okay. I see this as a real opportunity. Jerry's basically beginning over, you know, and me, too. It'll just be the three of us running the company. We'll be in on the ground floor—anything could happen." He looked genuinely excited about the prospect. "Besides, I need some way to get a cash flow going. I already owe you a week's rent."

He'd come down by bus, he said, bringing with him only a bag of clothes and the Telecaster, which leaned up against the wall by the TV in a brown vinyl gig-bag. SPIDERMAN DAN was stenciled slightly unevenly along the front of it in yellow paint.

I went downstairs, found my address book, and looked up Sally's number in Boston. On the second ring she picked up.

"Spencer, it's kind of late to be calling."

"He's here," I said.

"I know that—we talked on the phone. You guys are going to be roomies."

"I don't know what to do."

"There's nothing you can do. Let him stay."

"Really?"

"Why not? It's a temporary solution, anyway."

"You were right. He has a wife, and a kid."

"Are they nice?"

The question caught me a little off-guard. What difference did it make whether they were nice? Even if they were awful, they didn't deserve the kind of treatment they'd received. "The girl's name is Allegra."

"It's a beautiful name." There was a long pause. "Spencer?" she said, at last.

"What?"

"I'm going to come down with the station wagon to get my things. This weekend, okay?"

"Fine," I said.

"I'll see you then."

"Hey, we saw one."

"One what?"

"A moose."

"Good night, Spencer."

I hung up the phone and stared at it for a minute, then went back upstairs.

Spider had the Tele out and was plinking away, the snap of the unamplified strings as loud as the notes. "You're mad at me," he said. "It's to be expected. You'll get past it. Look at all your old societies, Europe, Asia—they all have households with parents in them. It's only in America that we make sure everybody goes off to separate places, and that's pretty sad, when you think about it. But listen, I really will leave if you want me to, and no hard feelings. Just say the word and I'm out of here."

"Of course you can stay," I told him. "I'm not going to put my own father out in the street."

16

Dear Mutronics, Inc.
   Enclosed is a questionnaire we hope you'll fill out and return to us. We have had a number of complaints about your company from dissatisfied customers, copies of which are enclosed. In our past experience, we've found that the businesses we contact are eager to do what they can to remedy any situations that may come up regarding such complaints. You may contact us, or contact the customers directly. In any event, we are certain you'll want to address these situations promptly.

> Sincerely,
> Molly Harbaugh
> Better Business Bureau
> Seattle, Washington

Dear Sirs,
   This past May, my client, Mr. Joseph Finstere, received a severe electric shock from one of your products, the "Talking Beaver." The enclosed lawsuit gives the details leading up to Mr. Finstere's eventual death in August as a direct result of this shock. We are asking for compensation, as stated in the suit, of $5,000,000, a figure based on pain and suffering caused to Mr. Finstere and his family, lost lifetime wages, and punitive damages.

I look forward to hearing from you or your attorneys regarding this matter as soon as possible.

>Sincerely,
>Howard Eisenbahn
>Cunliffe and Schwartz, P.C.
>Attorneys at Law
>St. Louis, Missouri

Dear Mr. Markus,

I am disappointed in YOU. Please think about this: YOU are free to do whatever you want. You walk around, you go to work in your nice office. You eat whatever you want, like maybe a grill cheese sandwich or WHATEVER. You sleep with your girlfriend. You don't look at CONCRETE all day long. You have a life.

My life is my music. I listen all day, even when I'm NOT near my tape player, because I can hear it anyway. Like now for instance when I'm hearing THIRD STONE FROM THE SUN (which is earth) even though I'm at work and just soddering. I hear this and I wonder if you are really all you are CRACKED UP to be. Rock and Roll is a spirit and you can't incarcerate a spirit.

I sent away to another company for strings and they sent me HEAVY gage because they knew I couldn't return them. I put them on ANYWAY and I can feel myself getting stronger. Hendrix could bend BASS STRINGS right across the neck. I believe this. And I am getting stronger.

Don't FORGET me. I haven't forgotten you.

>Furry Couch #C-563-2798

Part Three

17

M utronics had the look of an abandoned movie set. Inside the front entrance, blue barriers that read POLICE LINE, DO NOT CROSS lay stacked in a loose sort of pile. The union had been gone for weeks, but no one had thought to collect the signs. The offices themselves were empty and quiet, though evidence of frenzied activity was everywhere. Papers lay atop desks with pencils on them, as if the person writing had disintegrated in mid-stroke. The copying machine still had a schematic for a new product resting on its glass. In the technicians' area, each work station had a piece of electronics out, gutted.

My desk was the way I'd left it, except that the number of letters had multiplied by a factor of about four. There were now boxes of them, two on the desk itself, another three on the floor next to it. Apparently, it had never occurred to Jerry that I might not return.

I wandered out to the front desk and sat down in the chair from which Julie, the receptionist, used to glare out at the world, headphones on, drawing little cartoons. I'd seen something by her recently in an underground newspaper called *Scuzz*, which I picked up next to the register in a record store. A drawing of a square-headed man in underwear and a T-shirt, bent over, puking. Amid the vomitus were all kinds of oddities: musical notes, a tiny Michael Jackson, record albums and syringes, a couple of free-entry tickets to a nightclub. The caption read simply, HAPPY NEW YEAR. Sitting in her chair, I wondered where she was now, and if she missed her job. I punched the WATS line on the telephone and picked up the receiver. There was no dial tone. I tried another line but it, too, was disconnected.

"Babe," said a voice from behind me. It was Jerry. I got out of the chair.

He grinned and gave me an enormous bear of a handshake.

"I'm working deals, man. Working deals, every minute of the day. Come on, let me show you what's happening here. How's that head?"

As we walked around he explained that the business had been sold at auction two weeks earlier, and he'd bought it himself, minus any legal obligation to repay his debts.

"You can do that?" I asked.

"You bet. So long as it's a public sale and you put an ad in the papers. I was the only bidder."

I told him that surprised me, though given the state of affairs, it probably shouldn't have.

"Well," he admitted, "it was a very tiny ad."

He'd even bought the rights to use the name "Mutronics," though the new corporation was officially called Gryphon Research, Inc. "After the mythical beast that rises from its own ashes," he said, proudly.

I didn't tell him that he meant Phoenix, not Gryphon, because I couldn't see much point in spoiling his mood. Jerry was like a kid with all new toys. It didn't even seem strange to him that he was showing me around the same factory I'd worked in since the previous spring.

"Here," he said, stopping suddenly in front of a closed door. As I recalled, the room had formerly been full of junk, an unused office stuffed with random items: cartons of computer paper, hunks of old sheet metal, inactive files stacked in dusty cardboard containers. He gestured for me to put my face up against the smoked glass, through which I could just make out two blurred figures.

"Accountants," he said, with obvious distaste. "Goddamn

bean-counters. But I have to be very careful. I'm walking on eggshells here."

We continued the tour. Most of the time Jerry didn't say anything, although he occasionally cleared his throat as if he were about to. The lights were off throughout much of the factory. There was one on in the testing booth, though, and as we approached we could hear someone jamming away at a guitar, playing a minor blues full of diminished chords and nice tensions.

Spider had left well before me in the morning. There he was in Randy's old place. He turned on the stool and nodded hello. On the table in front of him was a whole tray of distortion boosters, built in the last days of the strike, shiny red and silver boxes with black knobs.

"Sounding good there," said Jerry.

He leaned the guitar up against the edge of the table and stood. Behind him, Randy's rock-and-roll posters still adorned the wall: Jimi, Eric, Carlos, and of course, her idol, Eddie.

"Spencer could probably use help with some of those letters," said Jerry. "You know, if you run out of things to test back here." He gestured toward the cardboard boxes stacked precariously all around the small room.

"Whatever he wants me to do." He stuck his hands into his pockets and leaned back against the battered plywood workbench.

Jerry looked back and forth between the two of us. "Yeah," he said, finally.

I followed him back down the long, dim corridor. Once inside, he sat in his thick leather-upholstered chair and faced me. I sat too.

"What I'd like is to use your picture." He reached into his desk and pulled out a box of surgical gauze. "I mean, if you don't mind. I want you to wrap this around your head, like it was just after the operation."

I stared at him.

"Not right now, necessarily. In a couple of hours. I can have a photographer here by about three. Then we use the picture on a mailing to every music store in the country." He was growing excited. "You'll be famous."

"Why would I want to do that?"

"I see your point. I'll pay you for it. I wouldn't ask you to do it for nothing. How much do you want?"

"I don't think I like the idea. For one thing, you're not going to sell products by making yourself look like a victim. That's not why people buy things, because they feel sorry for the company. You buy a product because it's something you want or believe you need. Besides, I don't really want my face all over the country wrapped up like a war injury."

He found half a cigar in the big ashtray on his desk and plugged the corner of his mouth with it. "You're right," he said. "But I need to reestablish good will with my customers. This is a critical time. You know the history of this company?" He found a match and ignited the end, sending a sour puff of smoke out over the desktop. "Back in 'sixty-eight I was playing R&B out on Long Island, where I'm from. The guitar player, a guy we called Buster, left this little device he'd come up with over at my house one day. A little power-booster, about a buck and a half worth of parts you could get at any electronics supply store."

"Your first product."

He squinted, knitting together a pair of eyebrows that looked like frayed rope. He seemed surprised that I would know anything about him. "I took ads in the music magazines. Did it all myself, you know? Hired a guy, set up a little shop in my house. A year later I had three products. The year after that, five. And you know why I was a success? Because I never forgot who it was out there that was buying my stuff. That's the key—I kept true to the spirit of rock and roll. That, and I supplied quality at a price people could afford, which is just good business." He stabbed at the ashtray with his cigar. He seemed to have finished. It was the most I'd ever heard him say at one time.

Here, I thought, was my chance, finally, to wield a little influence and try to help out some of the people I'd been lying to for months. "Then make good on all the back orders we owe."

Jerry pushed the ashtray aside. "What makes you think I wouldn't? That's what I want you to be in charge of, among other things. You go through those letters, and whatever you think is right, you do it. No refunds, though. I can't send back money. If they're waiting on products we don't have, offer them something else. We still have inventory on a lot of things, so go ahead and send it out. Just make sure it's legit." He ran a hand through his tangle of hair, only making it look even more like he'd stepped out of a wind tunnel. "And think this mailing idea over. I'd be willing to pay you, say, a thousand bucks. That's not bad for one photo." He dug around on the desktop and came up with a sheet of paper. "I've been working on the copy, too. Check it out, tell me what you think." He began to read:

" 'Dear Friend of Mutronics: As you may be aware, we here at the company have been engaged in a Life and Death struggle with the forces of Socialism and the enemies of Rock and Roll. For a while it looked pretty bad—they threatened us, they blockaded our factory, and, yes, they even beat our employees (see photo). But we had the courage of our convictions on our side, and . . .' " Jerry smacked at the page with the back of his hand. "Something else here, I'm not exactly sure yet. I've got some notes." He scooped up three more sheets of paper and gave them all to me. " 'Courage of our convictions.' That's my favorite part. That's what I want to stress, you know? Integrity."

"You want me to do this?"

"I got it started for you, just pick up where I leave off. A little history of the company, some stuff about our valiant fight against the union, that's all. We want 'em to know what happened here, that we're heroes, rock-and-roll heroes, and we're back on the block, this time for good."

"I haven't said yes to the photo."

"That's okay, think it over. We'll do the mailing regardless. But think hard. A thousand bucks, amigo."

It was a chunk of money, and also there were literally hundreds of people around the country who blamed me personally for ripping them off on behalf of Mutronics. A little sympathy didn't sound like such a bad idea.

He spun on his chair, then kicked his feet up onto the desk. "I can give you an extra two bucks an hour over your old salary."

"Make it three?"

He hesitated. "Okay, three. I tell you what, I feel good about this, really good. A couple of months, we'll have this place back on its feet."

"Who else have you got working?" As far as I could tell, except for my dad and the two accountants, we had the fifth floor to ourselves.

"Well, no one's exactly working. I've got some people coming in on a fee basis to do things—engineers and technicians and stuff. For the time being you and Spider are it, as far as staff goes."

I picked up a letter opener off the desk and ran a finger along its smooth, metal edge. "You hired him to be sure I'd come back, didn't you?" I asked. "To get the picture."

"Not true. Not true at all. I needed a tester, and I haven't heard anything from Randy. I want you, man. We all need each other. That's how I like to look at it." The phone on his desk rang and he answered it. I stood and watched for a moment as he barked at the person on the other end, something about a loan. When I made my exit from the office, he didn't even notice me leave.

I went back to the testing room. "I don't think this is going to work out," I said.

"What did Jerry want?"

"He wants to photograph me wrapped up in bandages and send out the picture to get sympathy. I'm supposed to write a press-release kind of thing to go with it." I didn't mention the thousand dollars.

"Need help?" he offered.

I stared at him. "I don't understand. Why would you sign up to work here, of all places? It's not going to last, you've got to know that—it can't. We're just going to tread water for a while, then drown."

He pursed his lips and considered, as if I'd asked him something to do with the nature of the universe. "Well, it's like this. I've never had a job I liked. I mean it, the whole concept of working just freezes me up. That includes playing, too, because there's only two levels to the business. Either you make it big and get to do whatever the hell you like, or you don't, and you spend your life drag-assing around to little piss-hole bars and Holiday Inns, playing wallpaper music while a bunch of noodle-heads shuffle around the dance floor hoping to get laid. Right now, I'm between things, and I need a few bucks. This place is just right—low-pressure, good atmosphere, no structure. It might be a chance to get in on the ground floor of something. Maybe we will drown, I don't know. Maybe we won't. We'll just have to see. In the meantime, I'm going to write some songs back here."

"It'll never work."

"I trust Jerry. He's got connections."

"He's also a borderline looney. You know that. He dresses up in superhero outfits."

"Lots of times, it's the crazy people who have the real vision."

I left him and went on my own tour of the offices, wandering aimlessly, trying to think. The problem was that I really had no other plans. If I walked out now, what would I do? Sit around the house waiting for the lawsuit to come through? Move someplace?

I found my way into Cat's old office. Jerry had mentioned in passing that Cat was now up on Forty-eighth Street selling guitars. I thought about how he used to dress, his one-piece black jumpsuits with yellow leather boots, parachute pants with tie-dye shirts. He'd worked for Jerry for years, had a relationship with the man that seemed almost like father and son, yet when push came to shove, he'd left with the rest of them.

I sat at Cat's desk and poked through his Rolodex. His writing was overlarge and forced, as if each character had taken a concentrated effort. On the inside of his closet door was a *Penthouse* centerfold. Another was taped to a typing extension that slid in and out of the desk, and showed a naked girl standing with her legs apart, holding a Rickenbacker bass by the headstock. I stared at it for a while. The rumble of air through the heating ducts sounded like a distant storm.

I went back to my desk and lifted one of the cartons of letters, then carried it back to Spider.

"Start sorting through these," I said. "Put all the ones from Better Business Bureaus together, as well as ones from state attorney generals, and anything else that looks official. The letters from individual customers are another problem. Some of these people have written six or seven times, so we need to get those all together too, so we understand what stage they're at with us—whether they ever got anything like a refund, or maybe their pedal back."

"What's the plan?" he asked.

"We're going to solve all these old complaints, case by case."

He stared uncertainly into the box. "There must be five hundred letters in there."

"And that's just for starters. We've got four more cartons."

He whistled, then dug in and extracted an envelope at random. When he opened it, a dollar bill fell out and onto the floor. " 'Dear Sirs,' " he read. " 'Please send me your catalog. I am a big fan of your effects. Signed, Rocky Casella, Big Foot.' Big Foot must be the name of his band."

I picked up the dollar.

"What are you going to do with it?" asked Spider.

"Send it back to him. The closest thing we have to a catalog is over five years old."

"Why not send him one anyway?"

"You don't understand. That's how we got in trouble in the first place. Half the things in the catalog haven't been in stock for years." There were some stacked up on the corner of the table, and I grabbed a copy to show him, first blowing the dust off it. "Look, a Deluxe Chameleon Guitar Synth. Not only don't we have any, I've never even seen one. Except in this picture."

"The kid wants the catalog," said my dad. "That's all, and since we have them in stock, I don't see the harm in sending him one. Let him fantasize a little."

I held up the dollar. "All right," I said. "But there's no charge for catalogs."

Spider took the dollar from me and put it in his front pocket. "Then this is pure profit, I'd say."

18

***

S ally came down on the weekend in her father's station
wagon. She arrived wearing jeans and a loose sweatshirt
from which the arms had been carefully ripped. I opened the
door partway. There was an awkward moment, then she leaned
forward and gave me a kiss. "Going to invite me in?"

"I don't know," I said. "Are you a thief?"

"I do plan to take all your belongings."

"That's all right, then." I held the door wide. She looked different, I thought. Refreshed.

Spider sat in front of the television while I helped move
boxes of books, her dresser, her clothes. We didn't talk much
as we worked. I still didn't quite believe it was happening.

We passed back and forth in front of Spider on the couch,
who stared into the set, ignoring us. He was in a bad mood because he'd answered an ad in the *Voice* for an R&B band that
needed a guitar player, but when he told them his age, they'd
said they weren't interested. I thought it was kind of funny, but
he'd been stewing all day.

"I really miss you," I said, as we loaded the final box of stuff.
Jutting out from the top were a pair of roller skates, an old
eight-track tape player, probably from the same stoop sale, and
her Ranger hat. The plastic lobster was in there, too.

"Well, I miss you. But that doesn't make this wrong."

I was suddenly aware that we were being observed from the

next stoop. A smallish, thin man with wire-rimmed glasses and a mustache sat smoking a cigarette, watching us. I glared at him, but he took this as an invitation and came down.

"You're a musician, aren't you?" he asked. He had on a checkered cap, and from the sides protruded tiny puffs of thinning, dishwater hair.

"Not really. Look, we're having a conversation here, if you don't mind."

"I don't mind," he said. "I'm Arnold Blickman. I'm a songwriter." He lowered his voice. "I've been hearing a lot of my stuff on the radio. I'm not sure what there is I can do about it. I thought I'd ask if you had any ideas."

Magnified behind his thick lenses, Arnold Blickman's eyes seemed out of proportion to the rest of his head.

"What do you mean, exactly?" asked Sally. I made a face at her, but she was obviously intrigued.

"I mean," said Arnold Blickman, "that other people are doing my material. Leonard Cohen, for instance. Bob Dylan. These are people you may have heard of."

"That's amazing. How do you think they got hold of your songs?"

He shook his head. "I can't say. Except that sometimes I write things just walking around, you know, on the street. I'm not as careful as I probably ought to be. For the longest time, I've had the feeling I was being watched." He stepped closer to me. "Contact microphones." He practically whispered it.

"There are directional microphones that can pick up the sound of a mosquito at a hundred yards," I said, helpfully.

He nodded—I'd confirmed his suspicions. "I've been writing since the first grade. Poetry, songs, you name it. I used to have a studio over a fabric store, and there was a band that rehearsed upstairs. At least that's what they said." He tilted his head. "Some guy named Winston. Ever heard of him?"

"No."

"When I packed up and left, so did they. Do you think Winston might have something to do with this?"

"More than likely," I said. "Maybe he's the one that's having you followed."

"Joni Mitchell did some of my stuff. A song I made up once when I was walking down Seventh Avenue, about four years ago. I distinctly remember making up the lyrics. I was feeling really down, you know? Suicidal, actually. Then, about six months later, there they were, on her album. Black Sabbath, too. You know the song 'Paranoid'?"

Sally sneezed.

"I wrote that. What I want to know is, what can I do? Do you think I have a chance going after these people? They're so big. The way I see it, I'm owed a lot of money."

"Arnold," she said, "the next time you write a song, copy it down on paper, then mail it to yourself and don't open the en-velope. You'll have dated proof that it's yours."

"Oh, everyone knows that. But you have to remember what it is you wrote long enough to get it onto paper." He held one finger in the air, as if testing wind direction. "That's the trick of it."

"It's a tough business," I said.

"You're telling me," said Arnold. "I just want what's coming to me." He went back to his own stoop and began polishing his glasses on his shirttail.

Sally and I took a walk through the park, where we ran into a couple of her Ranger buddies. I stood a few feet apart while the three of them caught up. She'd phoned in her resignation from Boston, and they were surprised to see her back so soon.

"It's getting weird out here," one of them, a tall, skinny black guy, said. "Found a goat's head the other day. All burned and shit. The voodoo people are getting serious."

"A goat?" Sally said.

"It ain't just chickens anymore." He leaned in a little closer and said something to her I couldn't hear.

"No, thanks, Luther," she said. "I'm cool."

"We all miss you, baby." He tipped his hat at me. "Have a good one."

We walked around for a while, finally ending up at the zoo, because she wanted to visit her favorite animal, the capybara. About the size of a large dog, it seemed to be made out of spare parts from other animals: a little pig, some wild rabbit, a touch of hyena. In fact, I think it was in the rodent family. It came and stuck its unfortunate face right up against the bars, and Sally gave it a piece of grass. When it wasn't interested in that, she offered a peanut M&M, which it took greedily.

"Smarter than your average capybara," she said.

I explained to her about Rick's going to New Mexico, and she listened with interest. "He's really kind of a romantic, isn't he?" she said. "I never realized."

"He just felt responsible. It is possible that the whole thing's a scam. In which case I feel sorry for her boyfriend."

"You think he'd do something violent?"

"Rick?" I thought about the way he'd been at Desmond's apartment, simmering with hostility, but definitely under control. "Probably not, but you never know. He doesn't like to be lied to."

"I think he's going to go out there and win her back. I think hearing she was pregnant made him realize that he really did love her. And I'm sure she loves him."

"How are you sure?"

"Why else would she tell him? It's so obvious."

I tried giving the capybara some licorice, but he wasn't interested. "It isn't obvious to me."

"Well," she said, "no matter how you look at it, it's exciting."

We made our way in silence through the bird house, then over to the monkeys, who screamed at us and flew into a psychotic spurt of activity. We made faces at them. I held Sally's hand and she didn't pull it away. Words kept spinning into my mouth, but I was unable to say them. In front of the rhinoceros enclosure I touched her cheek.

"Arnold Blickman," I said. "What a name."

She turned and stuck her hands in her pockets. "I'm seeing someone."

"How'd you like to be the lawyer he comes to with a claim? Bob Dylan, Joni Mitchell, and Black Sabbath. The guy is definitely an eggroll short of a pu-pu platter."

"Don't you want to know who it is?"

"I don't know. Do I?"

"My old boyfriend, Steven."

I remembered the occasional letters that came—typed ones, on bond paper. They'd always made me feel smugly superior. "Run out of fifteen-year-olds, did he?"

"He's totally straight, goes to meetings, all that. We go back a long way together. There are some people whose lives are just bound up with yours, you know? I don't think it's serious or anything, at least not right now, but it is what's happening and I thought I ought to tell you." I could see this was not a matter we were to negotiate; I was already just a blip on her radar screen, growing fainter with distance. "I haven't gotten stoned since I saw you last. I don't even want to."

The rhinoceros eyed me from between mud-splattered folds of leathery skin. "You're not going to blame me for that."

"I'm just saying this has been a good decision."

"There's still room here," I said. "You could move right back in. I'll even unload your stuff."

"What about Spidey?"

"Out in the street—just say the word."

"I don't know, he looked awfully comfortable to me. Hey, wait a minute." She looked up at me in surprise, her lips parting enough to show a glimpse of white, which for some reason, at that particular moment, struck me as impossibly sexy. "I just remembered something."

He was still watching when we came in. Sally pushed in the antenna while I unplugged the cord and wrapped it up.

"This is serious," he said, taking his feet off the coffee table. "What are we supposed to do around here without a TV?"

"We'll buy another," I said. "This one was getting kind of old anyway."

"This set," said Sally, "belonged to my grandmother, who only watched one channel. After Walter Cronkite retired, she didn't watch at all. It's in great shape."

I hoisted the television and followed Sally down to the car. "It ghosts a little," Spider called after us.

It was late afternoon, and a splash of crimson in the sky spread out behind the rooftops like an accident. I managed to squeeze the set in with the rest of Sally's belongings, though in the process I put a small tear in her headliner, which I didn't point out. We kissed good-bye, her arms around my waist, mine clasped lightly behind her back.

"You two try and stay out of trouble," she said.

I watched as she headed down the street. With her things still upstairs, I'd been able to maintain the fiction that she was only away for a while. This was different.

Over on the next stoop, I saw Arnold Blickman, sitting in the shadows, smoking a cigarette, staring straight ahead at nothing in particular. I wondered if he'd lived there all along, because I certainly didn't remember him. Perhaps he'd only recently been let out of someplace. More likely, though, he'd been there and I just hadn't been paying attention.

I took Jerry's thousand dollars and posed for the photographer, my head wrapped in gauze. I couldn't see why not. We did it at Mutronics, in Jerry's office, against a screen the guy brought with him. He took a whole roll of film, moving around me as if I were a fashion model, trying different angles, talking the whole while about some guy he'd photographed recently who won the lottery, and how this was the second time this had happened, that someone he'd shot had hit the number. "My advice to you," he said, "is after we're done here, go straight out and buy a ticket. I shit you not."

I didn't buy a Lotto ticket, but the next evening, with my cash from Jerry, Spider and I went down to Canal Street and picked up a beautiful new television—stereo, cable-ready, nineteen inches of the best Japanese technology. "This is a quality set," he assured me. He'd been at the public library poring through *Consumer Reports* all afternoon. He knew I was depressed about Sally's leaving, but he also seemed to feel that replacing the set would be a surefire cure.

We took our purchase back on the subway, hauled it up the steps to the apartment, and plugged it in. He took a step back to observe the picture.

"Nice, huh?" he said.

Actually, the picture wasn't coming in that well. I fooled with the antenna until there was more definition. "There," I said. "That's better."

He stared into the set critically. "You're right," he said. "That is better."

I left him standing in front of it and went to my room.

Jerry lost no time in having my photo reproduced onto a single-color flier, and he even hired some part-time help to stuff envelopes. I spent much of my workday trying to right various wrongs the company had committed against its customers, all the while making it very clear, as per Jerry's instructions, that those problems had to do with Mutronics, Inc., which no longer existed, and anything Gryphon did was strictly in good faith. I treasure-hunted through the crammed back rooms of the factory, poking under stacks of metal casings, empty boxes, old invoices. Occasionally I'd find something, a lost repair, for instance, or some old promotional item from the days when Jerry and his company were living the high life. In one room, I found a rolled-up poster of a younger, sillier-looking Jerry in bell-bottoms and flare-collared shirt open halfway down the chest, standing alongside "Miss Band-Aid," who wore two of them, one on each of her enormous breasts. I had to admire him, the young businessman playing at rock star, being outrageous not just to promote his business, but because he could be.

Mrs. Hong, the older, sadder-looking Mrs. Hong, who did repairs, had been rehired and taken up residence at her workbench once again. Where once there had been twenty people, now there was just her, and it was hard to tell how she felt about being back. She carried on the way she always had, working quietly with her soldering iron and oscilloscope, taking her half-hour lunch at her desk, usually something from home that she warmed on the radiator before eating. I brought her Nicky Dormer's distortion booster, which she examined. The screws were rusted in place from being kept outside. There was other work she was supposed to be doing for Jerry, but I made sure that she had a stack of priority repairs, too, items I'd managed to find for some of our most neglected letter-writers, and I put Nicky's effect on the top of the pile.

On a dusty shelf back in shipping, alongside a number of orphan pedals gathering dust, I found an item that looked like it might be a Gopher, though it had been spray-painted and had red glitter pasted all over, so there were no visible markings left. I brought it back to Spider, who was splitting his time between the letters and the testing room, where it was obvious he felt far more comfortable.

"I think this is Duke Davin's," I said. He turned it over in his hands, then set it on the bench and plugged in a cord.

"There's four or five letters from him. Where was it?"

"Just sitting on a shelf. No paperwork."

"Paperwork? This thing looks like one of Dorothy's ruby slippers. How could it get lost?"

"Let's just see if it works."

It did, and I mailed it back to Duke with a brief note of apology.

I tried to find a Gopher to send to Furry Couch, but even though they were one of the few items Jerry had managed to move through production during the strike, all of those units had been reserved for music stores, who were our first priority.

Spider and I had lunch across the street at Sun King Chinese Express, where glowering Asian men wielding long spoons served up steaming, colorless food out of stainless-steel trays. I had the pepper steak, while he opted for fried chicken wings on a bed of greasy rice. I dumped hot sauce all over my plate and stirred it in. He popped the top on a can of soda.

"Making any progress?" I asked.

"Oh, yeah," he said. "You bet."

In fact, I'd checked in on him earlier a couple of times, and as far as I could tell, he was doing almost nothing. He would read each letter through carefully, then stuff it back in the envelope and read the next. But I didn't want to criticize him.

"Look who's here," Spider said, pointing across the room. Seated over by the window, an untouched egg roll in front of her on a plate, was Randy. I waved, but she didn't see. So I stood and shouted to her.

This time she saw me, and she nodded in our direction. I motioned for her to come over, which she did, pulling up a seat, but not meeting my eyes directly.

"What are you doing?" I asked. There were circles under her eyes.

"Trying to decide whether to go across and ask Jerry for my job back."

"What have you been doing?"

"Nothing. Watching TV, collecting unemployment. I'm bored out of my gourd."

"Just do it. The worst he could do is say no. The other day he hired two guys to stuff envelopes."

"I'm not stuffing envelopes, and I'm not testing batteries, none of that shit-work." She looked out the window again, toward the entrance to the building. Her face seemed pained. "I've been walking up and down this block for the past hour and a half. I already had coffee around the corner. I even started up the elevator one time, then turned around."

"Why?" I said. "What are you afraid of? Jerry loves you." I thought how odd this sounded, as if I were preaching the gospel.

"I heard he hired a new tester. I guess I just can't handle the idea that I might get turned down for my own job."

"It's me," said Spider. "I'm the new tester."

She looked at him as if seeing him for the first time. "What do you know about testing?"

"I may not be Albert E. Einstein," he said. "But I guess I can tell if a fuzz box is working or not."

Randy gazed out the window. "I can't find a job anywhere. Been looking nearly a month. I'm an expert at what I do, but no one else needs me. I have a useless skill. Don't nobody else in this city make effects pedals. Hell, I'm not even sure there's any made in America anymore."

"I think there's a company out in Utah," I offered. "And I know there's a couple in California."

She shook her head and clasped her thick fingers together in front of her on the table. Jerry had said she'd lost a tooth, but if this was true, it wasn't obvious. "Oh, they got black people in Utah? I was born in this city and I plan to stay here. I just got to find me a job, and the sooner the better."

"Hey," said Spider. "Cheer up. There's work out there. And someone like you, I mean, you know. You're unusual."

Randy laughed. "Unusual. I like that. That's a good way to look at it."

"Capitalize," he said. "Make the most out of your situation. I'll bet there's twenty bands in this town that would love to have you on guitar. I mean, if you wanted to do that."

She sighed. "I'm forty-two and I'm overweight. I can't keep up with a bunch of no twenty-two-year-olds. And I don't like to stay out late—you miss all the good television. I liked my old job. I just want it back."

We convinced her to come with us and talk to Jerry. We all knew that with things as slow as they were, one tester was more than enough, and that if he did give her a job, it would only be out of sympathy. Spider began talking about how, if he had the money, he'd go to Europe and start a band, because Europeans were in love with American music. "I could be a star over there without having to do a thing. Just showing up would be enough."

"I kind of miss the crowds," said Randy, as we got on the elevator. "Say what you want about the union, they did liven things up around here." Colorful wires jutted out from where the emergency phone used to be, and on one wall someone had scrawled "Jerry Rules."

"What are the Jerry rules?" I said.

"The market is ripe," said Spider, ignoring me. "With the right act, you could clean up."

"If I had money, I'd go," she said.

"What do you know about Europe?" I asked him. It was the first I'd heard him on the subject.

"I've been reading up."

"Jesus," said Randy, as we pushed open the door and walked into the dark halls of Mutronics. "This is weird. It's so quiet."

I left Randy to make her own way with Jerry, went to my desk, and stared at the vast ocean of correspondence left to go through. It was hard to see any point to it with Jerry mailing out price lists again. Perhaps I could repair some of the damage, but what did that matter if new people were being suckered at the same time? I was too sensitive. I got up and wandered a little, finally ending up in testing. Spider was sitting at a desk in the dark, smoking a cigarette.

"Don't even think about it," I said. "Leave them alone. They don't want you bothering them. Cully doesn't, and Allegra's just a baby. I think if you're out of their lives, you're out of their lives, plain and simple."

"I know you think that. And I see you're making a real good showing with the women in your life."

"My breaking up with Sally had everything to do with your showing up and interfering."

"Is that right? Come on—you're so big on responsibility, take some yourself. Admit that you fucked up all on your own. At least don't get holy on me. I didn't say I was going anywhere. I'm just talking, you know?"

"That's where I think you should leave it."

He stubbed out the cigarette and drew a box off the pile to his right. "Look what I found," he said.

"What?"

"The fuzz box I sent in for repair. The one you wrote me back about, promising me I'd see it in a month."

"Is it fixed?"

"What do you think?"

I held it in my hand, punched the metal button a few times with my thumb. He'd had this for years, and I could even remember fooling around with it myself when I was little.

"You know what distortion is, don't you?" he asked. "Sound travels in waves out a speaker. If you push those waves hard enough they max out, square off into little boxes. 'Square waves.' They're what make your amp howl and scream."

"I know about square waves," I said, which was true, though only in the most general way. I suspected I knew as much about them as he did.

"Oh, yeah," he said, nodding. "I figured you did." He took the effect back from me. "Sometimes you have to take things to the extreme in other parts of your life, too. Out on the edges, with the howling and screaming, that's where the good stuff is."

19

K ravitch called me that evening at home. "What on earth do you think you're doing?" he asked. "You know, it's over now."

"What do you mean?" I'd just pulled a beer out of the refrigerator. My dad was in the next room with the television on. Along the underside of our cabinets, a slender, high-fashion roach tiptoed rapidly toward the stove.

"I mean," said Kravitch, nasal as ever, "that you allowed a photograph of yourself to be used in a mailing for Gryphon Research, formerly Mutronics. You've totally damaged any credibility you might have had. Did you accept money for this?"

"One thousand dollars. Jerry offered it to me." The roach was now directly over the edge of the stove, and I watched to see what it would do. The drop from cabinet to stove was three feet, probably the insect equivalent of leaping off a high building.

"This is what I'm talking about. Now you're paid publicity for Jerry, do you see that? It looks very bad, not to mention that any liability on the part of the company is out of the question."

"You mean sue Jerry?"

"That's right."

"I wouldn't want to sue Jerry. I like Jerry."

"Listen, Spencer, this is not a matter of like and not like. This is business. This is called, Can we get some remuneration for your injuries? I would have said that, having failed to provide adequately for your protection against the union, the company might be vulnerable. But that's a moot point now."

The roach did not jump. Instead, it rounded the corner of the cabinet and began making its way up the outside, going vertically toward our white-paneled ceiling, like a navy test pilot. "I bought a TV," I told Kravitch. "I still have about half the money. I could give it back. And I've located Randy Song, the other witness."

"It doesn't matter," he said. "You don't have anything going for you here, as far as I can tell. You didn't get me statements, and now you've allowed your image to be used as part of an anti-union publicity campaign. You'll be lucky if this doesn't end up *costing* you money. Look, I'm going to have to drop the case."

"That's it?" I asked. "Just like that?"

"I'm afraid so. There's no point in pursuing it—for either of us. I wish you luck, my friend."

I put down the phone, amazed. My potential fortune had disappeared in the space of a phone call. The roach, now two-thirds of the way to the ceiling, stopped suddenly, as if listening. I hit the side of the cabinet with my fist and he came tumbling down to the floor. Apparently, the foot-glue he had that allowed him to walk on walls wasn't that strong.

"My lawsuit is being dropped," I told Spider, settling in next to him on the sofa.

"You didn't want to go through with that anyway."

"Oh, I don't know. I was kind of looking forward to the money."

He laced his fingers behind his neck. "I got lawsuit money when I was your age and it spoiled me. Made me take the world for granted. Now someone else lives in my house." It was the first time I could remember him expressing any kind of regrets about what he'd had, what he'd lost.

"What exactly happened? You never told me."

"Some guy pulled out in front of me, that's all. I was going way too fast, of course, but he couldn't prove it. I had a broken collar bone, busted ribs, concussion, a whole bunch of stuff. You weren't much bigger than a wastebasket at the time."

"I do remember, though," I said. "At least I think I do."

"You couldn't possibly." He rubbed at one eye. "Anyway, sometimes I wish it had never happened."

"Is that why you wouldn't sign my statement? Did you think you were protecting me?"

"Not at all. I told you, I didn't actually *see* anything." He held up his hands in a gesture that said the whole business was beyond his control. "Hey, you want to play some cards?"

I took a breath, told myself not to get mad. What difference did it make now, anyway? "Cards?"

"Poker. Know anybody else around here? Maybe we could get a game together."

I could think of no one, but I didn't want to tell him that.

"There's this guy that lives next door," I said. "Arnold Blickman."

"Invite the man over."

I rang Arnold's bell, then stood staring at the flaking varnish on the huge old doors of his brownstone, the thick, beveled glass that must have been a hundred years old. After about a minute, he came down, examined me through the door, adjusted his glasses, and opened it. He was wearing a checkered bathrobe, but as far as I could see, underneath he was dressed.

"I'm glad it's you," he said. "The other day, when I told you I wrote those songs, I think I was experiencing one of my delusions. I get episodes. Especially if I don't sleep enough, or I malnourish myself. You want to come up?"

Arnold's apartment was a sterile place, with a table and two chairs, a single bed, neatly made, a stack of library books he'd been reading. They seemed chosen at random. I looked at the one that lay open, a history of the Cultural Revolution in China. Underneath was a book on paper airplanes, and under that a biography of Woodrow Wilson.

"Arnold," I said. "We were thinking about playing a little cards. Would you like to come play some cards?"

"For money?"

I hadn't thought about this. "Not necessarily," I said. "Maybe just pennies."

"Okay." He went to his bureau drawer and withdrew a sock that was filled with pennies. "I really am sorry about the other day. I'm not very stable. I get all worked up."

I wondered if I was going to regret getting to know Arnold Blickman. But it was too late now. I'd been challenged to come up with a friend, and I'd produced one. Arnold followed me back downstairs to the front door. "I should be all right," he said. "I had a can of soup about a half hour ago."

We played seven-card stud, with a little five-card draw mixed in. Spider wore his magnifiers down toward the end of his nose, adjusting them every now and then with his forefinger. Arnold was a terrible poker player. He had no sense of how to bet and you could bluff him forever. He just kept tossing pennies into the pot until someone called, and whenever it was his turn to deal, about half the deck would end up being wild. He'd bet on anything: a pair was as good as a full house to Arnold. The sock full of pennies grew rapidly thinner. I could tell my dad was pleased I'd brought over such a patsy.

In bits and fragments, Arnold's story came out. He'd dropped out of engineering school in the mid-seventies and had lived ever since off of the checks his parents sent him. He was thirty-seven, though he didn't look it. He ate no meat. His hobbies, he said, were reading library books and adding to his collection of vintage LSD.

"Vintage?" Spider asked. "How do you mean?"

"You know—dated. Mostly concert-related. I have everything marked with the place and year. I've got Windowpane I picked up at a Stones concert in 'seventy-two. I've got some White Lightning tabs from 'seventy-six when I went to see Mahavishnu. Let's see, Purple Microdot from the Allman Brothers at the Trenton State Fairgrounds in 'seventy-three. I just traded some pink UFO stuff with a guy out in Oregon who had blotter from Woodstock. Poor quality, but very rare."

"You do this through the mail?" I said.

"Federal Express."

"I used to trade baseball cards," said Spider.

"How can you possibly know that's where it came from?" It didn't seem unlikely to me that Arnold was experiencing another of his delusions.

Arnold shrugged. "What would be the point of lying? You've got to have a little faith. Faith and refrigeration. The stuff doesn't last forever." He scratched at the side of his head, then searched his pocket for a cigarette.

"I'll take one of those," said Spider. "If you can spare it."

Arnold held out a Camel. "In England, you're supposed to offer your cigarettes to everyone in the room. Did you know that?"

"Really?"

"I was there once."

"Is that right?" said Spider. "You see the Queen?"

"No, but I did see George Harrison. Outside a tube station. That's a subway over there. He was just standing, smoking a cigarette."

"Did he offer you one?" I asked.

"He would have," said Arthur. "If we'd been sitting around someplace, like a pub or something."

We played until one A.M. "Flaky," I said after Arnold had gone home. "The other day he told me he wrote some of Bob Dylan's songs."

Spider was stacking pennies on the coffee table. There must have been five hundred of them, all won from Arnold Blickman. "Don't apologize for him," he said. "Arnold's all right."

He'd never criticized any of my friends, but that was because, as far as I could tell, he'd never really paid any attention to who they were. I myself had been unwelcome in a number of other kids' homes. There were parents in our town who looked on me as someone whose family instability was potentially infectious, like chicken pox.

"Arnold is *not* all right," I said. "That's obvious. Anyone with a refrigerator full of old LSD has got something wrong with him."

"We've all got something wrong with us," he said, placing a tenth penny carefully onto one of the stacks to complete another pile. "It's just a matter of degree."

I finally called Judith. "I thought we could go out for dinner or something," I said. I felt awkward and at a disadvantage. "I told you I'd call," I added. "Remember?"

"Dinner?"

"Right." I tried to think of something clever to say. "That meal between lunch and 'The Tonight Show'?"

"What about your girlfriend?"

"Gone. For some time now, actually."

There was a long silence, during which I pulled about a foot of stray thread out of the sleeve of my shirt, before she said, "I think probably not."

"How about lunch instead? Less formal. We could have a picnic."

"Spencer," she said. "Forget it."

"Look, I'm sorry about the other night. How's Toby?"

"He's fine."

"Are you involved with someone? Do you have a boyfriend?"

"Well, thanks for asking. As a matter of fact, I have a couple."

I pictured young professional types with neat haircuts, shiny shoes. But the fact remained that, fairly recently, she'd invited me into her bed. That had to be worth something. I thought about what Sally had said, how there were some people you were just connected with, like it or not.

"I have to go. I'm being picked up. Please, do stay in touch."

I put down the receiver and stared at the dingy wallpaper on which, in Rick's handwriting, a couple of telephone numbers floated, their digits angling upward toward the ceiling. Then I looked up her address in the phone book, called a flower delivery place, and ordered a bouquet sent to her. Anything in particular? they wanted to know. Purple, I told them, remembering the general color scheme of her bedroom. Judith was partial to purple.

The holiday season was upon us, with its bell-ringers and fat magazines. I did my best to block it out. The temperature dropped into the twenties, and I marveled at the way New Yorkers refused to give in to the weather when it came to their clothes. For every person in a heavy coat, there seemed to be two bare-headed and bare-handed, with only their business suits to protect them against the winds whipping up the avenues. I bought myself a nice pair of leather gloves and promptly left them on the subway.

Two more bands refused to audition Spider on the basis of his age. "It's a fucking conspiracy," he said. "I'm not *that* old."

"Why don't you just lie?" I asked.

"That would be giving up. I wouldn't even think about it."

He had begun sitting in with the house band at a place called Chicago Joe's Monday and Thursday nights, a blues bar that got a big after-work crowd. The band didn't even have a name, and the players often rotated, the one constant being the guitar player, Lonnie Black. He was friendly, and the other musicians he brought in were generally solid players. Monday night was officially a jam night, and people who put their name on a list were invited up to play with the band. The bar was popular with Japanese businessmen who liked to get up one after another and sing "Stormy Monday." It drove me crazy, but Spider showed an amazing amount of patience.

"The way I see it, you can either be a snob, or you can give the people what they want," he said. "I believe in spreading happiness. Besides, they're big tippers."

Having a place to play seemed to brighten him considerably. He took to wearing sunglasses, not just when he was outside, but all the time. This didn't do much for his vision, and I noticed he walked a little more slowly, as if moving in a parallel, slightly less hurried universe from the rest of us. If Spiderman Dan had only been an idea of his when he was living in Maine, now it became a reality.

One evening when he was out playing, I wandered into his room and saw that he kept a small photo on the table by his mattress. I guessed it was the one Sally had seen. Cully in the picture seemed younger than the woman I'd met, less tired. She stared straight at the camera, not smiling exactly, but with a hint of amusement in her eyes, as if the person taking the picture were doing something unusual. It had been taken with a flash, and the faces were overlit, the background almost invisible. Nestled in Cully's arms, Allegra looked like a wizened old man, her face wrinkled and pink, her head hairless and all forehead— she couldn't have been much more than a few weeks old. I tried to think about them being my family. I imagined holding Allegra against my chest, feeling her hot baby-breath on my neck. I could see where it might be a little frightening.

I continued to scour every inch of Mutronics for things to fill orders with. In Cat's office there were a couple of units in the closet, a bit scratched, but they worked. I found other units in repair that had lost their paperwork and were simply collecting dust. By candlelight—we still didn't have electricity in the back—I carefully screwed their covers on and put them into boxes. There was a whole room of postal returns that I hunted through, products we'd shipped out a number of times, but that kept coming back undeliverable. No one had ever bothered to open these, so I kicked the mouse droppings off the cartons and razored through their packing tape.

Jerry had rehired Randy ("I was just waiting to hear from you," he'd said), and she was back in her old room, the company guitar across her knees, plugged into her beloved effects. With production at a virtual standstill, she kept retesting the same ones over and over, but she seemed relatively happy. If Spider minded, he was very good about not showing it, instead devoting himself even more fully to sorting through the never-ending piles of mail.

I gave Randy the units I'd found and she stacked them neatly next to her cigarettes and can of Sprite. She waved a hand toward the dim, vast emptiness of the technicians' area outside her window. "It's like a tomb. Where are all the people? I don't see how we can come back from this."

"Do you care?"

"Funny thing is, when I was unemployed and collecting, all I could think about was getting this job back. Now I'm here, I don't know. The place is different."

"It's a different place," I reminded her. "This is Gryphon Research now."

"Just what exactly is it we're supposed to be researching?"

"New and better ways of extracting money from the general public, I think."

She laughed. "You know what's sad? I used to believe that there was something special about what we did. Rock 'n' roll, rebellion, youth, all of that. I'm not stupid, I figured out pretty quick that this was just a factory, same as any other factory. That's why I have my posters up, to remind me. But after a while, when you look at it and you see it's all *just* about money, I don't know. Kind of makes you wonder what's the point. I never bothered to consider what would happen when I got to be this age. I don't think I really believed I'd *make* it to this age." She tucked her T-shirt back into the front of her jeans. She had on some dangly, African-looking jewelry.

"Are you really Korean?" I asked.

"I married one. He runs a fruit and vegetable place out in Queens. We didn't get along at all—I just couldn't keep up."

"Did you love him?"

"Who knows? I thought I did, but then I thought a lot of things back then, and over the years most of them have been proven wrong. How's your head? Looks like your hair's coming back in pretty good."

"I'm all right. Still a little weak, still taking my drugs." I wanted to ask her more about her husband, about why they were no longer together, but I couldn't tell if she wanted to talk or not.

"You know, I give a nice haircut. You could use one. Why don't I bring in my stuff tomorrow? I'll give you a special price. Five dollars, cut and style."

In fact, my hair had been bothering me. It had grown in exactly the same length all over.

"All right," I said. "But you have to promise to make me look good. I have a date Friday night."

"A date?" She ran a pocket comb through her own short, slicked-back hair. "You don't strike me like the date type."

"Me, either," I said. "But then, the girl in question doesn't know we're going out."

"Funny night for a date," said Randy.

"Why?"

"Well, most folks stay home Christmas Eve."

I left work early. When I got back, I took a load of laundry over to the Wash 'n Die (Sally's name for it, since the red plastic *r* in the word "Dry" had long ago disappeared from the sign over the door). A woman sat on the steps outside smoking a cigarette, talking to her dog, a pug. It was the strangest creature: a tough-looking little body, round, softball-sized head, big, bulging eyes. They looked like brown marbles.

"Okay, Vanessa," she said. "What do you want to do next?"

I pushed past her and stuffed my things into a couple of washers. From behind me, I listened as she continued quizzing the dog. There was something familiar about the woman, but I couldn't quite place it. She had a plain, round face and medium-length black hair. She wore a yellow T-shirt that said FASHION IS! on the front.

"Anything you want, Vanessa," she said. "Only, you have to tell me."

If Vanessa knew what she wanted, she wasn't letting on. The woman flicked her cigarette out into the street and came back into the laundromat to check her dryer. Then I realized who she was.

She saw me staring and smiled. "It's her birthday," she said. "One year old."

"Happy birthday," I said. I wondered if she still danced naked in her room. I was nervous, afraid she'd remember me as the eyes from across the street.

"Vanessa almost got run over last week," she said. "Ran right out into the road, into the path of a car. Do you know what? She's so small, the car passed right over her. I've been replaying it over and over in my mind ever since, and I'm convinced it was an act of God. If the driver had veered, that would have been it—the wheels would have got her."

"Lucky," I said.

"You're telling me." She rummaged in her purse for another cigarette, but came up with only an empty pack. "Lucky Vanessa. I'm going to take her out for ice cream, I think. She's a big fan of ice cream."

Vanessa had come into the laundromat and was inspecting the tops of my sneakers.

"Go ahead and give her a ride, if you want," said the woman. "She likes it. Just lift your foot very slowly, she'll hold on."

I took my foot off the floor carefully, elevating the toes first, then the heel. Vanessa wrapped herself around me. She weighed very little. I lowered her back to the tile floor and she hopped off.

"We're going to have to go get more smokes," said my neighbor. "Come on, darling." She left the laundromat, Vanessa trotting at her heels.

When she was gone, I stared for a while at her clothes, which were still spinning in the dryer. Every now and then some specific item would surface and become recognizable for a moment, a red brassiere, a pair of jeans, a washcloth, before jumbling up again with the rest. She was a remarkably ordinary person, this woman I'd watched from my window—plain, a little overweight, devoted to her dog. Yet I knew that occasionally, in the privacy of her room, she liked to take off her clothes and pose in front of the mirror, imagining herself as someone entirely different.

20

I 've decided something," Spider said to me, Thursday morning, coming out of the shower, a white bath towel of Rick's wrapped around his waist. "I'm going to Italy."

"Good for you."

"This is serious. I met a guy at the club who says he can line me up some gigs. Germany and Switzerland, too. I've never been abroad, and I figure it's about time. If I don't do it now, when will I ever?"

I sipped coffee out of an asymmetrical brown mug Sally had made in a ceramics class. "Look, what do you think is going to happen?"

"I'll talk to her, you know, explain things. At least see if I can. It's worth a shot, I figure." He sounded more or less indifferent, but I knew it was a pose. "Besides, it's what you think I should do, even if you won't admit it."

I ignored this. "What if she doesn't want you back?"

"I've been meaning to ask you about that. Did Cully say anything about me when you talked to her? I mean, did you get a sense of how she felt?"

"I think bitter might sum it up. Her brother would probably like to shoot you."

He tightened the towel, which had begun to slip. "Brian's a hothead, and he's always out of work."

"How soon will you go?"

"I don't know. I'll have to save for a while to get together air-fare and expense money."

"I just ask because I need to know whether to start looking for a roommate." Rick had sent me a rent check for January in an envelope from a motel in Las Vegas, New Mexico. It was beginning to seem like I'd inherited responsibility for the whole apartment.

"Soon," he said.

"You doing Chicago Joe's tonight?"

"That's right. Why don't you come down and sit in?"

I thought about it. I couldn't put this off forever. "All right."

Since there was nothing on Joe's menu for under ten dollars, we walked with our guitars over to a McDonald's after work and ate cheap, then made our way to the club.

Lonnie Black was surprised to see me with an instrument. He was very fat, with long, stringy hair he never brushed. "You gonna play?" he asked.

"If it's okay with you."

"Hell, yes, it's okay. Just say when."

"Earlier rather than later."

"With or without the Bruise Blothers?" He gestured toward a table of Japanese men, all of them in suits, all of them smoking.

"No difference."

"They want to do Elvis tunes." He snuffled a little. I had a feeling Lonnie did his share of cocaine before and after sets, possibly even during. "Doesn't matter what, just so long as it's Elvis."

"He wants to play with me," said Spider. "That's the idea here."

With the sound system jingling Christmas music at us, we sat and had a couple of whiskeys. Three extremely striking women came and sat two tables away from us.

"Models," said Spider. "They like to come in here. I guess four-dollar drinks and no tablecloths is their idea of slumming."

"What do you say to someone who looks like that?" I asked. There was one in particular I couldn't take my eyes off—a brunette, with sharply defined features and bright red lipstick. She wore a black stretch top off the shoulder, revealing a perfect, tanned expanse of skin below her neck. She cast her eyes around the room, surveying it, well aware that she was being noticed, and not just by me.

"Are you kidding? Anything she wants to hear." He got up and pushed in his chair. "Back in a second." With amazement, I watched as he made his way over to their table and began talking to them. He was gone about a minute, then returned and indicated that I should take my drink with me. "We're going to join them."

"How'd you manage that?" Looking past him, I could see that the three were talking animatedly about something.

"Just said the right thing. Come on. Oh, by the way, you direct videos."

Their names were Ursula, Britny, and Harley. Harley was the dark-haired one. Ursula was blond and pretty in a distant, orderly way; I could imagine her ice-skating someplace in a thick sweater with reindeer across the front. Britny had more of a small-town-in-the-Midwest type of beauty, the kind of girl who'd starred in all her high school plays, a bit simple, maybe, but with a great personality. She wore an embroidered shirt and gold half-moon earrings, and I got the sense that the other two only just tolerated her presence. Harley, with her commanding, dark looks, her restless eyes, was clearly in charge. She looked like she'd be at home at a film festival in the South of France, peering out at the world from behind dark glasses. All of them seemed, up close, strangely oversized. A slightly different roll of the genetic dice, smaller eyes or a bigger nose, and they would have spent their lives having people feel sorry for them instead of admiring them.

Spider introduced them all to me and we sat down. I had to hand it to him, I wouldn't have had the nerve. Britny was drinking iced tea, Harley a cup of coffee. Ursula had what appeared to be a glass of milk in front of her.

"I was telling these girls about our project," he said.

I remembered how Sally used to jump on me if I used the word "girl" to mean anyone the far side of twelve. These women, however, didn't seem to mind. It was their business to be girls.

"Ursula and I have both been in videos," said Britny.

"What's the band?" Ursula asked, leaning forward slightly. Her accent was thickly southern and not at all what I'd expected.

"The Purolators," said Spider without missing a beat. "A new group out of Texas. *Cojunto* music."

"Gesundheit," said Harley. When no one laughed she rolled her eyes. "All right, I'll bite. What's *cojunto* music?"

"Tex-Mex stuff. Button accordions. Sort of Mexican polka music."

Britny tossed her hair and looked at me skeptically. "Isn't Purolator, like, an oil filter or something?"

"That's right," I said.

"Are you still casting?" I could see she was interested.

"Absolutely."

"Do you know," said Harley, "that just about every third person I meet in this city is a photographer? Either that or a video director." She sipped at her coffee. "It's an amazing thing."

"You think we're lying?" said Spider.

"I know you are, Ace. It's okay, people lie to us all the time. But really, you ought to try and come up with something a little more original." She turned away from him and looked directly at me for the first time. Her eyes were the color of a sky just after a summer storm, flat, violet-gray. "No way you're a director."

"Oh?" I said. "Why not?"

"Because, you're too young, for one thing. And you don't have the look. Too earnest. I'd say you work in an office."

"Harley," said Ursula, "you're insulting these people."

"No, honey, these people were insulting us. You just didn't realize."

Harley took my hand in hers, surprising me. "You're pretty cute," she said. "In addition to being earnest, I mean." She let go and returned to her coffee.

Spider poked my arm. The drummer had taken his seat and the bass player was tuning. "Let's start with them," he said. "Come on."

"You're in the band, too?" asked Britny.

Harley nodded. "You do look more like a musician. Know any Christmas tunes? 'Santa Got Run Over by a Reindeer'?"

" 'Grandma,' " I said.

"Excuse me?"

"It's Grandma who got run over. In the song, I mean."

"I guess there's no chance of getting you girls' phone numbers," said Spider.

"Well, probably not," Harley said. "But thanks for asking. Hey, just between us, there is no Chicago Joe, is there?"

"How the hell should I know?" he said.

We left them, got out our guitars, and went up on stage. "I guess they get hit on a lot," Spider said. He handed me a tuner. "Here, use this. If there's one thing I can't stand, it's playing with someone who isn't in good tune."

We opened with a fast shuffle in A. I'd been afraid that somehow my mind would go blank when it was time for me to solo, but that didn't happen—I played as well as I ever had, which is to say, passably. I knew most of the standard licks, could string them together convincingly enough. I didn't try to go too fast, or to invent something new—I just stayed safe. Every now and then I'd allow myself to look at Harley, but whenever I did, I found her either talking to Ursula or staring off into space.

Next, he called a slow blues in F minor. I wondered if this was meant as a challenge. I was not in love with the key, since the only two positions I knew to use meant playing either very high on the neck or very low, and neither was particularly comfortable. I found a groove with the drums and bass, played a simple, Steve Cropper–style rhythm. As he worked over this, I watched his eyes close and his lips tighten. He was someplace else entirely.

"*Not bad,*" he told me at the break. The table of businessmen had just finished a serial killing of "Love Me Tender" and "Heartbreak Hotel." After my two songs, I'd stepped down and Lonnie Black had gone up. I'd had two drinks since. "How come you never told me you could play like that?"

"Come on," I said. "Don't shit me. I didn't make any horrible mistakes and I stayed in tune."

He shook his head. "I see something in your playing, I really do. There's a nice bite. Good overall feel, too. You're not a show-off like so many young guys. You play the *song.*"

"I'm not a show-off because I *can't* show off."

"Doesn't matter." He waved at the waitress to come over and take his order. To my disappointment, the table of models had left a few minutes earlier. "Think about Clapton. A great player who doesn't hot-dog. That's why they call him Slowhand."

"It isn't," I said. "It's supposed to be ironic. He was called Slowhand because he was so *fast.* For the sixties, he was. He just seems slow now because everyone else got *really* fast."

He looked at me with distrust. "Are you sure?"

"Pretty sure. But thanks, anyway. I just wish you wouldn't overdo it. I don't need to be praised to the roof. It makes me think you don't mean it at all."

The waitress made her way over with two whiskeys, which she put down on our table.

"Did you order these?" Spider asked.

"Nope," said the waitress. "Those three women bought them for you."

"Really?"

"Really." She tapped the edge of my glass with her forefinger. "Lucky guy."

"Not that lucky," I said. "I mean, they're gone, aren't they?"

"I suppose they are." She looked back and forth between the two of us. "Are you guys related, or what?"

"It's true," I said. "He's my dad. Don't tell anyone."

She was short, with reddish hair and a tough, don't-mess-with-me expression she wore like battle armor, but it dissolved at this news. "That is so *cute*," she said.

Christmas Eve, wearing a new haircut courtesy of Randy, who'd trimmed the sides tight around my ears while leaving some length in back, I boarded a train headed for the Village. In my hand I held a bag with two deep red roses I'd picked out. The car I got into had its heat cranked way too high. The effect was like a sauna and didn't help my flowers any. On the window next to me, someone had written a message with their finger, "Why are you so ugly?" I couldn't decide if the person meant this for other passengers who sat here and saw it, or if they'd been observing their own reflection.

Judith's apartment was in a relatively clean building with wooden pillars out front. I found her bell and rang, but there was no answer. Stepping back out to the sidewalk, I looked up at the different windows and tried to decide which might be hers. One had its shade drawn, but behind it was the distinct outline of a cactus, which didn't seem her style. In another, some books were visible, lining the sill, and I guessed that was the one. No-nonsense student quarters. She'd have a small stereo, a few classical records, some jazz. Scented candles in the bathroom. Art prints on the walls. I stared at the window for a long time, then decided I'd walk around for a while and come back.

I sat through the second half of a movie that was showing nearby, chewed my way through an entire box of Milk Duds. I was one of about ten people in the theater, and none of us were enjoying ourselves much. I stopped back and rang her bell again, but she was still out. It was nearly ten now, and I began to feel a little foolish. She was somewhere having a great time, probably with one of her two boyfriends, and here I was, pacing her neighborhood with a couple of flowers in a bag.

At a pizza place a few blocks away, I peered in and saw that the roses had begun to wilt. Too long without water, they had at best another few hours. A gnarled-looking old man with yellow skin and pants held up by packing twine stared in at me from the sidewalk, eyeing my slice. When I ignored him he stepped closer. I was about to take another bite when he put his tongue right up against the window and licked. My appetite, which thanks to the Milk Duds hadn't been great to begin with, fled. I waited for him to shuffle on, then left.

I bought a beer from a deli and drank it out of the paper bag while sitting on a bench in the park. A breeze brought the odor of marijuana from a group of huddled teens a few benches up the path. I heard people caroling. A man walking a small dog in a green knit sweater paused to let the animal sniff at my shoes, then yanked him along.

On my next and final pass by Judith's, I ran right into her. She had on a navy trenchcoat with padded shoulders, and her hair was done up. There was a man with her, nice-looking, with short wavy hair, dark, almost theatrical eyebrows.

"Spencer?" she said, squinting as if I were a fine-print text. "Is that you?"

"Hi, Judith."

She was trying to figure out if this was accidental or not, but I had the sense that she knew. Her companion stood silently at her side, smiling politely. He was about our age, maybe a year or two older. His clothes were conservative, but hip at the same time: dark shirt, wool overcoat unbuttoned and with the collar flipped up, slightly baggy pants. His face had the definition of an athlete's—he looked like he could drop and give you a hundred pushups on the spot.

"What brings you around here?" she asked.

"I was out at the movies." I fingered the bag with my two rapidly dehydrating flowers in it.

"On Christmas Eve?"

"Sure. No lines."

"What movie?"

"Oh, some dumb thing." I couldn't remember the name. "A cop-buddy movie."

"I hate those," said the guy. "They're all formula."

"This is my friend, Leon," Judith said. "Spencer and I went to school together."

"Really?" He offered me his hand. He had very straight, very white teeth. "In New Haven?"

I hoped there was a special place in hell for people who said "New Haven" when they meant "Yale." "Grade school," I said. "We used to chase each other around at recess." Get out of here, I thought. You've made enough of a fool of yourself as it is.

"Well," said Judith.

"Well," I said. There was nothing for it. I'd gotten exactly what I'd asked for. "I guess I'll see you."

"Nice to have met you," said Leon.

On their way up the stairs, she leaned over and said something to him and they both laughed. I strolled back to the subway stop as all around me, it seemed, young couples materialized out of thin air. It was as if a hundred theaters had let out all at once: everyone was beautiful, everyone had someplace to go. I thought I understood what it was that got into serial killers.

By the subway entrance, I saw the bum who'd licked the pizza parlor window. As I passed, he held out a grimy hand. I gave him my bag.

"God bless you, merry gentleman," he said in a voice that sounded like it was coming over a six-dollar telephone.

I didn't answer, I just hustled down the stairs. He probably thought I'd given him a sandwich or something. I remembered what his tongue had looked like, spread out against the glass—pink and wide and strangely healthy. It had surprised me, the way some dull-rinded fruits can surprise you when you cut into them and their insides glisten with color.

"Arnold's dead," said Spider. He was leaning back against the wall on one of my two dining table chairs. Our new television flickered across from him, tuned in to *It's a Wonderful Life*, the sound all the way off.

"I am not dead," said Arnold's voice from the sofa where he lay flat on his back, eyes bugged open, staring up at the ceiling.

They'd been playing more poker. I could see that from the empty beer bottles on the table, the little stacks of pennies on my dad's side. Next to Arnold on the sofa was a small black briefcase. I tipped up the lid and saw that inside it had been divided up like a jeweler's display case, and nestled into each neat, velvet-lined compartment, was a small glassine envelope.

"Feel anything yet, Arnold?" asked Spider.

"I don't believe this," I said.

He checked his watch. "It's over an hour now. You ought to feel something."

Arnold held his hand in the air and examined the back of it. "Heightened perception. Colors a little more vivid than ordinarily. Actually, I think it's safe to say I do feel something."

One of the glassine envelopes was out on the table. I picked it up. It was marked RETURN TO FOREVER, 1973. There were four white pills inside.

"Chick Corea's first electric band," said Spider.

"I know that," I said. "You haven't actually taken any of this."

"Not yet. Arnold is testing it out."

"Giddiness," said Arnold. "Lots of nervous energy."

Spider sniffed. "Probably cut with speed. That's often the problem with tab acid."

I went to the refrigerator and got myself a beer. A lone piece of pizza sat on a plate, uncovered, its cheese jelled and retracted into an orange moonscape.

When I came back in, Spider had one of the tablets in the palm of his hand.

"You're not really going to take that?"

"I really am. You want some? Arnold, what do you say? Can Spencer have some?"

"Of course," said Arnold.

"I don't want any. I'm in a bad enough mood as it is. I'd probably start seeing things."

"Hallucinations are pretty rare."

"Maybe for you," said Arnold.

"Well, here goes nothing." Placing it on his tongue, he made a face, then swallowed. He gestured toward my beer and I gave it to him. He poured a good measure of it down before returning it.

"What now?" I asked.

But they weren't paying attention to me. Spider nudged Arnold with his foot. "Money?"

Arthur sat up, cocked an eye at me, then stood. He was still wearing his checkered cap, and it occurred to me that I'd never seen him without it. I wondered what it was he thought he was hiding. He left us, went tromping down the stairs and out the front door.

"I won thirteen hundred dollars off Arnold," said Spider, stretching.

"And you really plan to collect it?"

"Why not? It's mine. And it's enough to get me started."

"You're crazy. Even if you go over there, she's not going to want to see you."

"Oh, I don't know. I'm sure she's mad. She's probably written me off entirely by now. But women are funny about things. They're not constant. One day you're dirt under their shoe, but then you send some flowers, show a little sensitivity, and everything's okay again."

"Maybe, but I wouldn't count on it."

"I think I can make this Spiderman thing go in Italy," he went on. "I really do."

I was short on patience, and having trouble digesting the fact that he'd just taken a tab of acid right in front of me. "You don't speak Italian. No one will understand you."

"What difference does that make? Music is international. Besides, you can always get by with English, if you speak it slowly and loud enough."

I picked up the glassine envelope with the remaining hits of "Return to Forever." A faint dusting of white coated the inside of the plastic. "When do you plan to leave?"

"As soon as I can get a ticket. This time of year, there's lots of deals."

"On Arnold's cash?"

He shook his head. "On mine. I won it from him, fair and square."

"If you can call it fair to play poker with someone who thinks his phone has been bugged by Joni Mitchell."

When Arnold returned, he said he wanted to go to midnight mass at one of the cathedrals, and Spider said he'd go along. I wasn't sure I should let them. They'd begun to laugh a lot and to turn a little red in the face.

"I'm serious," said Arnold. "I want to pray." He'd brought over thirteen hundred dollars in a small brown paper sack. Apparently Arnold kept a lot of cash around his apartment. I couldn't stand the idea that Spider was going to take this money from him.

"Isn't Blickman a Jewish name?" I asked.

"So what? I can still pray if I want."

"But this is *Christmas*."

He focused on me through the round lenses of his glasses. His face was earnest and a little pointy, like a terrier's.

"I pray," he said, "wherever and whenever I feel like it. You should come along, it might do you some good. Your soul is just like any other muscle, you know. You have to exercise it or it just wastes away to nothing."

"I think you two are having enough fun on your own. You don't need me. Besides, I just came back from the city."

He shrugged and stood up. "Suit yourself."

"Jimi," said my dad. "I hate to see you alone on Christmas Eve."

"I'll manage," I told him. "Go on out and pray. Have a nice time. Send up a few for me."

"There's eggnog in the refrigerator," he said. They left the bag of money sitting on the coffee table.

I watched television for a while, then shut it off and sat in the dark. Outside the wind had picked up and the panes of glass in the windows rattled in their crumbling moldings. The year was nearly through, and it almost felt as if I could hear it coming to a close, shifting heavily on its hinge, creaking with age and boredom at the sheer inevitability of it all.

I was still sitting there when the phone rang. It was Judith and she sounded angry.

"I want to know what you think you're doing," she said.

"How so?"

"Calling me up and asking me out. Sending me flowers. Hanging around outside my apartment."

"I just thought you might like to get together."

"You handle things in a very peculiar way, Spencer. That was embarrassing tonight. How would you like it if I did that to you? Just intruded on you like that?"

"I'm sorry, I guess I wasn't thinking."

Neither of us said anything for a few seconds. I could feel cold air pushing its way through the cracks in the walls. Every now and then the whole house shuddered in the wind.

"I shouldn't have been so short with you. But I just have to point out that even without your father around, you've grown up to be exactly like him, insincere, egotistic, thoughtless."

"Give me another chance," I said. "I'm really not like that."

"But you are, Spencer, you are exactly like that." She was

quiet for a moment. "Well, I'm glad I got that out. I feel a little better. Come over tomorrow afternoon. I'm having a few friends here for drinks."

"Are you sure?"

"Of course I'm sure. I wouldn't have invited you if I wasn't sure."

"Then I'll be there."

"I look forward to seeing you."

"That sounds so formal."

"I mean it that way. We're starting over, two old friends who haven't seen each other in a long time. I'm not promising anything else. In fact, I'm pretty much guaranteeing that's where it will stay."

I woke up in the morning to the smell of bacon frying. I pulled on some clothes, washed my face, and went upstairs. Spider was surrounded by breakfast makings. The coffee pot was full and there were eggs out and ready to go and toast already toasting. "I heard you coming," he said. "How would you like 'em? Over easy?"

"Where's Arnold?" I peered into the other room, half expecting to find him asleep on the sofa. Propped up against the wall was a small Christmas tree, its needles already more than halfway to brown.

"Took him home. He was tired and not making a whole lot of sense. How do you like my tree?"

"It could use some decoration."

"Picked it up last night, cheap. You'd be surprised how much you can save if you buy your tree on Christmas Eve."

"Aren't you tired?" There were obvious circles under his eyes.

He looked at me and wiped his hands dry on a towel. "Exhausted. But I still feel pretty good."

I noticed that the money was gone.

"I gave it back," he said. "You were right, it wasn't fair. But

I'm still going. Even if things don't work out with Cully, it will be worth it. At least I'll have given it a shot."

"That's the important thing." I was amazed that something I'd said to him had actually had an effect.

"You bet it is." He poured a cup of coffee and handed it to me. "Who wants to be boxed in to some ridiculous job just so they can take their credit cards to the mall on weekends? That's not a life, that's just sitting around waiting to get old. You have to take a chance or two. I tell you, Spencer, I envy you."

I couldn't see why. "You're the one with the talent."

"You're a kid. Nature's still driving you all by itself. You make your own talent. When you get to be my age, if you still want that kind of energy, you have to dig a whole lot deeper, if you can come up with it at all. Stuff gives out on you. One day your knees start to make noise, you notice your hair's a little thinner, you have to hold the paper three feet away to read it. When you go out, the women you try to talk to keep turning their heads instead of looking straight at you because they're wondering what else they're missing, and who's noticing that they're spending time with this old guy."

"You mean those models?"

"The hell with them. Walking coatracks."

We sat down to breakfast and I found I was hungrier than I'd thought. Neither of us said much, we just ate. Sunlight streamed in through the dirty windows, falling in bright patterns on the dark wood table. It was Rick's, along with much of our furniture. It occurred to me that at the age of twenty-two, I could probably fit all my possessions into the back of a station wagon.

"You want to do something today?" he asked, finally. "We could head into the city, catch a movie."

"I can't. I'm going over to someone's house for drinks."

"Someone?"

"A girl. From back home, actually."

"Not old Lucy Westbrook?"

I shook my head.

"Karen Jelliker?"

"No."

"Theresa what's-her-name? With the amazing hair?"

I couldn't believe he was coming up with these names. I'd never been convinced he knew the names of *any* of my friends.

"Judith Horner," I said.

He squinted, thinking. "Nope, don't remember her. She pretty?"

"I don't know. I guess you'd say she was pretty."

"The thing to do," he said, "is marry an ugly girl. You know that song?" He began to hum. I didn't stick around to hear it, but took my dishes in to the sink, then went back downstairs to shower. I wanted to look as good as I could for the party.

21

_____

D ear Mr. Markus,
I understand. I have been a fool, of course. You would think someone who stole MONEY would recognize another thief when he saw one, but not me, which is my OWN fault. Still, I am more disappointed than you can KNOW, because I gave you my FAITH and my money and YOU took off with both. I just hope you think about me sometimes and all the other dumb suckers out here you write to. WE think of you.

Sincerely,
Furry Couch #C-563-2798

Dear Mutronics,

Hey, heard about the strike. Just wanted to say keep up the good work and hang in there. I've used your products for years and I'm behind you one hundred percent. Sorry to hear about the guy that got beat up, too. America needs more businesses like yours. Have you spoken to "60 Minutes"? I think your story could easily be on television.

Brian Greenspan,
Raleigh, North Carolina

22

I t had already been going on for about a half-hour when I arrived. Leon was there, the guy I'd met outside her apartment,
though from the way he hovered around her, constantly offering to do things, laughing a little too hard at her jokes, I had to
figure that whatever relationship they had wasn't set in stone.
I talked for a while to another law student named Bob who had
red hair, a beard, and was doing his best to finish a bottle of
Crown Royal by himself. "I love this stuff," he kept saying,
holding the glass up and examining it against the winter light
slanting in through Judith's spotless windows.

Judith wore a red dress with a green pin in the shape of a sprig
of holly, and I couldn't get over how she could manage to look
sexy and proper at the same time. When I came in, she greeted
me briefly, then set me loose to mingle. From time to time she'd
catch me staring at her and smile back, but in general I was just
what she'd promised me I'd be: one of the guests, nothing more.

The apartment was small, but tidy, a living room with a futon
sofa, bookcases crowded with novels and poetry as well as legal
texts. In the back, I could just see into a bedroom where coats
were piled. There were some old photographs framed on the wall
outside the bathroom, and I studied them while waiting to get
in. One was of a couple who I guessed were her parents. Her father wore a top hat and tails, but they didn't quite fit him, and
he looked just slightly drunk, as if he were on his way to a cos-

tume party. Her arm linked through his, the woman I took to be Judith's mother smiled happily and leaned her head against her husband's shoulder. And yet—what, fifteen years later?—she had gotten up early one morning and put an end to her life. I wondered if somewhere in Judith there was a similar time bomb ticking, or at least if this was something she worried about.

I hung around and I hung around. I talked to Bob about the play-offs and whether or not the Bills had any chance at all this year. I let an overweight painter named Laura complain to me about the art world and the difficulty of getting a show. I was impressed with these people, impressed with myself for being at a party with them, for being able to pull off a reasonable impersonation of a young man leading a normal life. I was in the music business, I told them, the rock 'n' roll end of it, actually. After a couple of Crown Royals, I was telling them about the wildness that went on, the backstage parties, the drugs. I told stories about musicians I'd never met calling me at the last minute for equipment. After a while, even I was beginning to think that without the presence of one Spencer Markus at good old Mutronics, Inc., much of the popular music world would be unable to function.

"I had one of your pedals," said Leon. "A Groundhog, or something."

"Gopher," I said. "It's called a Gopher."

"Broke after about a week. I sent it in to the factory and that was the last I heard. That was two years ago. Wasn't there something about a strike?"

"Sure," I said, framing the scene with my hands. "Very bad news. A bunch of gangsters and thugs. I got beat up myself. But that's all over now. The company's back in business. It's a leaner, meaner operation." I thought of the empty halls of Mutronics, the gas generator rumbling away in the back room like some oversized, early Soviet version of an artificial heart.

"Wait a minute," he said. "You're the guy."

"What guy?"

"The guy on the flier I got in the mail. I thought you looked familiar. With your head all wrapped up in bandages, right?"

I admitted it. "Yeah, that's me."

"You don't look that bad."

"Well, the picture was taken some time ago. I recovered." I was looking at Leon and wondering what kind of guitar player he might be. I suspected great. I also guessed he didn't really care that much about it. He was going to be a successful lawyer. In a few years, he'd have a nice suburban home somewhere in Jersey, a wife, and a kid. He'd put together a home studio in his basement and make amazing, record-quality tapes, playing all the instruments himself. I hated him.

"You know, I'm in a little garage band kind of thing," he said. "Nothing that special, but we're playing Monday night at a place downtown, if you're interested."

"They're really good," said Judith, who'd appeared on the edge of this conversation. I watched stone-faced as she slipped an arm around Leon's waist and gave him a squeeze. I couldn't tell what was going on between them, and I couldn't help thinking that Judith was not only aware of this, but working it for all it was worth.

"What do you call yourselves?"

"The Pop Torts. It's a legal thing."

"I know what a tort is."

"It's meant to be ironic. Are you doing anything about that head injury of yours?"

"Like what?"

"Well, seems to me there's probably some kind of lawsuit potential."

"I suppose," I said. I didn't particularly want my legal fumblings scrutinized by a bunch of almost-lawyers.

"I think that's Spencer's business." Judith took the empty glass from my hand. "Refill?"

"No, thanks." I felt vaguely ill. "I should get a move on." It seemed important to me to appear to have places to go, things I was supposed to be doing. I pictured what was likely to be happening back in Brooklyn. Spider parked on the sofa, squinting at the TV. Perhaps Arnold would be back over by now.

"I'll go down with you," she said. "I want to get some cigarettes, anyway."

Leon looked surprised. I couldn't remember ever seeing her smoke, either, but I was glad for the company. I said good-bye, shook a few hands, got my coat from the bedroom, and then Judith and I were out in the hallway together.

"Awful, isn't it?" she said. "I'm so sorry."

"What do you mean?"

"My friends. That business about your head. I wonder what I'm doing with these people, I really do. I don't want to be a lawyer. I just don't think like one."

"Sure you do," I said, not certain at all this was what she wanted to hear. She wore a familiar perfume, and I wondered if she'd thought about me when she'd put it on. There was a moment where neither of us spoke. It wasn't uncomfortable, exactly. We just looked at each other.

"Leon?"

"What can I say? He's very persistent."

"But you seem to like him."

"I do like him. He's a good person. He's attentive."

"I can be attentive. Persistent, too."

We were standing on the landing outside her apartment door. I had one hand on the metal railing, but in spite of this, I suddenly lost my balance and nearly tumbled down the stairs.

"Spencer?" she said. "Are you all right?"

"Want to go get those cigarettes?"

"I have a whole pack upstairs. And I don't really smoke—well, sometimes. I just wanted to get you alone for a second. And to get out of there."

"Can I call you?"

She shook her head at me and smiled, the smooth, light skin of her cheeks turning visibly redder. "Of *course* you can call me. Only this time, why don't you do it, instead of just saying you will?" She leaned forward, gave me a quick kiss on the lips, turned, and went back inside.

I jogged down the three flights of stairs and out the heavy front door of her building. Outside, I barely noticed that the temperature had dropped another ten degrees. I was going to get another chance with Judith, and this time I intended to do it right. I could be attentive. I'd leave old Leon in the dirt when it came to attentiveness. I tried out her name with my own: Judith Markus. Spencer and Judith Markus. This was the kind of thing adolescent girls were supposed to do, but I didn't care. Okay, maybe I was getting ahead of myself; after all, I didn't even know the next time I was going to see her. Still, I thought, this was how love was supposed to feel. Not like a chore, not like a decision you might later regret. Like you'd been pumped full of helium. Like it was Christmas.

I'd sucked down a lot of Crown Royal, and I found myself having a little trouble keeping a straight line. I was afraid if I rode the subway now I might puke, so instead, I started walking uptown, figuring at least to clear my head.

Outside of a topless bar on Sixth Avenue, not that far from Mutronics, I saw the guy who'd hit me. I recognized him more from Rick's photo than I did from actual memory, but there was no doubt it was him. He stood with two other guys, smoking cigarettes and passing a bottle of something. He had a green New York Jets cap pulled over his ears and wore a cheap, blue nylon parka.

I stopped dead on the sidewalk and stared. I was across the street from them, and they hadn't noticed me. I didn't recognize the other men, but it was definitely the guy. One part of me wanted to run over and punch *him*, bang his head hard against the sidewalk a few times, let him know all the trouble he'd caused. I was also acutely aware of how drunk I was, and that I needed to think twice before doing anything stupid. Still, I felt I had to do something. I crossed the street.

"Excuse me," I said, approaching them. They didn't seem to notice, so I repeated myself, louder. "Excuse me."

"What?" said the tallest of the men. He was better-dressed than the others, in a long, leather coat, and he wore no hat. His ears had turned bright red in the cold.

"I just wanted to know if you remember me." I addressed my man, ignoring the others. He looked at me, then turned to the tall one and said something in Spanish.

"Remember you how?" asked the tall one.

"From this fall. I worked at Mutronics, just a few blocks from here. Your friend knocked me unconscious." As I spoke, I stared right at him. I could see that he was genuinely trying to place me, but couldn't. I knew him, though, the heavy brow, the mustache, the pockmarked cheeks, the head so squared off it seemed almost to have been flattened in a vise grip. He conferred again with the tall one. The third man, who held the brown bag they'd been passing, just stared at me. He had a wide boxer's nose and needed a shave.

"My friend says you must have him mistaken for someone else."

"Mutronics," I repeated. "Last September. He was there for a couple of weeks. He remembers me."

He turned back and said a few things more, including the word "Mutronics." His voice moved rapidly over the syllables like boiling water skipping around in a pan. The short guy suddenly began to nod.

"He says he remembers."

"Does he work for the union?"

"Sometimes, maybe. He works here, he works there. What do you want?"

I didn't know. What difference did it make, anyway? What could this person possibly do for me? I looked at him, right into his eyes. He seemed completely unconcerned, almost happy in a way, to have been noticed for something he'd done. "I want to know *why* he hit me," I said.

They talked again for a moment, the tall one translating my question.

This time, the short guy spoke directly to me. "My job," he

said, grinning. He took his hands out of his pockets and gestured toward his chest with stubby fingers, then out toward me. "Your job," he said. "My job." Then he took the bottle from the hands of the man standing next to him, who had continued to stare all this while, and offered it to me. "Scotch whiskey," he said.

I shook my head. My drunk from the party was turning into a general numbness, and I was losing touch with my toes. The wind had picked up in the time I'd been standing there, and the men in front of me were beginning to shift back and forth to keep their blood moving. "Forget it," I mumbled.

"What did you expect?" asked the tall one. He took a deep drag on his cigarette, tossed it to the sidewalk.

"I don't know what I expected."

He exhaled a great, blue cloud of smoke. "You never know what to expect. My friend says he has no hard feelings."

"He's got no hard feelings. I've got holes in my head."

"*Si?*" He stepped forward. "What do you mean, holes?"

"From where they drilled." I touched my scalp, feeling the indentations for myself, as I often did these days. It was turning into a sort of nervous habit.

The tall guy took off a glove and reached out his hand to feel, too. He beckoned to the short one, the one who had hit me, and he, too, touched my head.

Two women in miniskirts, tights, and very thin jackets moved past us, hurrying against the cold, and we all turned together to watch. They kept their eyes focused straight ahead and didn't speak at all, obviously concerned that the four of us were in some way dangerous. For a moment, I was one of these men spending Christmas Day drinking out in the cold. My nose was beginning to run, my eyes to tear. My stomach hurt.

"*Feliz Navidad,*" said my attacker, with a toothy smile.

"Merry Christmas," I said, and walked on toward the next subway entrance.

I threw up while waiting for the train, but luckily there was no one around to watch. I did it right over the edge, looking down into the black, trash-strewn track bed. Every now and then a rat scurried out from under one rail, ducked back behind another. The temperature seemed to be dropping a degree every five minutes and my head hurt from the cold. My train, when it finally came, was blissfully warm, though, and I dozed all the way back to Brooklyn.

23

I *slept for* a couple of hours after I got back and woke up a little after seven with a slight headache. I downed three aspirin in the bathroom, then headed upstairs.

Spider was sprawled out on the couch wearing a college sweatshirt of mine that was too small on him. His wrists extended out from the sleeves a good three inches.

"I guess that was some party."

"I drank too much."

"It's healthy to overindulge every now and then. How's old Judith?"

"She's fine." My mouth felt dry and I tried swallowing. "More than fine."

"Are you in love?"

I shrugged. "Maybe."

He sat up straighter. "That's great. Knowing who you love is like knowing where you live. It's basic information you need to get on with your life. Without it, you just spin your wheels. Look at me. I haven't had a handle on either of those things for some time now and the result is— Well, you can see the result. I'm all for this. Now, is she gorgeous, or what?"

"No, she's not gorgeous. Nice looking, you could say. Anyway, why do you care so much?"

"I want pretty grandchildren."

I went over and flicked some brown needles off our tree.

There were two packages underneath it. "What are these?"

"What do they look like? Santa came while you were out."

I picked up the one with my name on it. "Too small to be steaks."

"Very funny. Just open it."

They were cassette tapes—I could feel them through the wrapping, which was a red and white candy-cane motif. His package was larger, a wrapped-up shoebox, and I brought it to him on the sofa. I tore open mine. "All right," I said. "Albert Collins." I turned the next one over. "Buddy Guy." The last tape looked different. "*Bouzouki* music?"

"I wanted something Italian, but all they had was vocal stuff, so I settled on Greek."

"Thanks." I put them aside and watched as he opened his. It hadn't crossed my mind that we'd do presents, and now I felt bad that he'd had to go out and get his own.

"Look," he said. "What do you know."

The box was full of money. "I thought you gave that back."

"I did. This is different money."

"It looks the same to me."

"It may look the same, but look harder. This money is a *loan*. I'm borrowing it from Arnold, and I plan to pay back every cent. Tomorrow, I take this down to the travel agent and buy a ticket to Italy. How does that sound?" He was grinning now, almost giddy about the prospect. The money was in bundles, all different denominations.

"Good. Wish I could go."

"I'll see if Arnold can front you some too, if you want. Nothing I'd like better than to travel with you."

"That's okay. I've got a lot to do here at work. And there's Judith."

"I'm going to help. Don't think I'm going to run off and leave you stranded there. I'm going in tomorrow and start busting away at those letters. I'll leave in about a week or so, I figure. Between now and then, I can get a lot done."

I couldn't see where it would make much difference, considering how little he'd done up until now. But I understood, too, that this was part of our conspiracy. He always wanted it to seem as if we were embarked on some adventure together, no matter how much evidence his actions offered to the contrary. And I would let him. I always had, and I knew, staring at him on that sofa, that I always would.

"Now," he said. "How about we order up a pizza to go with the big bottle of Chianti I bought?"

We ate in front of the TV. I was getting sick of pizza, but he dug in like a starving person. For dessert, he produced a package of Milano cookies. "An all-Italian meal," he said. We each had two. Then he announced he wanted to go up on the roof.

"It's freezing," I said.

"Freezing is what it is up in Maine. It's freezing in Toronto. This is what I'd call chilly, and that's being generous. Of course, you need to take on a certain amount of antifreeze." He drained the remaining wine from his glass.

"Seriously, it's like ten degrees out."

"Are you coming or not?" He handed me the bottle, which was still about half full, then unplugged the boom box that functioned as my stereo system. His face was a little red and he needed a shave. I put on my jacket and gloves and followed him up.

With the cold had come clear weather, and the night was alive with contrasts, the lights from the river sparkling in the distance, the lack of moisture in the sky reflecting little or nothing of the streetlights back down. Between the bright stars there was only blackness.

"Let us *bouzouk*," he said, popping in the tape and cranking the volume up high. There were a few seconds of hiss and then some happy shouts as the music kicked in. He held his long arms out, palms toward him, fingers toward the sky, then began a reasonably graceful impersonation of a Greek dancer.

"That's good." I dug my hands into my pockets.

"You must *bouzouk* with me. One cannot *bouzouk* alone."

"I don't want to *bouzouk*."

"Are you too cool to *bouzouk*? Is this what you are saying?" He kicked one leg out, then the other, did a little half turn.

"Not cool, cold. Oh, hell." I took a long draw on the wine, threw my arms in the air, and tried to imitate what he was doing. It wasn't hard; the music had a happy, constant rhythm that you could do pretty much anything to and feel like you were dancing. We moved around solemnly. I tried not to think about what damage we might be doing to the roof.

"You *bouzouk* well, my son," he said. "You are true Greek."

"I am truly freezing, if you want to know the true truth."

"This is only a state of mind." He did a sort of pirouette.

"It's a state of toes, ears, and nose, too." The tape was slowing from the cold, the notes beginning to quaver, the pitch to descend.

"Think of warm, tropical nights, hula girls, the ocean breaking on the sand."

"Hula girls?"

"The hula is originally Greek. Not everybody knows this." He took my hands and made me spin around in a circle with him four, five, six times—I lost count. I began to feel dizzy. Finally, I broke free, went over to the chimney, and leaned up against it. It was warm and smelled faintly of gas.

"I'm done," I said. "Can't *bouzouk* no more."

He shut off the tape. "Is good," he said, exhaling and stretching his arms out, fists clenched. "I feel alive."

I left *Spider* in front of the TV and went downstairs to call Judith in private. I kept thinking about what he'd said, about how knowing who you loved was like knowing where you lived. You just made a decision and you stuck with it, but the important thing was that you did in fact *make* it in the first place. I stood in the hallway and surveyed my surroundings—the frayed red carpet, thick with dust (we'd never invested in a vacuum cleaner, and I could still see Rick, bare-chested, a T-shirt tied around his face for protection, working away with a straw broom, the air around him disappearing in a dark cloud), the peeling wallpaper, the radiators that clanked all night like disturbed spirits, but never gave up any real heat. I picked up the phone.

Judith was home, but she didn't seem to want to talk. I told her how much I'd enjoyed the party, said a couple of other things I thought were polite and cordial. I wanted to seem thoughtful, but not overly pushy. Attentive. She answered me distractedly, and finally I asked her if there was something wrong.

"It's Toby. I talked to my dad this evening and he wants to take him to the vet."

"What for?"

"To have him put down. Toby had four fits last night, and he thinks it's just not worth it anymore. I don't know what to do—I can't think about anything else. I'm probably going to go down there, but there's not much hope. I already tried talking him out of it and he just says he's sorry, but I'm not the one who has to live with him, and that's true."

"Why don't you take him?"

"I would if I could. I'm sure I could make him more comfortable. He's more my dog than anyone's, and he always perks up when he sees me. But I can't have a dog here. They're not even allowed in the building, and my apartment is a sublease anyway, so I have to be careful. I'm not legal myself."

"He can come stay with me," I offered. "There's a park right nearby, and I don't think there's any rule against pets here. The place is pretty torn up as it is."

"Spencer, that is really nice, but think hard. Taking a dog in is a big responsibility. Toby's got real problems. He's not going to live that much longer, no matter what. He's almost thirteen."

Just for a moment, I pictured myself carrying Toby's lifeless body down our stairs. But I knew how much he meant to Judith. "Don't worry about it, he can stay. That is, if you want to do that. I mean, I expect you'll come and help out and all."

"My God, Spencer, are you serious? Of course I will! I'll be there every day. You'd really do this?"

"Toby and I go back a long way."

"I could kiss you! I will kiss you!"

"I'm holding you to that."

"I'll call my dad back right now. Can you go with me tomorrow? I'd like to pick him up as soon as possible. I can borrow a car and we can drive down in the morning. Could you do that?"

"I'm supposed to work, but it's not a problem. I pretty much make my own hours."

We agreed that she'd pick me up around nine-thirty, and after another round of her thanking me and telling me how grateful she was, we finally hung up. I went back upstairs.

"We're getting a dog," I said to Spider. "Or I am, I guess."

He was surfing channels, the remote held at arm's length as if it were the handle of a fencing sword. "Dogs are good."

"Then why didn't we ever have one?" I asked. "I would have liked a dog."

"Your mother didn't want pets. I'm not exactly sure why. I once did bring home a dog for you, a spaniel or something. Back in the pound in less than twenty-four hours. Jan couldn't sleep with him in the house. She's a nervous woman, your mother." He looked at me. "How about you? Are you nervous?"

"I don't think so," I said. "I mean, I worry about things, I guess. Is that what you mean?"

He settled on a channel that was showing downhill skiing. "I don't know. I just wonder sometimes how much of me went into you and how much of her went into you and how much is just you, on your own." He tossed the remote to me, surprising me, but I caught it. "It's a parent thing. Doesn't mean much in the overall scope of the world, but you still want to know. Kind of like when you're near a mirror and you can't help but look in." He kicked his feet up onto the coffee table and folded his hands behind his head. "You pick something," he said. "I'm tired of making decisions."

I found an old movie that had just started, with Claudette Colbert and Don Ameche as a Hungarian cab driver. I'd seen it before. "This is good," I said.

"Then let's watch it." He yawned, rubbed his eyes. I could see he was fading. "I feel pretty good about the way things are taking shape," he said.

Within minutes, he was fast asleep, tipped sideways on the sofa, his head supported by the arm of it, his mouth slightly open. I watched about half the movie with him beside me like that, then went and got a blanket from his room, put it over him, and went downstairs.

24

———

J udith and I drove down to New Jersey the next morning in
a sporty blue Honda. I was pretty sure she'd borrowed the
car from Leon, but I didn't ask and she didn't make a point of
telling me. Toby was happy to see her, the front and rear sec-
tions of his body wagging back and forth in such a way that they
seemed almost not to be attached to each other. When he was
done, he gave me a friendly snout to the crotch, then hustled
off into the kitchen to eat his kibbles before I could get to them.
He was slow, though, and on his way he lost his balance and
tripped, legs splaying to all sides. For a moment, he just lay
there, defeated. Then he heaved himself to his feet and continued on to the dish.

While he ate, we packed his belongings up into a grocery bag:
leash, collar, pills, peanut butter, hairbrush, flea shampoo.
When he'd cleaned out his bowl, Judith rinsed it in the sink and
we headed out to the car.

I'd brought along a new Golden Possum phase shifter for
Nicky Dormer, and I had Judith swing around by the church so
that I could deliver it. "Nicky Dormer?" she asked. "That strange
guy with all the shirts? I haven't thought about him in years.
Whatever happened to him?"

"Nothing," I said. "Not a thing, that's his problem. He just
stayed exactly the same and moved out into the woods. He's
waiting for the revolution."

"*These* woods?"

"Last I knew."

"The revolution better come soon, then. These are all going to be cut down. They're going to be condominiums, I think, or an office park. My dad's doing some design work for the developer."

We walked out to Nicky's tree, but there were no signs of habitation. We had to crouch to get under. The rich smell of pine seemed to emphasize the cold.

"Maybe he has another place to hang out in winter," she suggested, shivering. "Maybe he moved."

"I just saw him here a few weeks ago." Looking up, I saw a bundle wedged in among the branches: Nicky's sleeping bag. "That's his." I'd brought the unit in a small plastic garbage bag, and now I tied the end around a branch. "There," I said. "How many other companies do you know of that give this kind of service?"

By *noon we were* at my place. At first, Toby just looked at the stairs and I was afraid that it wasn't going to work. I hadn't considered the mechanics of moving him up and down when I'd made the offer. After looking up at Judith as if to say, "Really? You want me to do this?" he began gamely to climb them. We followed behind, ready to catch him if he fell, but he didn't. At the upstairs landing he sighed, turned in a circle twice, then settled to the carpet. We had to step over him to get past.

"What do you think?" I asked.

"I think it's going to work," she said with confidence. "At least I hope so. It's got to. Do you hear that, Tobe? This is your new house."

"You want coffee or something?"

"It's okay. Why don't you go on in to work. I'll stay here with him, keep him company. I brought books to read and everything."

"I don't have to go in."

"Well, I really need to do this reading. I mean, I can't do anything else, if you know what I mean."

"Did I suggest anything else?"

She tapped her knuckles against my forehead. "No, but I can hear your libido clanking away in there. Go on, go to work. I promise you, I'll be here when you get back."

"You will?"

"Yes, I will. We can have dinner, something nice and civilized like that. I want to move slowly this time so we don't have another disaster. Just because you're taking in my dog doesn't necessarily mean that I come with the package." She put her arms around my waist and we kissed. "Go," she commanded, breaking away. Toby looked up, as if this were directed at him. "Just leave me a key, okay?"

I arrived at work at the same time as a stocky guy with blue sunglasses and a round, inexpressive face lightly peppered with freckles. He carried a black briefcase and wore a blue parka with orange lining in the hood. We stood silently together, waiting for the elevator to creep down to us. The blue police barricades were still in the hall, leaning up against the corner wall. I had a feeling this guy must be on his way up to our offices, but I didn't feel like asking. If he had a complaint, I didn't want to know about it. The elevator came, we got on, and sure enough, when I pushed the button for five, he kept his hands around the briefcase.

"You work for Mutronics?" he asked. His voice had a kind of catch in it, as if he didn't quite have enough breath to get all the words out.

"There is no Mutronics," I told him. "I'm with Gryphon Research and Development, though, which bought the company." The door opened and we stepped out. "We're not exactly open for business. Can I help you?"

"I want to talk to Spencer Markus."

I'd figured as much. "Your name wouldn't be Void, would it?"

"Excuse me?"

"Never mind." I pushed open the door into the empty reception area. "As you can see, we're just getting things started back up here. There was a strike a few weeks back." I noticed that he had a cloud tattooed across the back of his hand.

"I know all about it," he said. "Can I see Spencer Markus?"

I picked up the phone from the front desk and pushed the intercom, then punched a couple of random numbers and waited. "He doesn't seem to be at his desk. Maybe there's something I can help you with?"

"Who are you?"

I held out my hand. "Randy Song. I run the switchboard here, mostly. Listen, we're not really open, strictly speaking. The holidays and all. Why don't you come back sometime after the new year? Or if you want, you could leave a note for Mr. Markus. He's very good about getting back to people."

But he shook his head, and I was glad to see that I'd discouraged him. "I guess I'll just get along, then," he said. He didn't leave, though. He simply stood, staring at me.

"Is there something else?"

"It's these shoes."

"Shoes?"

"I just got them and they don't fit right. I thought they did, but now I think I was wrong. They're too big and I'm getting blisters."

"Take them back." I looked down at his feet. He had on plain black lace-up shoes. They did look new. In fact, much of what he was wearing looked new. His dark green work pants had sharp creases in them that said they had yet to be washed.

"You think they'll take them back? Shoes?" He seemed fascinated that I had such faith in the essential good nature of the retail world. His breath smelled strongly of onions. "They won't take back shoes. Not after I've worn them."

"I don't know. They might. Depends on the store, I guess."

He nodded. "Never in a million years," he said. "But thanks. I'll be back."

"Don't mention it," I told him.

Spider was sitting at my desk, typewriter on, a stack of open mail in front of him. "I'm solving problems right and left. You know, not all of these are complaints. There's a lot of letters of support. All right, there's your odd lawsuit mixed in, but on the whole, things could be worse. Right now, I'm typing a letter to this guy who wants a schematic for our wa-wa pedal."

"We don't make a wa-wa pedal."

He snapped his fingers. "Exactly what I'm telling him. Okay, it's an easy one, but it'll be one less for you."

"Did you order your ticket?"

"I did. I can pick it up anytime. How's the dog?"

I leaned against the edge of the desk. "Hard to say. He's back at the house with Judith."

"Really?" He pulled a bandanna out of his jacket pocket and blew his nose loudly. "Is she going to be staying with us, too?"

"I doubt it. But things are going pretty well."

"You kissed her?"

I scratched with my thumbnail at a bit of dried correction fluid on the desktop. I didn't particularly feel like giving him details.

"Come on, did you or didn't you?"

"Sure, I kissed her."

"Yes!" It was as if I'd scored a go-ahead basket with time expiring. Addressing an imaginary audience, he said, "He kissed her." He turned back to me. "Anything else?"

"I think that's my business." There was a touch of ice in my voice, and I was a little surprised to hear it. He was just trying to be funny.

He adjusted the typewriter roller up a few notches. "Two weeks' time and you'll have that place all to yourself. I had to wait that long for the cheaper fare. I'm in with a consolidator—

these guys buy up whole blocks of seats, then resell them. There's all kinds of rackets out there, you know? Everybody's got some kind of scam."

"I'll take over," I said, picking up a letter and stepping around to his side of the desk.

"Relax. You want to do something useful, go get your old man a cup of coffee, light, three sugars. And a Ho-Ho or something like that." He pulled out three crumpled dollar bills from the front pocket of his jeans. "Get something for yourself, too."

It wasn't a real workday anyway; I was here to get out of Judith's way for the afternoon. And I realized that I resented the fact that he was really leaving. Had things only gone a little differently, it might have been me making plans to travel right now, along with Sally, perhaps financed with an enormous settlement from the union. Though I knew it was pointless, I couldn't quite get past wanting to blame him.

I took the elevator back down and walked to the corner coffee shop. Twenty-third Street was clogged with traffic and people honking their horns. Someone had opened a hydrant near the Sixth Avenue end of the block, and cars were slowing to crawl through it, water spewing out from around their tires. It was still well below freezing, and this was likely to become a skating pond in a few hours. I liked the idea.

The elevator had just left when I got back, and I had to wait again with the police barricades as it crawled up and back down. I couldn't understand why, after all this time, the barricades had never been retrieved, but it said something about the inefficiency of the system. It was a small thing, certainly, but the fact was, they'd been forgotten. The tile floor was a swirl of muddy footprints, and I felt a dampness in my sneakers from having stepped across the stream from the hydrant. There was a broken stub of a cigarette smoking in the floor ashtray and I watched it smolder, almost hypnotized as the last traces of the white collar of paper turned to ash, leaving only the filter.

Randy sat up front by the phones eating a big deli pickle that was quartered and spread out in front of her on butcher paper.

She seemed surprised to see me. "I thought you were back at your desk," she said.

I held up the bag. "Coffee. One for me, one for Spider. Sorry, I should have asked if you wanted some."

"Don't sweat it, I got my pickle. And I had my limit on coffee already today. Wait a minute. What happened to that guy?"

"What guy?"

"The guy I sent back to talk to you a couple minutes ago. I *spoke* to you."

"Not to me you didn't." I felt suddenly nervous. "Did he say his name?"

" 'Fuzzy.' Something like that."

"Furry?"

"That's it."

"Furry *Couch?*"

"I don't know."

I put down the bag and started to run. As I did so, I heard the first shot. It didn't sound like much, really, just a loud popping, but it froze me. Then there was another, like someone clapping hands around a blown-up paper bag. I was in the hallway outside Jerry's office, and I just stood there, unable to move. Jerry's door was a few feet away, and now it flew open.

"What the hell is going on?" he said. His eyes were puffy, as if he'd been asleep.

"There's a guy in there with a gun."

He nodded, but showed no signs of the panic I felt. It was almost as if he'd been expecting something like this all along. "Come into my office. Has anyone called the cops?"

"No," I said. My entire body was shaking.

"Who else is out there?"

"Randy, up front."

"Well, get in here. I hope she's got the sense to take cover." He turned, moved quickly to his desk, and picked up the phone. As he did so, there was a third shot, though this one sounded oddly muffled and farther away.

I leaned sideways against the wall, directly opposite Jerry's clawfoot bathtub, my stomach shrunk to the size of a pea. *Randy Song. I run the switchboard here.* I thought I might be sick. I also knew instinctively that the crisis was now past. I heard Jerry's voice talking to the operator, though only in fragments. I heard "emergency," "shots," and "ambulance." I left him there and continued down the hall, praying that what I knew had happened hadn't.

The first thing I felt was the cold. Spider had been shot once in the forehead and again in the lower cheek. The impact had carried him backward and out of the swivel chair—my swivel chair—in which he'd been sitting. It lay alongside him, while he leaned with his back against the green cardboard filing boxes full of invoices, arms limp at his sides. He might have been resting, except that he wore a dark mask of blood and he was clearly dead. An awful burnt smell hung in the air. At the far end of the room, the fire escape door was open, the source of the draft. It was held that way by Furry Couch's body, which sat in a similar position to my dad's. He'd shot himself in the mouth, and from the back of his head there arose a tiny trail of gray vapor. Apparently, he'd started to leave, then changed his mind.

I walked out into the hall, took a breath, then reentered the room. Nothing had changed.

"Jesus," said Randy, coming up alongside me and putting a fist to her mouth. "Mother of God."

"He thought it was me," I said. I was surprised by how calm I was. "He came to kill me."

"Why?"

"Because of a fuzz box." I thought about the bag I'd left hanging from the branch of a tree only this morning. "He ordered one a long time ago, and we never sent it. He's been writing letters since last spring."

Jerry came in carrying a baseball bat. "I called the cops. There's an ambulance on the way." He looked around, took in the scene, and fell silent.

"It doesn't matter," I told him. Randy was crying, and she tried to take my hand, but I didn't want to be touched.

"You told me to send him back," she said. "I swear to God, you did."

The next morning, shortly before dawn, I took Toby out to the park. Judith had stayed the night, sleeping next to me, Toby parked a few feet away on a bunch of old blankets I'd given him. I was unable to do any real sleeping, and around five-thirty I quietly dressed and motioned to Toby to get up. He was skeptical at first, but once I put my shoes on he began to show some enthusiasm, licking my hand, staring at me expectantly, tipping his graying face to one side.

"This was in no way your fault," Judith had said to me before we went to bed. "It's just a stupid, crazy thing, a one in a million chance."

I tried to believe her. The police had been able to explain, after a few phone calls, what had happened, more or less. Furry Couch had been released from prison the week before and sent home to Chicago. It was early parole, given to him as a reward for his exemplary behavior, and in light of the upcoming holidays. He'd done five years of a fifteen-year sentence for holding up a fried chicken place, a robbery that netted him a little over three hundred dollars, but in which he'd carried a gun—a .38. A habitual criminal who'd been in and out of jail since he was sixteen, he'd been sent down to a federal penitentiary, where the time would be harder, and the place had seemed to have a good effect on him. The gun he'd used to shoot Spider and himself was a .22, the kind of cheap handgun any idiot with two hundred dollars and the desire could pick up in Manhattan.

I had not cried last night. I'd gone along to the hospital in a police cruiser. I'd answered questions, filled out forms. As a crime victim, Spider's body had to go to the morgue first. There was quite a bit of paperwork, apparently. I could pick him up in twenty-four hours. I talked to a series of police officers, was given a number to call if I decided at some later date I might want counseling. Through it all, I moved in a kind of haze. Even back at my apartment, with Judith holding my hand and crying, I felt as if I had morphine in my veins.

Toby and I made our way along the dim paths. In the shadow light, forms began to take shape, the world appearing gradually. Dark lines of trees, a building under repair, the Swan Boat pond, a stand of reeds. I would stop and wait for him as he investigated some smell or another, marking this lamppost, the corner of that bench. Everything still felt unreal to me. I was supposed to be dead right now, at least according to Furry Couch's plan, but he'd shot the wrong man. I was alive and breathing. It was about ten degrees out, but it didn't bother me. I was on bonus time, it seemed, out of regulation and into extra periods, a dead man, walking.

We were deep into the long meadow when Toby started to growl. I looked around but could see nothing threatening. I told him to cool it, but he kept it up, his front legs lowered, hackles high. He was looking back into the mist in the direction from which we'd come, and now I saw the outline of a figure headed toward us. For a moment, I was scared. Perhaps the world was not so random a place. People won the lottery two weeks in a row against odds in the billions. It seemed possible that I was deep in a trough of some waveform pattern of violence from which I had no real chance of escape, other than locking myself away until time carried me back out of danger. I thought of Judith, warm in my bed. I'd been stupid to come out here.

Toby barked twice, threateningly, and the figure stopped about twenty yards away. It was a man, wearing a cap and a heavy parka, and for a second I was sure it was Furry Couch, even though I had watched his bagged body being loaded onto an ambulance with my own eyes. Then I realized that it was Arnold.

"Hold the dog," he said. "I don't want to get bit."

"What are you doing?"

He approached and froze as Toby investigated him. Deciding he was harmless, the dog moved off to sniff interesting patches of the frozen ground.

"I saw you leave and I couldn't sleep, so I followed you."

"You saw me leave?"

He looked slightly embarrassed. "I've been staring out my window all night. I'm afraid they're going to come for me, too."

"Who, Arnold? Who would come for you?"

"I'm not sure."

"Did you forget to eat? Is that it?"

"I don't know," he said. "Maybe I'm irrational. But I've been followed before."

I'd stopped over last night to let him know what had happened. He was the only person I could think of to tell. He'd brought out herbal tea and bottled water and insisted on making me some because it was "soothing and good for stress." To humor him, I'd drunk the tea, which was dark and tasted vaguely the way mulch smells.

"Look, don't go crazy on me," I said. "I don't have the patience. Whatever demons are after you, you're just going to have to fight them off alone."

"It's not demons," he said.

"Well, good. I'm glad to hear it."

"What was the guy thinking?" Arnold asked. "If I knew, maybe I could settle down. I just don't see what he could have been thinking."

"He was thinking that we let him down. That I let him down. He sat around a prison cell and began to believe that the only reason he wasn't a big success was that a guy named Spencer Markus hadn't sent him his stupid fuzz box. That's what he was thinking. There's no mystery."

"Beginning with an illogical premise, he acted in a logical way—that's what you're saying?"

"The guy was convinced he was supposed to be a rock star." I could see he was thinking about this in terms of his own sheltered life, his own irrational fears, odd moments of inspiration. It struck me that given the people around me—Arnold, Rick, Spider, Nicky Dormer—I was surprisingly normal. I saw this now as a kind of lucky accident.

"Whose dog?" he said, gesturing toward Toby.

"Friend of mine's. He'll be staying with me for a while, it looks like."

"The friend, or the dog?"

"The dog. I don't know, maybe the friend. It's a she."

"Pees like a male," he observed.

"The friend, not the dog."

He nodded. "Are you okay, then?"

"I think so, Arnold, I think so."

He stood looking at me in his big blue mittens that could have doubled for oven mitts, his glasses slightly frosted over. "You know, at the church?"

"What church?"

"The other night? When we went for Christmas services. You might want to know this. Spider said a prayer."

"A prayer? Really?"

"He wished for somebody for you to look after."

"You mean someone to look after me?"

"No, no, the other way around. Somebody for you to look after."

"He *prayed* for that?" If there was one thing he was *not*, it was religious.

"Maybe prayed isn't the right word. It wasn't actually in the church, it was later, down by the water. We rode the number one down to Battery Park to see the Green Queen. The Statue of Liberty—that's what I call her. It was more like a wish. 'Give my boy somebody to look after,' he said. Or something like that. I mean, that was the gist of it. We were tripping, remember."

"Do you know what he meant?"

"I don't. But now you've got this dog. You could even say it came true, the wish. It's good to be depended on. I mean, I guess. Nobody's ever depended on me for much."

"Spider did. I think you were about his closest friend."

"*You* were his closest friend."

I had to turn my head. Toby had found a stick partly frozen

271

into the earth and was trying to yank it out. I didn't particularly feel like letting Arnold Blickman see me cry. To his credit, he seemed to sense this and left me alone, heading back up toward the Ninth Street exit out of the park. Then I found my way to a bench and allowed myself to fall completely apart.

A couple of reporters called me, but I told them I had nothing to say. To my relief, Jerry didn't try to figure out some way to make the incident work to his advantage; he saw that it was more than likely he and the company would come out looking bad. So, although Furry Couch made the evening news, and there were short articles in most of the papers in which he was called a "madman" and a "deranged ex-con," within a few days it had all blown over.

I contacted a funeral home in the neighborhood. It was expensive, and I had to ask Hal for a loan. He and my mom came up for the ceremony, standing quietly beside me, hand in hand, she in a navy dress, he in a brown suit and tie, looking respectful and, I thought, solid. When the coffin, plain pine with no handles, was lowered slowly into the ground, I glanced over at her and saw she was biting her lip so hard it appeared she might break the skin. I'd always suspected that in spite of everything she'd said over the years, her absolute refusal to look back with anything but a feeling of relief that she'd gotten out of that marriage while she still could, a part of her had continued to love him. I think Hal knew that, too. It made me admire him all the more.

New Year's Eve, Rick called. Judith and I had spent the evening watching television and drinking tall, festive rum drinks she concocted out of three different kinds of fruit juice and a little tonic water. She'd bought a pack of colored umbrellas and she speared pineapple slices with them, then hung them over the edges of the glasses. She'd decorated Toby, too, and he lay on the floor by us, having long since given up trying to shed the red and blue ribbons from around his neck.

Rick was using a pay phone at a bar, and it was hard to hear him over the background noise. "The situation is weird," he said, "but under control. I'll be staying for a while."

Susu *was* pregnant. She hadn't been that crazy about having an abortion, just positive she wasn't ready to raise a child. She was definite about its being his, and they'd worked out a plan where Rick would stay on the property in a small guest cottage–type place, help out with expenses. When she delivered, they'd both take care of the kid for a while. As soon after that as possible, Rick would take over completely. "It's workable," he said. "Maybe not ideal, but definitely workable."

I didn't tell him about Spider. He was so excited. I tried to sound happy for him, though I'm sure something of my mood shone through. I kept hearing myself say things like "Well, if that's what you want, then I guess it's great." I asked if he was coming back any time soon.

"No reason for it," he said. "I don't have anything essential there, really. I've got a sleeping bag, clothes, my checkbook, and credit cards."

"What about your screenplay?"

"Brought it with me. But, to tell you the truth, I think I'm going to dump it anyway. I've got something better to write about now."

"What?"

"This. What's happening to me, this whole thing. Shit, if this isn't a movie, I don't know what is."

I promised to box up a few things and send them to him, including his ceremonial sword from military school and a desk lamp he wanted, and to forward any important-looking mail. We agreed that I'd look around for another roommate, and this made it seem final. After I hung up, I walked in and out of all the rooms on the floor. I decided it had never been a place to live, to set down roots, but rather just a spot to land for a little while on the way to somewhere better. I felt stupid for not having seen this much earlier.

"You didn't tell him *anything?*" Judith asked when I returned to the sofa.

"I couldn't see any reason. He's got enough on his plate."

She reached down and stroked Toby. "Strange, isn't it? You want to tell people, but at the same time, you don't. It's not a matter of getting pity, or even sympathy, really, though that's about all anyone can offer. It's just that connection you need. Reassurance that there is a world out there and that it does make sense. At least most of the time."

"Is that what you believe?" I asked her.

"Yes," she said. "It is."

I gave Arnold back his money, still in the same box. Among Spider's things I discovered a small life insurance policy, recently taken out, with Allegra as sole beneficiary. I wrote a letter to Brian explaining this, and he wrote back with Cully's address in Italy, where I sent the policy, along with a note about what had happened. I never heard back, but this didn't really surprise me.

About three weeks after the funeral, an envelope came in the mail for me at work. Inside there was a carefully typed note that read:

Dear Mr. Markus,

We are terribly sorry about our boy's misdeeds. He was not a good person, and we have no intention of trying to make excuses. Mr. Couch and I may be to blame in some way, I don't know. Certainly, we are more than sorry for what has happened.

These are some things of his I thought might interest you. Whatever Albert became, he started out a normal child, I think you'll agree.

Sincerely,
Claudia Couch

She had enclosed a second-grade class picture with a little boy in the third row circled in black marker. He had that same moon face and freckles, ears that jutted straight out to the sides like radar dishes, and he was smiling, showing off a set of wildly unsettled teeth. Also included was a small certificate of good citizenship for participation in an Earth Day cleanup of a park in Chicago, dated April 1975. And there was a painstakingly printed list, on graph paper, divided into two columns. The one on the left was headed "Girls I Like," and underneath there were three names, Wendy Cippone, Denise Larson, and Bitsy Koppelman, with an exclamation point after this last one. The other column was headed, "Music I Want":

> All of Hendrix (YES!)
> Led Zep 1, 2 and 3
> Sgt. Pepper's
> Robin Trower
> Cream

Check marks had been made in pencil after all the entries, indicating, I guessed, that he'd gotten hold of the albums, either by buying them or stealing them. I wondered where old Bitsy Koppelman was today, and if she'd had any idea that Furry Couch had loved her from afar. I left the list and the picture out on my desk for a few days, but they made me feel sad, and I finally slipped them back in the envelope and tucked it away into my desk drawer, out of sight.

I continued working for Jerry, sending out the products that began coming off the assembly line upstairs slowly, but regularly, still with lots of bugs and defects. Mornings and evenings I took Toby for long walks in the park, sometimes with Judith when she could make it over, but mostly alone. We'd doubled his phenobarb, and for a while it helped, but then in February his fits became more frequent, and the effect on his body and spirit was apparent. He just began to look weary. One night in early March he had six in one night, and in the morning I couldn't get him to stand. I tried to call Judith, but only got her answering machine saying that she was at the library, working. I didn't go in to my job, choosing instead to sit with him, stroke him, talk to him. He died that afternoon with me watching, my *Bouzouki* tape on in the background. It was nothing. He just closed his eyes and let out a deep sigh. That evening, Judith and I took him into Prospect Park and buried him in a wooded area, just the other side of the fence from a graveyard that dates to colonial times.

What else is there to say? I went through a couple of different roommates, each a worse disaster than the last. My heart just wasn't into the selection process. I took in, in order: one re-forming junkie on public assistance who left hypodermic needles out in the bathroom and paid his rent weekly; one newly divorced man who found a new girlfriend within two weeks and left without even saying good-bye; two macrobiotic members of a women's softball team who filled my refrigerator with foreign-looking substances and hated me with their eyes every time I passed by them on the sofa, where they spent all their time watching television and holding hands. There was a bout with roaches, a subsequent bombing, a lot of sweeping up dead bodies. Al DiGrassi came through for me, and after a brief hearing before a judge, workmen's comp agreed to pay my bills and even reimbursed me for some lost wages. I began to think of places to go, ways to escape. When Judith got a job interning with a firm in Atlanta for the summer, I decided to follow her.

Judith and I attended my mother's wedding together in May, looking for all the world like the happy young couple, me in a suit I'd bought on Fourteenth Street, Judith in a stunning blue dress that made her easily the most attractive woman there. But even then, whatever we'd had was rapidly falling apart, and we both knew it. The burden of our two tragedies, rather than bringing us closer, was instead like some oversized anchor, keeping us from moving in any direction at all.

I found a job at a music store and moved in with two Georgia Tech students who had a spare room and four cats. Through the hot, soggy summer, I did my best to keep the relationship alive. I met Judith every evening at the office building where she worked, thought up things for us to do: the World of Coca-Cola, the High Museum of Art, trips to funky barbecue joints. None of it made any real difference. By the end of the summer we weren't seeing that much of each other anyway, and when we did, we spent most of our time arguing. When she left, in August, I stayed.

I continued on at the music store, selling guitars mostly, but electronics, too, even a drum kit from time to time. We had a couple of old Mutronics boxes in stock, a Gopher and an Iguana octave doubler, but people weren't lining up to buy them. With money I borrowed from my mother, I bought a cheap car at auction, an old Dodge Dart with a backseat that had been torn to pieces by feds looking for drugs.

Every now and then, it would occur to me that I wasn't supposed to be here—that my very existence was a lucky accident—and I'd feel as if I'd returned to my body after an extended, mindless absence. On a number of occasions, I found myself in places I did not expect to be, with no real memory of how I got there: in the middle of Piedmont Park, for instance, or at a strip bar out near the perimeter. I'd think as hard as I could, trying to put my hands on the last solid facts I knew to be true—where I'd had lunch, what I'd done after leaving the store. Eventually, it would come back to me, but with an odd sort of distance, as if my actions and their results were not conscious choices, but rather the meanderings of some child chasing a puffball in the wind.

Rick and his boy, Grant (after Ulysses S.), moved to L.A., where he began waiting tables and taking scriptwriting classes at night. Two months after he arrived, he married an Irish girl who was working illegally at a bar. They bought a small house in the Valley and started sending me cards inviting me to come out and see them, none of which I ever answered. I kept promising myself I'd get around to writing back, but in fact I was too jealous. I was eager to start something solid of my own, something that would last and allow me to prove to myself and the world that I could be counted on, that I was the kind of person who could see things through. I didn't begrudge him his happiness, but I didn't particularly want all the details, either.

I met a German girl on assignment with the German consulate, another lawyer, or about to become one anyway, back home. She was only in town for a few months, and she was beautiful: big eyes, long hair, puffy lips, and a smile that just took you by surprise. She bought a harmonica from me—she wanted to learn the blues—and I worked up enough nerve to get her number. Our first date, I took her to this black club down near the stadium. Five different guys hit on her almost immediately, and I began to worry that I was going to have to stand up to someone if we stuck around. So after about a half-hour, we went to another, safer bar where I drank too much beer and watched her chain-smoke. "We have nothing in common," she said, midway through her third pint, "except that we both want company." Still, we saw each other a few more times. When she left a month later to go back to Germany, she gave me a phone number in Berlin where I could reach her, but the one night when I was feeling lonely enough to try it, I just got some recording telling me it was nonworking. At least that's what I think it said.

There's a fair amount of blues down here, which I suppose is true of the whole country these days, and I guess it's pretty good. I'll go out and listen every now and then, but the sad truth is that I get bored quickly. It's "Stormy Monday" and "Crosscut Saw" and Stevie Ray Vaughn covers no matter where you go. Every now and then I remember that this is where the Allman Brothers are from and I get a touch of that old excitement. The other night, for instance, I wandered into this club in Buckhead, a new place, very upscale, the men in suits and ties, the women looking moneyed and corporate. I went in because from outside it sounded like the tightest band I'd ever heard. It turned out to be two middle-aged guys, one on guitar, the other on piano, playing along to a digital tape machine on which they'd prerecorded the bass and drums. The guitarist was overweight and balding and wore a black vest over a red shirt, a cigarette tucked into the corner of his mouth. He picked up a slide and kicked into a version of "One Way Out" that just made me grin. Then they did "Statesboro Blues," and it was like listening to the record, not just the notes, but the energy, too. I left before the end of the set—I didn't really want to talk to the man, I'd just liked watching him. He looked solid, dependable, happy to be where he was, to be able to do what he did with such ease, such control. He was so normal-looking, he could have been a car salesman. When I got outside, I could still hear him. I walked to my car thinking how good it was to see somebody that talented who'd managed to survive where so many others had given in, one way or another. Probably you could argue that he'd made a dumb choice, spending all those years on what was basically mimicry, but I don't know. There's so much emphasis on originality in the world when the truth of it is 99.9 percent of us are as indistinguishable from each other in our daily lives as supermarket eggs. And I think that despite what we want to believe, we also know this, deep down. It's why so many people are unhappy—they're fed on dreams until they grow fat with desire. The world dangles storybook lives in front of them until they can't help but see their own as failures.

It had begun to rain lightly, as it does here a lot, and I got into my car and fired it up. Even though I was now blocks from the bar, underneath the dull flap of my wipers I swore I could still hear the music.

I can hear it now.

About the Author

Geoffrey Becker is the author of *Dangerous Men*, a collection of short stories that won the 1995 Drue Heinz Literature Prize. A guitarist as well as a writer, he is a graduate of Colby College and the Iowa Writers' Workshop, and has taught creative writing at the University of Iowa and Emory University. He has received a number of awards for his writing, including a James Michener grant, the Nelson Algren Award from the *Chicago Tribune*, a PEN Syndicated Fiction Prize, and an NEA fellowship. He currently lives in Iowa City, Iowa.